THE LONG
JOURNEY HOME

Other books by the author

Michael Gilbert

THE LONG
JOURNEY HOME

1817

HARPER & ROW, PUBLISHERS, New York
Cambridge, Philadelphia, San Francisco, London
Mexico City, São Paulo, Singapore, Sydney

E

A HARPER NOVEL OF SUSPENSE

THE LONG JOURNEY HOME. Copyright © 1985 by Michael
Gilbert. All rights reserved. Printed in the United States of
America. No part of this book may be used or reproduced in
any manner whatsoever without written permission except in
the case of brief quotations embodied in critical articles and
reviews. For information address Harper & Row, Publishers,
Inc., 10 East 53rd Street, New York, N.Y. 10022. Published
simultaneously in Canada by Fitzhenry & Whiteside Limited,
Toronto.

FIRST EDITION

Designer: Ruth Bornschlegel

Library of Congress Cataloging in Publication Data

Gilbert, Michael Francis, 1912-
   The long journey home.

   I. Title.
PR6013.I3335L6   1985   823'.914   84-48600
ISBN 0-06-015430-6

85 86 87 88 89 10 9 8 7 6 5 4 3 2 1

THE LONG
JOURNEY HOME

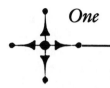

One

There were three distinct reasons for letting the charter flight go on from Rome without him. The single question that John Gabriel Benedict debated was which was the most important reason of the three.

The first was that he had no incentive to go any farther. His cousins in New Zealand were expecting him and had written, with simulated enthusiasm, to say how splendid it would be to see him again after twenty long years. But he had a suspicion that their real thoughts must be turning on the question of who was going to have the chore of meeting him at Auckland International Airport and which of them would be expected to put him up until he found himself a house.

Then there was Italy.

In truth, the piece of it that he could see from his corner seat in the upstairs bar at Fiumicino Airport was not attractive, consisting as it did of macadam roadways and advertising signs. But behind them lay all the sun-baked, vine-covered, cypress-shaded mountains and valleys of the country he had come to love. Most of his visits to it had been to the north, on business for his company, to Milan and Verona. He had made trips to Florence and Venice and, once or twice, to Rome. But that left nearly half the country unexplored: the southern half, the romantic half of which his father had spoken more than once.

"Charter Flight ABZ for Bahrain, Bombay, Singapore, Darwin and Auckland boarding now at gate sixteen."

The clinching reason was a practical one. He had begun to distrust the aircraft. It was an aging Tristar, hired by the charter firm, he guessed, from one of the Gulf airlines. But it was not so much the age of the aircraft he distrusted as the attitude of its crew. John had been seated near the front, in the first class section. At the moment before their departure from Heathrow, when the no-smoking notice went on, the door of the flight deck happened to swing open and he had seen two of the stewardesses deep in conversation with the captain and the first officer. All of them should have been busy with their many obligatory checks before takeoff. Nor had the chief steward yet put in an appearance.

John had traveled often enough on different airlines to recognize a slack and undisciplined crew. Perhaps this was to be expected on a charter flight when fares had been cut to the bone. What really worried him was the thought that there might have been the same lack of attention to the standard maintenance routines of the aircraft itself. He was an engineer, and it seemed to him that there might be troubles ahead. Either they were in the hands of an inexperienced captain or one of the portside engines was not running at the same power as the other; there had been a momentary heart-stopping unwillingness of the aircraft to leave the runway at the end of its run up. None of the other passengers had seemed to notice it. Possibly their attention had been distracted by the stewardesses, who had elected to emerge from the flight deck and start taking orders for drinks. If members of the crew had had to move about at that particular moment, John considered they would have been more usefully engaged in checking that all seat belts were fastened.

"This is a final call for passengers on Charter Flight ABZ."

But did it add up to a reason for forfeiting a substantial sum of money? If he abandoned the flight at Rome there would be no question of any part of his fare being remitted or returned to him. The conditions of the charter flight were clear on this point. But then, again, was money important? After years of hard living, he had found it difficult to adjust to the idea that he was rich. Not stinkingly rich. Not quite a millionaire, but the possessor of enough money for all foreseeable contingencies. Ingrained habits of economy die slowly. He still found himself taking a bus when taking a taxi or hiring a car would be quicker and a lot more comfortable. Come to think of it, was it not that same instinct which had led him to prefer the reduced fare on a charter flight to one of the regular airlines?

From where he was sitting he could see the aircraft parked on the apron about a hundred yards from the terminal building, and he watched the file of his fellow passengers being shepherded toward it by one of the stewardesses. This was it. He would have to make his mind up soon. The next thing would be an announcement directed at him personally: *Will Mr. Benedict, passenger on Charter Flight ABZ, report forthwith to gate sixteen?*

When that summons came, would he obey it, or would he go on sitting where he was, finishing his second glass of beer? He did not think they would wait for him very long. He was in a state of indecision that bordered on indifference. Perhaps he would get out a coin and spin it. Heads, go on. Tails, stay put.

As he was thinking about this, he noticed that one of the small electric tractors which fussed about the apron had backed up to the flight of steps at the rear of the Tristar. While he watched, it was hitched on and the steps were drawn away. The steps leading up to the first class section in front were still in position.

Surely the summons must come now. John found that, for no particular reason, he was holding his breath.

A second tractor appeared, was hitched up and drew the front section of steps away. Almost immediately the Tristar began to move, swinging ponderously out toward the runway.

The decision had been taken for him. In a final demonstration of inefficiency, his defection had gone unnoted and the aircraft was proceeding without him. John settled back in his corner seat, waved to the waiter and ordered another glass of beer.

His absence was not noticed for nearly two hours.

It was not unusual for passengers to change their seats, particularly in the first class section, which was only two thirds full. Before the flight left Heathrow, in the absence of the stewardesses, John had helped a middle-aged lady who seemed puzzled by the operation of the seat belt, and he had subsequently moved over to talk to her, learning that she was visiting her grandchildren in New Zealand and that it was her first experience of air travel.

Other people moved about as well. After the takeoff from Rome, two of the first class passengers made their way back to talk to friends in the tourist section, and others joined a party at the bar at the back of the front section of the aircraft. It was only when everyone returned to their seats for the service of afternoon tea that the possibility first arose of passenger J. G. Benedict's not being on the plane.

The lavatories were inspected, but these were empty. A check through the tourist section showed that he was not there. The chief steward reported the fact to the captain, who had too much on his mind at that moment to do more than say, "His fault, not ours."

The outer port engine was giving trouble. The second pilot, one of whose jobs it was to scan the massive bank of dials and indicator lights, had drawn his attention earlier to the gauge that showed it had begun to overheat. The flight engineer had diagnosed a block in the oil feed, which might clear itself. The overheating was now approaching danger point. There was no alternative. That engine had to be shut off. They could get along, at reduced speed, on three engines. When they reached Bahrain the emergency maintenance team, which was on call twenty-four hours there, could have a look at it. It would be a nuisance if it turned out to be a long job, because this would involve the trouble and expense of putting up all the passengers at a hotel for one night at least; more, if the fault was a serious one.

"However," as he remarked to the flight engineer, "that's not my headache. All I've got to do is fly the bloody crate."

The flight engineer, who was by far the oldest of the four-man crew and had no very high opinion of his captain, said, "Just as long as you get us there, skipper."

"Do you think there's any doubt about it?"

"I'm not too happy about the inner portside engine. If the oil block's farther back than I thought, we could be in for trouble there too."

The two men looked at each other. The same thought was in both their minds.

"Take nearly as long to go back as to go on," said the captain. "Maybe longer. We've got a tail wind helping us. It would be dead against us on a return trip."

The flight engineer said, "So long as we don't run into anything rough, we ought to be all right. We'll have to hope the inner port holds up. Even if it packs up altogether we could make it on two engines, with the wind behind us."

He did not sound cheerful. He had been long enough at the game to know that when you had any sort of trouble with your engines, this was always the moment when you ran into further trouble. "Sod's Law," he said to himself.

It came fifteen minutes later. The sky above them was still the same metallic blue it had been since they left Rome, but visibility ahead was worsening. At the moment it was only a fine haze, flung like a veil across the horizon.

The radio operator, who had been busy on his set, looked up and said, "I've just had a met warning, skipper. There's a sandstorm blowing up ahead. It's reported as a big one. The advice is, best go over the top of it."

"Bloody good advice, with two and a half engines," said the captain. "Find out if we can get round it."

The radio operator buried himself in his set again and started to draw a diagram on the pad in front of him as he listened. Then he said, "If you make a deviation onto course one-five they reckon you can clear the worst of it, but you'll have to get a move on."

The captain said, "Then don't let's frig about."

The great plane banked as it swung nearly a quarter turn toward the north.

"And put on the seat-belt sign." He picked up the hand microphone. "This is your captain speaking. I hope that change of direction didn't upset too many drinks. We've been warned about a sandstorm ahead, and we're going a little out of our way to avoid it."

As his training dictated, the captain's voice had been calm and noncommittal, but it sent a shock of apprehension through his passengers so definite that it could have been picked up on a seismograph. This was the moment all travelers, however experienced, secretly dreaded: the moment when what had been a first class carriage was transformed into what might be a well-appointed elaborately equipped coffin.

Outside, the windows were first blurred and then obscured, and the aircraft began to buck a little as it felt the force of the wind currents that were driving the sand in an upward spiral. Suddenly they seemed to be going very slowly, limping forward into a nightmare of sand and darkness.

The middle-aged lady who had spoken earlier to John caught hold of the arm of the stewardess as she hurried past.

"We are going to be all right, dear, aren't we?" she said.

"Of course we are," said the girl. But the look in her eyes deprived the words of any comfort.

As soon as Charter Flight ABZ was overdue at Bahrain International Airport, emergency routine swung into operation. The alarm had been sounded when the aircraft went out of radio contact.

The last recorded signal had been from the captain at 17:35 hours, local time, when he reported that his speed had been reduced by the loss of his port outer engine and some malfunctioning of the port inner engine. As a result he had been unable to take the avoiding action recommended, but he hoped he would be able to sidestep the worst of the storm.

The surveyors were already beginning to plot his likely course and position, but they were hampered by the fact that he had omitted to report the exact deviation from his flight path. Even at the reduced speed at which he was flying, a difference of 10 degrees would make a difference of between eighty and a hundred miles on the ground.

The nearest air force station in a position to help was the RAF base at Akrotiri in Cyprus. Possible alternative positions of the Tristar were notified to them, and they undertook to send up a Canberra from the Photo Reconnaissance Unit. By the time they had got the signal, there was no more than an hour of daylight left. They could not hold out much hope of success before the following day.

It was three days before the scene of the crash was finally pinpointed and photographed. By this time the whole international search organization was in operation. As soon as the location had been confirmed, a Chinook helicopter, equipped with long-distance fuel tanks, was sent out by the American Third Battle Fleet off Beirut.

When the sergeant pilot in charge landed his machine beside the ugly blackened framework of the Tristar, he felt no urgent desire to get out and look closer. As it hit the ground the plane had split in two, scattering bodies over a wide area. Those remaining inside the aircraft had been incinerated.

His orders were to recover the black-box flight recorder and report. He climbed out and walked across, taking care not to tread on the things and pieces of things that lay around, some already half covered by the drifting sand.

He did not envy the men who would come after him to try to sort out and identify the bodies. In his view it would have been better to have left it to the desert to finish what it had started. He said to his number two, "One more good sandstorm would do the job for us." His second-in-command nodded. He did not feel like talking.

They found that on impact the plane had embedded its nose into the side of a sandhill and this had served, to some extent, to protect the bodies of the crew in the front cabin. They were recognizable as human. To get at the black box, two of them had to be shifted. The sergeant wondered whether they, at least, ought to be buried but decided that this was outside his orders.

As a professional, his sympathy was with his fellow professionals rather than with the two hundred civilians who had entrusted their safety to the crew's care and expertise.

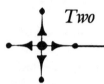

Two

"Ah bin thirty years in the States," said the tubby bald-headed man. "Detroit, Michigan; Pittsburgh; Houston: all over. Wherever work was, I went there."

"Plenty of it in those days," suggested John.

"That's right. Postwar boom. But lemme tell you there's one thing to watch out for with booms. Sooner or later, they bust." He took a pull at the tumbler of red wine that John had bought for him, wiped his mouth with the back of his hand and added, "Howsomever, this one held up for quite a while. Soon as I saw it was going to bust, why, me and my wife we packed our traps and headed for home. The kids wouldn't come with us. Thought they knew better than the old man. Last I heard, they were on public assistance." He took another pull at his drink to wash away the taste of filial stupidity. "You got children?"

"Unmarried," said John. "Not that that proves anything these days, of course."

"Maybe not where you come from, mister. But in these parts a girl doesn't have kids before the wedding bells have sounded. No, sir. We're real old-fashioned here."

Old-fashioned, thought John, was hardly the word for it. The tiny village of San Vito, which he had reached that morning, looked as if it had been hewn out of the top of the hill and could have stood there unchanged from the Middle Ages. The stone-flagged main street ran between houses that crouched forward until they almost touched overhead. Most of their windows were shuttered or barred. The drainage system was a single narrow channel down the middle of the street.

He was sitting in the only bar in the village, a drinking den in the square at the top of the street. It was not the sort of place where you lounged about under striped blinds. Its thick walls had been designed to keep the sun out in summer and the warmth in in winter.

The interior was cool and smelled of wine and cheese.

It was a village in the foothills of the Appennino Napoletano some fifty miles west of Naples as the crow flies, maybe twice as far on the twisting roads of the Campania, a country of limestone rock and uncleared forests of cork oak and chestnut and streams that dug deep beds for themselves when the rains of winter brought them into spate.

He had spent only a single day in Rome, changing some money and replacing the small personal items that had gone on in the aircraft. So far as clothes went, very little had been needed. He was a man who believed that comfort came a long way before elegance in air travel. He had been wearing an open-necked shirt, corduroy trousers and a well-worn pair of shoes. Now he had changed his jacket for a waterproof wind-cheater and bought himself a stick and a haversack.

To get clear of the city as quickly as possible, he had taken a local train to Colleferro and from there had headed northwest, crossing the Simbruini hills and setting his sights on the peak of Monte Rotondo. He had slept in cottages, farmhouses and barns and had found very little use for money. As soon as his farming hosts discovered that he understood engines, they had pressed him to stay and overhaul the tractors and agricultural machinery which they had bought from persuasive salesmen and soon found subject to breakdowns beyond the skill of the local mechanics to repair.

"That's Americans all over," said his bald-headed acquaintance. "They sell you a machine you doan unnerstand and cain't look after. So what happens? You doan treat it right. Soon it's kaput, no good. Then you buy another one. That's good business, eh?"

9

"I think it's sharp practice," said John. "Surely they could produce something simple that would work in this sort of country."

"It's good business for you. Now you can go where you like. They all want you."

This was true. The knowledge that there was a traveling mechanic on foot in the Abruzzi who had a miraculous way with machinery had spread rapidly. His course was now dictated for him as he was passed from farm to farm.

To more sophisticated or inquisitive people it might have seemed curious that a man of his obvious abilities should have been quartering the countryside like a traveling tinker, but his hosts, with the natural politeness of countryfolk, rarely asked him what he was doing or why he was doing it. The women, once the ice had been broken, wanted only to know whether Signor Gabriel—he had adopted his second name for the time being—was married and how many children he had. An idea which became current, and which had increased their discretion, was that he was a businessman running away from his creditors. This had gained him nothing but sympathy. As a consequence it was assumed that he would wish to avoid any unnecessary contact with the police, and one farmer directing him to another would indicate minor roads and tracks that would keep him clear of such dangers.

It had taken John some time to realize that people regarded the police, openly and without qualification, as enemies.

"Bastards," said the bald-headed man. "No better now than they ever were. People tell you Musso's caribs were worse. Doan you believe it. All bastards, all out for what they can get. You want my advice? Keep away from them."

"I've managed to do it so far," said John. There was one embarrassing aspect to this fugitive role, which, otherwise, he was enjoying. If the time did come when he had to produce his passport, it might be difficult to explain to the authorities why Mr. Benedict had been passing himself off as Mr. Gabriel. However, that was a difficulty which could be dealt with if and when it occurred. He was too happy to worry about contingencies which might never arise.

It had been an unforgettable two months.

He had been baked by the summer sun and soaked by the summer rain. He was feeling fitter than he had been at any time since those faroff days when he had won the high jump, the pole vault and the long jump for Otago in the All New Zealand University Sports, with records in all three events, and had been under consideration for an Olympic trial. Looking back, he was not sorry that such ideas had come to nothing. The life of a top-class athlete was brief and ultimately unrewarding.

In fact, it had been on the very evening of that day of glory that he had made one of his sudden decisions: to come to England and set up business as an electronics engineer.

It was a bold decision.

He had known no one and had very little money. All he had to sell was an idea, the Benedict flexible disc. Before he could begin to set up his own business he had to take such jobs as were offered in other engineering shops. This had its useful side. He had been able to learn his trade from the workbench upward, live rough and save money. It was five years before he had scraped together enough to rent a small workshop and sales office in an industrial development near St. Albans. His first assistant had been an equally serious-minded young man from the North London Polytechnic. (Satisfactory to think that fifteen years later, when he sold Benedict Engineering to MBA, that same young man should have gone to America and set up his own firm.)

It had been a long hard fight, and many normal and desirable things had had to go by the board, among them any thought of marrying and setting up a home. At a time when his business had achieved a turnover of a million pounds, he was living in two rooms in a small private hotel. Forget sport, forget fast cars. His holidays had been snatched affairs, a week or ten days spent walking through the roughest country he could find, usually not too far from his place of work.

In the early years he had acted as his own salesman. His principal markets had been in the north of Italy in the growing computer industry based in Milan, to whom the Benedisc, as he had named his brainchild, was at that time a novelty. He had

11

taught himself to speak very passable Italian, finding an affinity with that soft, liquid language, and had learned enough law and accountancy to enable him to talk sense to solicitors and accountants. This was necessary, since as the business grew he discovered that the emphasis had switched from making and selling the Benedisc to protecting it from poaching rivals. This had involved a plunge into the morass of international patent law: eighteen-hour days of planning, thinking and worrying. It was lucky that he was a sound sleeper; otherwise the months leading up to the final sale of his business would have finished him.

Now, as he strode along the ridgeway of the Monti del Matese, he had a feeling that some of the youth he had so wantonly thrown away was being offered back to him. Often, in a day's march, he met no one. He had time to think and time to observe.

Once, getting up very early one morning, for the simple pleasure of seeing the sun rise out of the mist in the east, he had watched an eagle swoop down and take a day-old lamb from the side of its mother. Intrigued by this, he had started to observe the other subjects of the kingdom of birds. There were the carrion crows, with their watchful eyes and long curved beaks. Bullies, but not lacking in courage. He had seen three of them mob an eagle and steal his prey. And there were the magpies, thieves and villains but amusing too. They reminded him of the currawongs he had watched in his youth in New Zealand.

The bald-headed man said, "You seem sad."

John realized that he had been silent too long for politeness. He said, "Not sad. I was just thinking."

"Of something not pleasant?"

"No. As a matter of fact, I was thinking about birds."

"You are a naturalist?"

"Not any sort of instructed naturalist. I just like to keep my eyes open on my walks. I have always wanted to see this part of your country, you know."

"You had never been here before then?"

"I had never been south of Rome. But my father used to talk about it. He was in the army."

"Ah ha! The Ottava Armata."

12

"Right. He landed with them in September 1943. He was in the New Zealand Division, under General Freyberg. Perhaps you have heard of him?"

The name of the redoubtable New Zealand V.C. meant nothing to his acquaintance, but he had brightened up at the mention of the Eighth Army.

"General Monty," he said. "Ah ha! What a man. I recall him well."

"You met him?"

"I was only a boy. Twelve years old. Thirteen. I remember him very well. He parked his caravan for the night in *our* farmyard."

John expressed appropriate surprise. During his walk he had already met three farmers in whose farmyards General Montgomery was alleged to have spent the night. It occurred to him that this was the modern equivalent of "Queen Elizabeth slept here."

He said, "The place I am making for next is a farm owned by a man called Genzano. I spent last night with a cousin of his, near Mirabella. He told me that Genzano was badly in need of help with his tractors."

"That would be Battista Genzano."

"I expect so. His place is between Morra and Montenello. At least, I think they were the names. I sometimes find it difficult to understand the local accent."

"Morra is right," said the bald-headed man judgmatically. "For Montenello, he should have told you Mattinella."

"Then you know the place?"

"Battista Genzano? I know him. Yes. In some ways a curious man."

"Oh?"

"When I say curious, I doan mean nothing adverse to him, you unnerstand. He is a good farmer. Has many machines. Makes good wine. What is curious about him is his ideas. He has had some bad experiences. Bad experiences give a man curious ideas."

John agreed that this might be so. He waited for further information, but none was forthcoming. When he rose to go,

13

the bald-headed man went through the motions of offering him a drink. John, with equal politeness, said, "I have a long walk ahead of me. I must be getting on my way."

The bald-headed man did not dissent. He accompanied him out into the little piazza to give him some final directions.

"Keep to the road which runs down the river, but when it turns left to Carile, keep straight on. There is a police post in Carile. I have heard stories of the sergeant in charge. An untrustworthy man. Soon you will come to the Bisaccia road. Cross that and make your way up one of the tracks into the mountains. There it will be better for you to ask again. Remember, Mattinella, *not* Montenello."

John promised to bear this in mind.

The first part of the way was easy to find. After he had crossed the main road he kept his eyes open for help. The first man he encountered was a shepherd who professed to know the Genzano farm and gave him directions. John knew, by now, that it was no use asking him how far it was. In the mountains distance was measured in time.

"*Una mezz'ora,*" suggested the shepherd.

Since half an hour might mean anything from one to three miles, according to the speaker's standard of walking, John lengthened his own pace. September had turned to October and he had no desire to spend a night in the open.

Fortunately, this *mezz'ora* was a short one and the Genzano farm easy to find. It would have been difficult to overlook, being on top of a hill and surrounded by a fence tall enough and stout enough to be called a stockade. It reminded him of one of the old Maori forts near his home in South Island. As he approached it the noise started. It was the deep baying sound of hunting dogs.

A shutter in the front gate was opened and a boy looked out. He said, "Are you the man who makes the machines work?"

"That sounds like me," said John cautiously.

A voice from inside shouted, "Open the gate, Guido," and, to the dogs, "Quiet, all of you."

The dogs went quiet, the gate swung open and John stepped into the yard. The man who came forward to meet him was carrying a shotgun under one arm. This was Genzano, no doubt. He had a halo of gray hair, a jutting gray beard, a beaklike nose and, as John observed when he got closer, brown eyes behind which a flame seemed to burn.

An Old Testament prophet, thought John. One of the fighting kind. Elijah, not Jeremiah.

"Signor Gabriel. I am glad that you should have arrived safely. Guido, inform your mother."

The boy scuttled off. In that household children and dogs did what they were told. He came back with Signora Genzano, a stout placid woman who had been at work in her kitchen. Her forearms were powdered with flour. She said, "I hope you can eat polenta." John said that he was very fond of it, which was only partly true. It depended on how it was cooked and what it was served with. On this occasion it turned out to be excellent.

After supper they sat in the living room in front of an open fireplace which was large enough to take a tree trunk. The boy Guido and his sister sat together on a sheepskin mat in front of the fire, smiling when he caught their eye. The room was lit by a big pressure lamp, which afforded a good light and gave off a buzzing noise like the sound of bees on a summer day.

"As you see," said Genzano, "we are not blessed with electricity. For years we have been promised it. But the promises of a government are paper, to be thrown into the discard as soon as they become inconvenient."

"Not only in your country," said John.

"Politicians speak always of progress. Sometimes it seems to me to be progress in a backwards direction. We are told that mechanization will save our labors. We buy machines. In the showroom, where they are covered with red and gold paint, they look very beautiful. I think they are constructed to work in flat country. Here we cultivate hillsides. In my father's time we used bullocks. They could pull a heavy plow up a slope as steep as that." He indicated with his hand. "A tractor may be of five horsepower or of ten horsepower, but it is not equal to two bullock power."

The engine troubles, which he described, seemed to be the endemic ones. John said, "If it is the fuel flow or the ignition, I can deal with it easily enough. If it is the gearbox or the clutch, it might be necessary to send for spare parts. Where is the nearest town which would have an engineering works?"

"Calitri, perhaps. Or maybe Rionero."

"There is a blacksmith in Calitri," said his wife, "but he knows nothing about motors. It is time you children were in bed."

The children raised the normal objections to this suggestion. Their objections were overruled. Signora Genzano went with them, leaving the two men alone in front of the fire.

Genzano had evidently been turning over in his mind how to introduce a painful subject tactfully. In the end he said, "I am told, Signor Gabriel, that you have had business troubles."

For some reason John felt disinclined to lie to this man. He said, "That is just a fairy story which the people of these parts have made up about me and which I thought it amusing not to contradict. I have had no business troubles. In fact, I have no business. I sold it to a large corporation for a satisfactorily large sum. I decided I had earned myself a holiday, so I took it."

Genzano said, "Truly our people love a romance. It adds a little interest to their lives, which are sometimes not entirely happy."

John remembered what the bald-headed man had said. He wondered what bad experiences this fierce Old Testament figure might have suffered. He was to learn.

"You may have wondered," said his host, "at the precautions we take here. The barred gate, the gun, the dogs. They are unhappily necessary. You read in the papers about the kidnapping of rich industrialists or their sons. No one has much sympathy for them. Five billion lire are demanded. Let them pay. They can afford it. But unhappily such easy methods of making money have spread downwards."

John shifted uncomfortably in his chair. He said, "Surely you don't mean—"

"In this district alone, in the last three years, there have been seven cases of kidnapping from families living in the countryside. Small farmers, for the most part. On the first occasion the father refused to pay. His two boys, one aged seven, the

16

other aged nine, were strangled and left in his yard. It was done as a warning. After that, people paid. When Guido and his sister Domenica were taken last year I found the necessary payment. It was two million lire. In your money that would be—what? Eight hundred pounds. The profit of a year or more of my labor, yet not too much to pay for two lives. It was not only the money. Guido soon forgot about it. He is a tough boy. But Domenica, I do not think she has recovered yet. She has great difficulty in sleeping. We have to use drugs. Maybe she will never get over it entirely."

There was a long silence in the comfortable firelit room with the lamp purring in the background.

In the end, conscious that he was saying something stupid, he said, "Couldn't the police do something about it?"

Genzano said, "No police force is of any use when its members are ruled by fear. Fear for their own families if they are too efficient. Fear of what their superiors will do if they are efficient in the wrong way. When a police force is afraid to act, the people are better without it."

If this was one of Genzano's curious ideas, John felt a good deal of sympathy for it. He found some difficulty in expressing his views in his limited Italian. He said, "You cannot have nothing. A vacuum. There must be some force to protect the people."

"If the police fail, the people will make their own force. This happened a hundred years ago, in Sicily. The Mafia was, at the start, just such a body as you describe. The Honorable Society, it was called. It lived up to its name. Now it is that no longer. It has been corrupted by money. Its services can be bought by people and corporations whose purses are long enough to pay for it. The Mafia operate in the cities and on the coast. They will not bother themselves with poor farmers in the mountains."

"And if neither the police nor the Mafia will protect you, what then do you suggest?"

"It is the right of any man to defend himself and his own. If he finds that the authorities he would naturally turn to, the politicians, the army and the police, cannot help him, he must help himself. A man who yields weakly in the face of wrongdoing is himself a wrongdoer."

John said, "I understand that. I come from a country where, in the memory of my grandfather, homesteaders had to fight for their own. How do you suggest that it would operate here?"

"We would need to form a citizen army. The men would be armed and would have means of keeping in touch with each other. Each district would appoint a capo, on Mafia lines, a head over twenty or thirty men. A careful watch would be kept on all strangers. If a kidnapping was attempted and the men were caught they would be chained to their car, which would be driven to a high place and set on fire, so that the flames could be seen by all in the area."

As Elijah dealt with the prophets of Baal, thought John. Aloud he said, "You think that terror can be fought with terror."

"That is what I think," said Genzano. "I also think that you have come far today and will be tired. I will show you your bed."

John was tired and his bed was unexpectedly comfortable, but it took him some time to get to sleep.

The next morning he was waked by the sound of a motor horn. He rolled out of bed and went across to the window. A large open touring car was standing in the courtyard. There were five children in it already. As he watched, Guido and Domenica came running out and somehow managed to pack themselves into it. The young man who was driving waved to Signora Genzano, and the machine lurched out of the gate and started down the winding track toward the valley.

John thought that it looked extremely dangerous. He dressed and went downstairs. Signora Genzano gave him his breakfast in the kitchen, of warm milk, bread, butter and jam.

"All our own," she said. "Even the jam. We make it from berries which the children collect on the mountains." She told him the name in Italian. John thought they might be bilberries. He said, "That was quite a carload I saw going off."

"There will be two more children before they get to Mattinella. That is where they attend the school. The men take turns doing the driving. Another man watches the track. Both are armed, of course."

"Of course," said John. He went out to look for Genzano and found him in the tractor shed.

"This is the one which gives real trouble," he said. "I have had it only six months, would you believe it? Now it seems that the wheels are locked."

John spent the morning dismantling the axle. He found, as he had expected, that the trouble was in the differential. Two teeth had been stripped off one of the cogs. He said, "We shall need a replacement."

"We will get nothing like that around here, I fear. It will mean driving to Salerno, or perhaps to Naples. Even then they might have to order the new part. It could take many weeks, and I need the tractor for the autumn plowing. Is there nothing you can do?"

John thought about it. He was holding the damaged cog-wheel in his hand. He said, "If there is a garage around here—one that carries out repairs—it is possible it might be able to produce a replacement. It would not perhaps be of exactly the right size, but it might be filed down and serve as a temporary expedient. It would be a tricky job, but I will try it if you wish."

The job was indeed a tricky one and took three days. Guido, on his return from school, proved an enthusiastic helper. He liked nothing better than getting his arms covered in black oil up to the elbows.

On the afternoon of the third day, the tractor was moved out of its shed and into the yard. Its mechanics were observing it proudly when they heard the sound of a car coming. From where they were standing they could see the last hundred yards of the track.

It was a smart little two-seater, painted a vivid scarlet. Genzano said, "I thought so. That is the Paoli car, and it is Anna who is driving it. I suspect that some further work lies before you, Signor Gabriel."

Guido had already run to open the gate. The little car came bouncing into the yard and the driver got out.

It was a very beautiful girl.

19

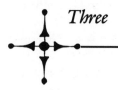

Three

In the warm light of that October afternoon he saw the face of the Italian Renaissance. The face that had enchanted Dante and charmed Donatello. The high forehead, the small straight nose, the short upper lip and generous mouth, the eyes with a hint of mockery and a hint of melancholy. The face of the unknown Florentine model whom Botticelli had used impartially for the goddess Venus and the mother of Jesus.

If Anna was aware that he was staring, she showed no sign of it. She jumped out of the car, said to Guido, "You are filthy; don't dare to touch me," and smacked him on the bottom, picked up little Domenica and greeted Genzano, who was advancing toward her, with a kiss in the middle of his forehead.

He said, "I fear that you have come to steal away our mechanic. He is, I promise you, a wizard. With his own hands he has constructed a new part for my tractor. It now marches beautifully."

Anna had swung around and was examining John. She said, "We have heard great accounts of his skill."

"Exaggerated, I'm sure," said John. "If I am indeed to leave you, I must do my packing. It is not elaborate." He went back into the house. The truth was that he wanted time to get his breath back. The sudden appearance of the girl had knocked him off balance.

If her face was cinquecento, her appearance was definitely twentieth century. In the previous months he had seen plenty of pretty girls, but they had been dressed either in their workaday farm clothes or the shapeless black that was their Sunday uniform. Here, suddenly, was a girl wearing a neat gray skirt, a striped boy's shirt and a sleeveless plum-colored waistcoat.

"Pull yourself together, John," he said as he washed his hands and forearms and packed his few belongings into his haversack. "She's just an ordinary modern girl. It's the contrast. Nothing more than that."

When he had stowed in the car the ham and the bottle of homemade grappa which Signora Genzano had pressed on him and taken an affectionate farewell of all the family and they were bouncing down the winding track that led to Mattinella, Anna said to him, in good if stilted English, "If it is true that you can make any machine operate, then I assure you that you will be as welcome at our farm as the archangel whose name you bear."

"Are they all in such bad condition, then?" He said it, without thinking, in Italian. Then, when she smiled, repeated it in English.

"That is better," said Anna. "Speak English all the time. It is good for me to practice on you. No. The machines are not all bad, but we have so many of them. I should explain that we are a most unusual household. The farmer is my grandmother."

"Your—?"

"Yes. My grandmother. She is helped by two boys who come in every day to do the rough work, but she is the one who runs the farm. My father and I are away all the day, down at the factory. It is on the coast, near Battipaglia. A big factory. I work in the office; my father is in charge of all the—I have forgotten the word. No. Don't tell me. Dynamos. He is in charge of the dynamos which produce the electric power."

"A big factory, near Battipaglia? Do you mean, by any chance, the MBA factory?"

"That is correct. You have heard of it?"

"Certainly I have heard of it," said John thoughtfully.

"It is the largest in Campania. Perhaps the largest in all of southern Italy. Ten years ago there was nothing but wasteland. The Piana di Paestum. Now there are buildings which spread over more than ten hectares of land."

She swung the car neatly around the corner and into the valley road.

21

"You drive very well."

"That is from practice. Every morning I drive my father and myself from our farm down to the factory. To start with, it was he who drove and I was nervous. Now I drive, and if he is nervous he does not say so."

John laughed, and that made her smile. She smiled, he thought, like an unself-conscious schoolgirl. He wondered how old she was. Not more than eighteen. Perhaps even younger.

He said, "Tell me more about your farm."

"You will understand that there are so few hands to do the work that we have to rely much on machinery. In the house as well as the farm. Fortunately, we have electricity. Really, we are like an electrical showroom. We have a machine for washing dishes, a machine for washing clothes, a machine for drying clothes and a machine for mixing food. Then there is a storm in the mountains and the electricity is cut off and we go back to primitive times and use our hands."

She took both hands off the steering wheel to demonstrate the return to manual operations and got them back again just in time to avoid a goat which had appeared around the corner, towing a small girl on the end of a rope.

John said, "And your farm is mechanized as well?"

"But certainly. Everything that used to be done in the old days by hand is now done by machinery. The digging and the planting and the reaping. We have two boys who come in daily. They enjoy racing around on our machines."

"But do not spend much time looking after them, I imagine."

"That sort of work is not so appealing to them. And that is why the machines break down so often. There will be much work for you to do. You will have to stay with us for a long time."

As long as I can, thought John happily.

They had topped the crest which divided the headwaters of the Ofanto from the Sele and were now on a road which followed down the stream. John could see the coastal belt ahead and caught a glimpse of the sea. Then the car swung to the right and started to climb a track even narrower and rougher than the one which had served the Genzano farm.

"This must," he said, in a series of gasps, "be very"—*bump*—"hard on your tires."

"Murder," said the girl. She was handling the little car with a lightness of touch that John found enchanting.

"What happens if you meet a car coming the other way?"

"Fortunately we are the only car owners who use this track. Old Valori, who has the farm below ours, uses a motorcycle. Not far now."

As they swung around a final hairpin bend, he saw the Paoli farm, a house and a spread of outbuildings filling a cup in the hills, with its fields around it on the slopes on three sides. Anna's father, Ermino, came out to meet them. He had bright blue eyes and a brown, good-natured but worried face. Some of the worry seemed to be connected with Anna.

"She drives too fast," he explained. "I keep telling her. On these roads there is only one safe method of progress, the method of the snail. He may be slow, but he arrives."

"Unless someone treads on him first," said Anna. "I must go now and change into my working clothes. On Saturday we are all farm laborers."

From somewhere behind the farm John could hear a high-pitched voice raised in expostulation.

"That," said Anna, "is my grandmother. She keeps those two boys hard at work. Behind her back, they call her names. But not to her face."

When John got to know Grandmother Paoli better he believed this. Most Italian families were matriarchal. The force and fortitude which was sometimes lacking in the males seemed to be concentrated in these formidable middle-aged dragons. He wondered whether the breathtaking beauty of her granddaughter would one day harden into the same mold. He found it difficult to believe.

He spent the afternoon making a preliminary examination of the farm machinery. It was good stuff, used roughly and cared for not at all. He soon saw that all that was necessary was to strip and clean the working parts. However slowly he worked, he could hardly justify a stay of more than two or three days. However, he was granted a respite. The next day was Sunday, and Sunday at the Paoli farm turned out to be strictly observed.

"Those who labor on the Sabbath," said Grandmother Paoli, "are unblessed. Their labor will not be of benefit to them."

She had put on her Sunday dress of black silk and departed, after breakfast, in the car with Anna to go to the church in Colliano, on the other side of the valley. Ermino settled down to his farm accounts. This, not being manual labor, was apparently permitted on the Sabbath. John decided to go for a walk.

He set off down the track and arrived, after about half a mile, at the Valori farm. It was smaller than the Paolis' and seemed to be devoted to root crops: parsnip, turnip and beetroot. There was a barn beside the farmhouse, and as John peered into it a large dog came out. Half Alsatian, half God knows what, thought John. But if its parentage was doubtful, its intentions were not. They were clearly hostile.

John decided to stand still. The dog examined his ankles, making up his mind which one to chew.

A voice from inside the barn said something which sounded like "Bruto." To his relief, the dog turned about and trotted back into the barn. When it came out again the owner of the voice was with it. A boy or, perhaps, a young man? It was difficult to tell the age of someone with a face so vacant of expression or meaning.

John said, "Good morning. That is a fine dog of yours."

The boy grinned and patted the dog's head but said nothing.

"Are your father and mother at home? Or have they perhaps gone to the church?"

The boy opened his mouth. The sound which came out might have been yes but could equally have been no. It was halfway between a cluck and a moo. John wondered if the boy was dumb but remembered that he had at least been able to make the dog understand him.

24

At this moment, to his relief, the front door of the farm opened and a man whom he presumed must be Valori came out. He was quite small, and a deformation of his shoulders that threw his head forward made him look even smaller. He had a stick in his hand, which he leaned on as he hobbled.

He said, "You will be the man who mends our machines for us. I am Pietro Valori. I am glad to meet you. Please enter."

He took no notice of the boy, who was smiling and tickling the dog under one ear, and led the way into the farm kitchen. He motioned John to a chair. His wife appeared, smiled at John, opened a bottle and filled two glasses from it. Then she retired to another room. The wine was white and a bit sweet for John's taste, but quite drinkable.

Valori said, "My son, or I should more precisely say my stepson, Stefano, is not at ease with strangers. To us he talks quite freely. To others, until he knows them well, he finds it difficult to speak at all."

"Some children are like that," agreed John.

"To his dog, also, he speaks, and I believe that Bruto speaks to him. Until the weather becomes too cold they sleep together on the haystack in the barn."

"Certainly they seemed to have a rapport. He is a remarkable-looking dog."

"I would surmise that one of his ancestors was a wolf."

"You have wolves in these parts?"

"Not for many years now. In the mountains of the north, the Marche and the Gran Sasso, I believe there are still a few. Here they exist only in the imagination of the children. However, they serve a useful purpose. They keep children from wandering too far from home."

"We had wolves, not long ago, in my home country," said John. "Vicious creatures. When I was young I was terrified of them. I wouldn't care to meet one even now."

"The blessed Saint Francis," said Valori, "spoke to them as his brothers, and they did not try to harm him."

"You need exceptional talents to do that," said John. He accepted a second glass of wine. This would have been bad manners in a bar but was correct when the wine belonged to your

25

host. Then he made his way back up the hill. As he passed the barn, Bruto and the boy were looking out. The boy's arm was around the dog's neck.

When he got back, Ermino had finished his calculations and was typing out the results, using a modern machine of the golf-ball type that John had admired before. It was an unusual thing to find in a farmhouse kitchen, but it was an unusual farm altogether.

When he mentioned the Valoris, Ermino said, "You will have seen his son. He is touched, poor boy. They say he has been like that since birth. Possibly he was dragged rather roughly into this world."

"His dog seems to understand him all right."

"Bruto is a most intelligent animal. He acts as a guard to both farms. We have to take certain precautions here."

John had noticed the bars on all the windows and the stout doors with their elaborate locks and bolts which Ermino fastened at night.

"We have also an alarm, which is connected with the police post at Colliano. You may think such precautions overly elaborate when there is so little to steal."

"I don't think I should worry too much about burglars. You keep a gun handy; you could deal with them long before they could get inside the house."

"Ah. You were thinking, perhaps, of kidnapping. Genzano will have spoken of it."

"Yes."

Indeed, at the back of his mind was already the thought that Anna and her grandmother had been gone for nearly three hours. The run down to Colliano would take no more than a quarter of an hour. A little more for the return journey, maybe. Roman Catholic services lasted longer than English ones, but surely—?

Ermino, who had noticed him glancing down at his watch, had read his thoughts. He seemed unworried. He said, "Always when women come out from church they spend much time talking. It is a natural release of the spirits." He walked across and opened the door. "And here, I think, they are."

The first thing they heard was a bark from sentinel Bruto, down the road, then the sound of the car. John was surprised at the relief he felt when he heard it.

26

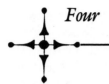

Four

Breakfast next morning was a hurried meal. Ermino and Anna had to leave before eight to be sure of reaching the factory in time.

"It's not the roads down the mountain," Ermino explained. "It is the last section, along the autostrada. You can be held up for twenty minutes."

"Father dare not be late," said Anna, grinning at him. "Always he has to set an example to the workers."

Ermino grunted, swallowed his coffee too fast and burnt his mouth.

When they had departed, the work of the farm began. The two assistants arrived. They were the sons of a fellow workman of Ermino's called Giacomo, who lived across the valley at Valva. They were a cheerful pair. In England, John thought, they would have been at school. Here, they worked a nine-hour day with a two-mile walk at each end and seemed to thrive on it. The grandmother appointed the tasks and oversaw the work. When she had her sharp black eyes on them they worked hard. When she went back into the house they took things more easily.

That morning John made a closer inspection of the machinery. There were two tractors. One of them was obviously a recent purchase; the other was middle-aged and looked as if it had had a hard life. There was a mass of equipment. It included a disk harrow, two plows, a mechanical dibbler and an old-fashioned reaper and binder. As far as he could see there was nothing mechanically wrong with any of them, but they were all rusty and all looked as though they could do with thorough lubrication. The main job would be the rejuvenation of the second tractor, a good vehicle that had been sadly abused.

He started to map out the work in his mind. Taken deliberately, it might be made to span one working week but no more. Helped by the boys, he manhandled the second tractor out onto the hard ground in front of the barn and started to dismantle the engine.

After a day or two a certain routine had established itself. They worked all morning and broke for a midday meal at noon.

During the morning the grandmother was busy with her household work, cleaning the house and cooking the midday meal. After the meal she would relax for a brief period and was inclined for conversation. John found her easy to understand, since she spoke with the deliberation of an old lady who had seen much of life and did not want her observations on it to be missed. Most of her talk was about the countryside and the old ways. Occasionally it was more personal.

Ermino, she said, was conscientious in his work. Sometimes this was good. Sometimes it got him into difficulties.

John said, "He told me that he looked after the power plant at this factory. If he does that conscientiously, surely it should get him nothing but credit."

"If that was all he did, you would be right. Unfortunately he has another function. He has become a man of confidence."

John thought about this and said, "Perhaps you mean that he is what we should call a shop steward."

"Possibly. What he has to do is to represent the views of the other workers to the management. Sometimes those views are not agreeable to the management. In particular, to the head of the management. Sergio Faldo. He is—" Here the old lady used a word which was new to him. She said, "I mean that he is Mussolini, he is Julius Caesar, he is God Almighty."

"Yes. We have them like that in England too."

"He is an unpleasing man. Unpleasing in his outlook. Unpleasing in his character. I much regret the fact that Anna has to work for him."

"She is his secretary?"

"She is his personal secretary. She sits in a little room outside his office. She does not, I am certain, sit on his knee, although no doubt that is what he would like."

"Such a situation is not unknown in other countries," said John.

"She is a good girl." The old lady paused. She had an important observation to make. She said, "It is easier for a girl to be good when she is attractive than when she is unattractive."

She then signified that the conversation was over by rising and throwing all the dishes into a tub of boiling water.

After supper there was more general talk. John described what progress he had made with his repairs. Ermino discussed factory politics and gossip. A new computer, the 555, was in its last production stage. There was a similar one being produced by IBM. It was important that their model reach the market first. This gave the union a weapon they had not been slow to use. A pay increase was in course of being negotiated.

"You may consider this wrong of us," said Ermino, "to use the difficulties of the management as a lever for obtaining more pay, but in truth our rates of pay are the lowest in Italy and well behind the other countries of the West. As for America—" He spread his hands to indicate his feelings. "They pay such high wages that I wonder how they compete in manufacture at all."

"One thing the West Coast factories do," said John, "is to send components down to Mexico to be assembled."

"Why would they do that?"

"Labor is so cheap there that they reckon it pays them, even after adding in the cost of transport there and back."

Ermino thought about this. It was a new idea to him.

John said, "With smaller components, watches and transistors and pocket calculators, where they can use air freight, they can even send them to places like Taiwan. No unions to bother about there."

He became aware that Ermino and Anna were looking at him. Ermino said, "I did not realize that you were an expert in these matters, Mr. Gabriel."

"I'm not an expert. But computers were my business. I sold out early this year to your people."

"To our company?"

"To MBA. Yes. Their headquarters are in London. That was where the deal took place. We had some patents which were still valuable. Before I entered into negotiations with them, naturally I made it my business to find out something about them."

"They are a large corporation, are they not?"

"The second largest in England, but said to be overhauling ICL fast. Perhaps the third largest in the world. They are truly multinational, for they do *all* their manufacturing abroad."

Ermino said, "They have a factory as large as ours in the south of France and a smaller one in Corsica. That much I know. There is talk that another is being set up in Scotland— that is a part of England, is it not?"

"For some purposes," said John cautiously.

"It was sensible to set a factory up here. It is an area declared by the Istituto per la Ricostruzione Industriale to be an area of special development. The site of the factory was given free, the services, water and electricity were there already and there were many concessions. Freedom from rates and from taxes for a certain period. It was the same in Corsica and, I understand, also in France."

"In some parts of Scotland, no doubt, as well."

"There was one other advantage," said Ermino sadly. "No doubt they had it in mind. Labor could be obtained cheaply. When it is a poor area with little work available and a big corporation comes along and offers hundreds of jobs, you may imagine that men are glad to have them."

"Women, too," said Anna. "Much of the work is done by women. They are cheaper than men."

"That's not right," said John. "If they do the same work, they should have the same pay."

"Try to convince that pig Faldo," said Anna. "He would laugh in your face. If all the women went on strike today, he could replace them tomorrow."

This was the topic of many evening conversations. John gathered that the life of a shop steward in a south Italian factory was not a happy one. He did not realize at the time quite how unhappy, but he thought it must account for the patches of white in Ermino's hair and the lines on his good-natured face.

On Friday evening, Ermino said, "You have worked all week. I declare tomorrow to be a holiday. Anna shall take you for a drive and show you the Appennino Lucano. It is not the highest, but some say the most beautiful of our mountain ranges."

"It will be a last chance," said Anna. "I think the weather is going to change soon. The wind has started to come from the north."

The grandmother put up a basket of provisions for them and they set off at ten o'clock, going first down the valley and then taking the main road toward Taranto. This was an offshoot of the Autostrada del Sole, which runs from Genova to the west coast of Italy and all the way down to Reggio di Calabria. Like all Italian superhighways, it was beautifully engineered, and they made quick progress down it until they were clear of Potenza. After that they struck up into the mountains, taking the twisting road to Tolve and on and up until they reached a point on the crest from which, on a clear day, it was possible, Anna assured him, to see both the Adriatic to the east and the Mediterranean to the south.

John, who could read a map, doubted this but did not contradict her. The day was far from clear and the wind was bowling along the tops of the mountains, chasing a flock of gray clouds. It was too cold to think of picnicking outside, so they backed the car off the road, turned on the heater and made themselves comfortable.

John said, "If the Apennines are the backbone of Italy, we are sitting on the ankle, looking down at the big toe."

"They are wonderful mountains," said Anna. "The most wonderful in the world."

"But not the highest."

"They are not monstrosities, like the Himalayas, no. But they are higher than anything you have in your own country."

"That's just where you're wrong," said John, his eye on the map. "I see there's nothing here which goes much over three thousand meters. In South Island, near my home, we have Mount Cook. That's three thousand seven hundred and sixty-four meters."

"You're sure about that?"

"Certain."

"I mean, it couldn't, just possibly, be three thousand seven hundred and sixty-three?"

John saw that she was laughing at him. Being laughed at by this beautiful girl sitting close beside him filled him with an almost irresistible urge to put his arm around her, pull her closer and tell her that he was head over heels in love with her, dizzy with the realization that he had never met anyone like her in his life.

He resisted the urge. There was a wall between them that he could not climb. It was the difference of nearly twenty-five years in their age. If he had married at a sensible age, she was just as old as his own daughter would have been.

He said, "Of course I'm sure. I measured it myself."

"Tell me about your country."

John sank back in his seat. He had been walking on the edge of a precipice but was now back on firm ground again.

He said, "I was born and brought up on a farm, near a town called Cromwell. That's in the north of Otago Province, in the foothills of the Southern Alps. I could see Mount Cook from my bedroom window."

"All three thousand seven hundred and sixty-four meters of it."

"Not quite all of it, but a good deal. Because the mountains on that side are bare and almost barren, like yours."

"Our mountains are *not* barren."

"Arid, then."

"Arid in summer, perhaps."

"But when you get to the crest and look down, you see something quite different. That is the wet forest. Very heavy, tall bush. Enormous trees and deep chasms you can look down into, with little lakes at the bottom like blue stones. It is all dark greens and blacks."

"It sounds creepy."

"It is creepy. Woodmen who went to work in it and were supposed to camp and stay for a week or so used to come out after a few days. They said it was the silence that got them down. I think it was more than that. It was the feeling that they were at the tip of the civilized world."

Anna shivered and said, "That's enough about scenery. Tell me about you."

"About me?"

"About your family and your farm. Was it like ours?"

"It was much larger. The farms out there are mostly sheep farms, and that means a big spread. Ours went right up to the foothills. It had been in our family for three generations. It was my great-grandfather who carved it out of the wilderness. They must have been exciting days. The Maoris had not got reconciled to the idea that white people were taking over their country."

"Maoris? I have read about them in the newspapers. They play rugby football."

"In those days they played rougher games. If you were taken captive, very probably you would be eaten."

"Goodness!" The idea seemed to fascinate Anna. "Fancy being eaten. It would be very strange." She thought about it for a bit. "Tell me some more about your great-grandfather. He was not eaten?"

"No. He managed to avoid that. He must have been a remarkable man. His men called him Bareknuckle Jack. He had a very explosive temper, and when he lost it, he liked fighting with his fists. My grandfather inherited a little of his temper and my father a little less, though when he did lose it we children all ducked into cover."

"And you?" said Anna, looking at him out of the corner of her eyes.

"Oh, I'm a very placid person. I can only remember losing my temper twice in my whole life. Once was when I was very young. The other time was when I was at University. That was not agreeable. I wanted to kill another man and perhaps I should have done so if I had not been stopped. I think I was as frightened as he was."

"*You* were frightened?"

"It is always frightening to lose control of yourself."

Anna shifted slightly in the driving seat. She said, "I do not think that you often lose your control now, do you? You are very much—I do not know the exact word—very much in command of yourself."

"I hope so."

"For instance, a little time ago, you wished very much to kiss me. But you did not do it. I can assure you that any Italian man I know would have been pawing me all over. I am glad that you did not do that."

Before he could say anything she had released the hand brake, switched on the engine and was guiding the car back onto the road.

That night, as he lay in bed, John made his mind up. He said to himself, very firmly indeed, You nearly made a fool of yourself in the car this afternoon. If you can't control yourself, my lad, there's only one thing for it. You've got to move on.

He decided that he would allow himself Sunday on the farm and take his leave on Monday. He felt little enthusiasm for the idea, but his mind was made up.

Fate, which had already played a significant hand, now turned another card. Late on the following evening, as he was coming down the outside steps of the barn carrying a log for the fire, he slipped and fell awkwardly. When he tried to get back onto his feet he felt an agonizing pain that started behind his right heel and ran like an electric shock up the back of his leg. He knew what had happened. He had done it once before, when training for the pole vault. He had either snapped or strained the Achilles tendon in his right foot.

Five

"Excellent," said Ermino. "Now you will stay with us for a long, long time."

"It doesn't look as though I shall be able to move for a few days," agreed John.

The doctor had called, had examined John's ankle and had encased his right foot in a huge lump of bandages and plaster. He was not only unable to use it, he was hardly able to lift it.

"Not days," said Ermino. "Weeks—months. In any event you would not wish to be traveling the mountains in weather like this."

The north wind had brought with it a cold, misty rain. Gone were the warm spice-laden southern breezes, the long summer days. It was not full winter yet, but a warning note had been sounded. Certainly it was preferable to be seated in front of a log fire, to listen to the winds rattling the casements and to eat the excellent food of Grandmother Paoli.

Much of his enforced leisure he passed in reading the books and papers Anna brought him from Salerno, but since he liked occupation for his hands as well as his head he set himself to master the crafts of the farmhouse. He hobbled into the kitchen and watched the grandmother make pasta. She mixed a paste of flour and milk and egg, rolled it on the table top until it was almost as thin as tissue paper, folded it over and over into a tight square and sliced it up with a big knife. The result, which looked by now like a tangle of knitting, was thrown into an iron pot of boiling salt water.

"More tasty and more digestible," said Grandmother Paoli,

"than the ready-made macaroni and spaghetti you can buy in shops."

John agreed with her. It was delicious. After a bit he was even able to help prepare the rabbits that were their prime source of meat. These friendly animals ran where they liked but returned to the farm to be fed. Grandmother Paoli would catch one, break its neck with a karate chop and bring it into the kitchen still warm and kicking.

"Now we skin it and draw it," she said. John had to overcome a certain squeamishness at dealing in this manner with what was almost a household pet.

After a number of failures he mastered the art of making butter and cheese and even became moderately proficient at the simpler forms of weaving. The grandmother watched him at work and said, "If you persevere, you will make a good husband."

With these occupations time could be killed. But the moment John waited for each day came in the early evening. First, a single bark from sentinel Bruto down the track. Then the arrival of the little car. Anna would jump out, kiss her grandmother and run upstairs to change out of her working clothes. The fire in the living room, which had been smoldering red, would be fed with dry sticks. Ermino would toss a bulging briefcase of papers into the corner and sit down in front of the cheerful crackle to savor his first drink of the evening.

Just like any businessman coming home in suburbia, thought John. The only difference was that the drink was wine, not whisky or gin.

Now that John was an accepted member of the family circle, the talk ranged more widely and became, at the same time, more intimate. He heard a blow-by-blow account of Ermino's dealings with the different workmen's committees and their neverending but undeclared war against the management, interspersed with sharp comments by Anna, who viewed matters from her seat in the managing director's office. It was like seeing two sides of the same picture at once. It was not a happy picture.

He learned about the Mafia. Ermino said, "We have, to a

36

certain extent, their friendship. Such friendship can be bought by those whose purses are long enough. It is not exactly a question of corruption. It is a question of business. They have power. You have money. The one can be bought by the other. You understand?"

"I understand the theory very well," said John, "but how does it work in practice?"

"I will give you an example. You spoke to me once of the fear of kidnapping. You wondered why we did not take the same sort of precautions as the farmers in the backcountry. It is because it is known that we have the protection of the Honorable Society. In the early days, when the factory was being established, there was always the danger that one or another of the head men might be held for ransom. That did happen—once. Sergio Faldo was taken when he was on a shooting trip in the mountains."

Ermino paused as if he was choosing his words carefully. Anna was watching him.

"A message was conveyed to the kidnappers. I do not know by what method it was done. But a message was certainly sent. No money was paid, of that I am sure. Faldo was returned unharmed."

"Except in his feelings," said Anna scornfully. "Do you know what was his chief complaint? That he had not been allowed to shave or have his hair attended to before they let him go. This was particularly distressing to him because his pictures were in all the papers, and he wished to appear at his best. I will show you."

She got an old newspaper out of the desk and unfolded it. John saw a thick-set, wild-haired, unshaven man scowling importantly. He looked at the banner headlines.

"He seems to have got a good deal of publicity." He looked at other photographs. Even when shaved and tidied up, it was not a pleasant face.

"Oh, he made a great story of his experiences," said Ermino.

"In which he was naturally the hero," said Anna.

"You mean that he dined out on it."

"Dined out? What is that?"

"It's an English expression. It means that it would be his favorite topic of conversation whenever he was invited out to dinner."

John could see Anna making a mental note of this. Her colloquial English was improving as fast as his colloquial Italian.

"My daughter's plan," said Ermino, "is to take herself off to England and work in the office of the company in London. In its headquarters. No doubt she thinks she would encounter there a rich and handsome English businessman who would marry her."

"A smooth type," said Anna with a grin. "That is what you say? Smooth?"

"Smooth is exactly the right word," agreed John.

"I tell her she would be unhappy in London," said Ermino, "and would return in a month."

John felt that, unhappy or not, Anna would be an unquestionable sensation in the City, but the topic was one he felt disinclined to pursue. He said, "It seems to me, then, that you pay these people in exactly the same way that you would pay premiums to an insurance company."

"In some ways, yes. Except that they perform functions which would be beyond the power of any insurance company."

Again John noticed the slight tension between father and daughter. It was as though she knew that Ermino was going to tell him something and was not sure she wanted him to.

Ermino said, "You noticed that fine typewriter I was using. In fact it belongs to Anna. It was a gift for her."

"It's an excellent model," said John, "and must have cost you a lot of money."

"It was not I who gave it to her. It was the man Faldo. Nor did it cost him anything. He had a dozen or more at his disposal."

Anna nearly said something but refrained. It was clear that Ermino had a story to tell and that he was going to tell it. He said, "It was five years ago, when our factory had not been long in production. It was understood by all that it was most important that profits should be made. We had been developing a

38

market in North Africa, particularly in Tunisia, where their new oil wealth had led to the setting up of a great number of offices. They needed typewriters and tape recorders and calculators. As with all such things, it was the first to arrive that would benefit. It was good strategy to swamp the market with our products. We loaded a fine selection of our latest models into the *Lucania*. A day before she sailed from Naples, we got the news. An American ship was already in Tripoli and had unloaded machines of exactly the same type, in every particular, as our own. They were on sale in the shops and were being eagerly bought. Our informant produced a price list. Not only were the machines identical, but in every case they were, by a small amount, cheaper than our own."

"Shrewd tactics," said John. "I suppose you had then to cut your own prices and take what was left of the market."

"Now we might be able to afford to do so. Not then. Our economy was too nicely balanced to absorb a loss of that dimension. London would have been very angry. Faldo would certainly have been replaced. Other senior men, too."

"So what did Faldo do?"

"Strictly speaking, he did not do anything. One might say that Providence intervened on his behalf. When the S.S. *Lucania* was five hours out of Naples, a fire started."

"I see. In the cargo hold, I suppose."

"That is so."

"Typewriters are not normally fire risks."

"There were other items with them. Paint and varnish. And wooden office furniture."

"They could make quite a bonfire if they got going."

"Evidently the captain considered so. He turned back to Naples. By the time he got there the fire was under control. The cargo was taken out and stored in a locked warehouse until it could be inspected by the port authorities."

"And—?"

Ermino hesitated. "We did not, of course, see the report, but it appears that the inspector declared the whole cargo to be a ninety-five percent writeoff."

"I imagine that it was insured."

"Fully."

"And the insurance company paid up?"

"They had little option. As soon as the inspector's report was received, the damaged cargo was offered for sale locally. That is normally done in such cases. In this case it was perhaps done rather more speedily than is usual. Our own company bought back a number of the items from the assessor. For a tenth of the proper price."

"Then you were able to judge the damage. Was it serious?"

"The machines looked bad. But when you come to examine them, the damage was quite superficial. They were covered with a black oily deposit, but once that was cleaned off they were really as good as new. The greater part of the machines are still in use."

John was examining the typewriter with interest. He said, "And this is one of them. It seems to me to be a very healthy survivor. Did it need any mechanical repair?"

"None at all. Only cleaning."

"And since the cargo was fully insured—by which I assume you mean overinsured—instead of taking a crippling loss the company made a handsome profit and was able to reequip its office at knockdown prices into the bargain. It leaves a few questions to be answered, doesn't it? Such as who started such a very convenient fire and who twisted the wrist of the port inspector?"

"There was one other question that had to be answered."

"Father," said Anna, "must you? It was horrible. Nothing was ever proved."

"The question," said Ermino steadily, "was a simple one. The American opposition could not so effectively have copied our exact products and timed their arrival in North Africa without inside information. In other words, they had planted a spy—two spies, to be exact—in our factory. They were identified. And when we came to work one morning we found them hanging by their heels from the arch at the main entrance. Their throats had been cut. They were not an attractive sight. We have had no spies planted among us since."

Anna still looked distressed. She said, "Was it necessary?

Industrial espionage is an offense punishable in our courts. The men should have had a chance to answer."

"And would have been found guilty. Possibly. And if found guilty, punished with a fine. That would not have stopped others from coming after them."

"It was effective, I agree. Maybe it saved us some money. But is money as important as human life? You were not happy about it yourself at the time."

"I was shocked, yes. Brutality is always shocking. But if espionage had been allowed to continue unchecked, we should always have been a few weeks or a few months behind our markets. At that time our future was in the balance. If we did not make profits, our masters in London would have closed us down. They have no moral attitude in the matter. To them profit is right and loss is wrong."

He sounded so angry that John guessed he was not really happy about it either. He realized, too, that it was an old argument between father and daughter and that he was expected to give his opinion.

He said, "I think the truth is that the people at the center are able to be ruthless because they do not see the results of what they do. They are like the generals in an old-fashioned war, tucked away in their châteaux, miles from the front line. If men get killed and wounded as a result of their orders, it does not disturb their sleep at night."

It was a sort of answer, but he knew that it did not satisfy either of them.

This was on a Saturday.

It was the beginning of a spell of better weather, a very late St. Martin's summer, a last moment before winter closed down. John spent some time after breakfast examining the family car, which had been proving difficult to start. In the end he decided that what it needed was a new coil. It was the turn of Ermino to drive the grandmother to church. John said, "When you get there, leave the car pointing downhill. Then you can start it with a push." Ermino looked doubtful but promised to try.

As soon as the churchgoers had departed, encouraged by

the sunshine, he resolved to carry out some repairs on himself. The plaster on his foot had served its purpose and was now doing more harm than good. It was time to remove it. He and Anna tackled the operation in the kitchen, using a saw-edged bread knife, a carving fork and a spatula. It took them half an hour to chip away the last of the plaster and unwind the bandages. John flexed his ankle cautiously. It seemed to be in working order. He sat on the table swinging his leg, while Anna swept up the pieces. He knew her well enough, by now, to know that she had something on her mind. He suspected that it arose from their conversation of the night before, and he was right.

She said, "You must understand that my father is in a most difficult position. He has to retain the confidence of his own people. I think that the women are more difficult than the men. They have friends who work in other parts of Italy. Some have relations who have gone to America. They hear from them about wages and conditions. They *know* they are underpaid. Of course, small pay is better than no pay at all, but they do not like the idea that the management is taking advantage of them. Do you understand?"

"Perfectly. It must make it very difficult for your father when he wants to get tough with the bosses."

"It is more difficult than you think, John. The man who had the job before him, Giovanni Segno his name was, he would have been described as a hard man. The management was not as firmly established at the start as it is now. He fought them all the way and won many concessions for the workers. Then, about two years ago, it came to the point when one side or other had to give way. Giovanni was quite determined that, if necessary, the men would strike. It was an important question about overtime rates. He was determined not to give way. But then, one morning, there was a change. Father was a member of the strike committee. In many ways he was acting as number two. He and the others were astonished. Giovanni Segno had now turned about. He was in favor of compromise. He would not advocate a strike. He preferred negotiation. When the others would not support him, he said, Very well, since I have lost your confidence I can no longer act as your leader. I suggest that Ermino Paoli take my place. And he walked out of the room."

"Awkward," said John. "Like a general quitting on the eve of battle. What did your father do?"

"He accepted the position, very reluctantly. Such things are much a matter of personalities. He was not, then, well known to the workers. He had not built up his position. He doubted whether they would follow him."

"So the strike fizzled out."

"What does that mean?"

"Like a firework that doesn't take off."

"Fizzled out. Right." He could see her making a note of this. "There was no strike. But that was not all. It came to light why Giovanni had changed his mind. He had been visited."

"Visited?"

"On the evening before, by two men. It was said that they came from Naples. They were with him for an hour."

"One hour's talk, to change the convictions of a lifetime. One wonders what arguments they used."

"It would not have been a threat to himself. Giovanni was not a coward. But—he had a family."

"So what happened then? Your father took over?"

"Gradually, yes. He had to proceed very carefully. He built up confidence and has gained a number of concessions. But I am not sure that he can continue much longer. The difficulties are now personal ones, in addition to all the others."

"Faldo?"

"That pig. Yes. Since he was released by the kidnappers he has started to think of himself as above the law."

"Mussolini, Julius Caesar and God Almighty," said John.

"Now things are coming to a crisis. Our new model, the Five fifty-five, it is a fine machine and they say it will make much money for us, but it has been expensive to produce. The men in London have been getting worried about the cost. I hear these things. You understand?"

John said, "I understand very well." He was thinking about his own early struggles. The phases of planning and de-signing; the machine tools, the jigs and the prototypes; money flowing out, nothing coming in. The solemn warnings from the bank. For one whole year his chief assistants had been on half pay and he had taken no pay at all, and this had just tipped the balance.

Anna said, "That is why the management is fighting so hard against the new pay scales which the union put forward. I am sure that Faldo's own future depends on this matter. If the new model fails, he goes down with it, and this time there will be no one to rescue him."

"And would you be sorry about that?"

"For myself, I would be very glad. He is an unpleasant man. For the company, I am not sure. I know many of the senior people. I cannot think of any one of them who could take his place. I suppose it's better to have an unpleasant man who makes things work than a pleasant one who lets things slide."

John was to remember that remark later.

It was soon clear that the removal of the plaster had been all that was necessary to restore the mobility of his ankle. He tried it out cautiously around the farm on the following day. To give it a real test, he decided to walk down the track that evening to meet the car. Sometimes Anna and her father came home together. On other occasions, when he had an evening meeting at the factory, Anna would come back alone. Giacomo, the father of the boys who worked on the farm, was a member of the committee and could be relied on to give him a lift back later.

The sky was clear. All the stars were showing, and there was a semicircle of new moon in the sky to the east. John walked cautiously and arrived at the foot of the track without so much as a twinge. When he got there he looked up the road for headlights. It was then that he noticed the car, drawn into the left-hand side, a few yards farther down.

He had never seen a car parked there before. It was a big, new-looking four-door model. As he moved toward it, he had an impression of some sudden violent movement inside the car. Then he heard the noise, halfway between a shout and a scream. He moved up quickly until he was level with the car on the near side. The two people in it were too busy with their own affairs to take any notice of him. He recognized the man from his photograph and went into action.

He opened the near side door, put one hand in, grabbed Faldo by the hair and banged his head twice, hard, on the steering wheel. Anna was holding together her dress, which had been torn down the front.

She said, "Have you killed him?"

John said, "I don't know and I don't care." He moved around to the other side of the car.

Anna said, "I tried to open the door, but it seems to be locked."

"It will be some sort of safety catch. Wind down the window."

He put in his hand, found the catch and released it. Then he got one arm around Anna and helped her out. She had started to say something when they heard another car coming. It swung around the corner and stopped with a jerk as its headlights lit up the scene ahead.

It was Giacomo, driving her father home. Both men jumped out.

Giacomo took a quick look at Anna and John, moved across to the other car and peered inside.

Anna said, "Is he dead?"

"He is still bleeding," said Giacomo indifferently. "He will no doubt come to his senses soon. He will have to explain away his face in the morning."

"He will make a great story of it," said Anna. She seemed to have recovered some of her composure. "It will have been another attempt to kidnap him. Valiantly repulsed by our hero."

"I will take you all up to the house in my car. What has happened to yours?"

"This evening, finally, it refused to start. All the late shift turned out to push it. No result at all. Then this pig offered me a lift. I could hardly say no with all those men listening."

Giacomo said, "I see." The rest of the story needed no embroidery. "Come along, all of you, then."

John noticed that the only person who had not spoken was Ermino. His face was white and set. When they had reached the farm and thanked Giacomo, he strode in ahead of them. Anna ran up to her bedroom to change her dress. As soon as they were alone, Ermino spoke.

He said, "That is enough. It is more than enough. I shall tell his superiors in London that Faldo must go."

"Will they listen to you?"

"If they do not remove him, I shall publish the truth about the S.S. *Lucania*. And certain other matters concerning the activities of the Mafia."

John said, "I see. Certainly they will have to pay attention to that."

Six

"If we learned one lesson from that cock-up in the Falklands," said Air Commodore Loveday, "it was that we *must* control our own defense technology."

"Agreed," said Brigadier Fildes. "And I've got Bob's proxy on that. We were all glad when you removed the last bits and pieces from the factory in the south of France, Tom."

"So was the government," said Tom. "Very glad." He was Sir Thomas Chervil. The fact that his colleagues on the board of Multinational Business Aids all called him Tom did not diminish the respect they felt for him. The easy and agreeable front was a by-product of Eton, a short service commission in the Irish Guards and diplomatic posts in the Middle East, but they knew that behind it was a framework of steel. You had only to bump into it once to recognize it. You took care not to repeat your mistake.

He said, "Jim and I finalized the arrangements last week. When I pointed out to the Ministry of Defence that all our hardware for the defense control systems and the nuclear plants was now being centralized in our new factory in Scotland, they stopped making difficulties about the modest grant we were asking for. Macintyre—he's the new Minister of State at the Scottish Office—told the Chancellor that if he didn't stop dithering he'd resign and publish the reason for it."

"Good show," said Loveday. "I was never easy about that stuff being in French hands. Even indirectly. Can't trust them. The next war, for all we know, they might be on the other side."

"It wouldn't be the first time we've fought them," agreed Fildes.

"I think the prospect of a war with France is fairly remote," said Chervil with a smile. "Almost as remote as the possibility of a war with Scotland."

"We might even have that," said Fildes. "If the more extreme Scottish Nationalists had their way."

"However," said Chervil, in a tone of voice that brought the board back to business, "we have to face the fact that the government grant, although it's very welcome, won't pay the whole bill. I think we shall have to go back to the public. I asked you to think about it, Mike."

Michael Hanna was the senior partner in Harriman, Hanna, the merchant bankers who advised MBA. He was a big man, in his middle sixties, the oldest of the seven men around the table. He said, "I have done so. Broadly, this is the position. Our four subsidiaries are all in balance, but they've none of them much to spare. Corsica is about the best. The French results have been affected by being forced to hand over a sizable part of their production to Scotland."

"And Scotland hasn't quite absorbed it yet," suggested Chervil.

"That's right. A case of financial indigestion. Temporary, we hope. That leaves Italy. Normally we'd be looking to them for help, but I understand there's been a bit of trouble."

"Potential rather than actual," said Chervil. "I hope to do something about it before it becomes serious. I shall be talking to Henry about it later today. It seems, then, that if we need immediate cash we shall have to look to the City."

"No great difficulty," said Hanna. "The institutions love us. We saw that when we had our first public issue two years ago. With only one bank debenture, and no loan stock, our loan–equity balance is remarkably favorable. I think we could arrange a fifteen-year bond at a coupon between six point six and six point seven."

"As low as that?" said the small coffee-colored black-haired man at the end of the table. This was Yussuf Benami, who represented the three Middle Eastern banks, all of which held substantial numbers of shares as nominees for their clients.

"I don't see why not," said Hanna.

"Might I remind you that the Finnish government had to offer seven point two one on a ten-year bond."

"No doubt, Ben. And Portugal, I seem to remember, had to make it seven point two four to attract any buyers. The fact is that the City seems to think we organize our finances better than most governments."

This produced a laugh.

"Right," said Chervil. "Let's have the details."

Hanna had opened a folder of papers, and Brigadier Fildes allowed his attention to wander. He had no head for figures and was prepared to leave them to people who understood them. His own field was the computerized control of weapons. Most of his recent service had been at the joint-service research stations at Chobham and Blandford Forum. In a number of projects he had worked with Loveday, who had been in charge of the air force establishment at Farnborough.

No question, the MBA board was a working board. Its members had not been selected for title or rank, but solely for the contribution each could make. The naval member, absent that morning, was Captain Bob Hunter, R.N., whose last active command had been a nuclear submarine. He had finished in charge of the closely guarded outfit on Loch Cree. The universities were represented by Professor Lampe from Cambridge, who was tall and thin and silent, and Dr. Brinsley Pope from Oxford, who talked a great deal. Much of what he said went over the Brigadier's head, but he had a fund of dirty stories that seemed even funnier when related in the doctor's clear and academic voice. Lampe was a mathematician. Pope was a physicist. On that occasion only Lampe was there.

A working board, thought Fildes. But not an executive board. When it came to the crunch, the decisions that mattered were made by Tom Chervil with Henry and Jim, the two friends who had helped him to set up MBA in the early seventies.

"Henry" was Henry Ligertwood, the only son of Abel

49

Ligertwood, founder of the Ligertwood Pharmaceutical empire. He and Tom Chervil had met when they were both subalterns in the Irish Guards. They had abandoned the army on the same day, Chervil to go into the Foreign Service, Ligertwood to join Wontners, the advertising firm. He had been made a director at the end of his first year with them and had left them three years later to found his own firm, taking some of Wontners' best clients with him.

"Jim" was James Ferrari. He was a different proposition altogether. At Winchester, a school that distrusts precocity, he had been recognized as a mathematical prodigy. At seventeen he won a top scholarship to Kings, took the highest honors in the mathematical tripos and was offered a Fellowship at the age of twenty-two. This was the turning point. Ahead of him beckoned the Sadleirian Professorship of Pure Mathematics and a life of academic distinction. Instead, he had turned to industry. After a spell with the English Electric subsidiary of Marconi, he had become head of research at the data processing wing of English Electric. In 1968, when English Electric were taken over by International Computers, he had left them and set up as an industrial consultant. One of his first clients had been Tom Chervil.

The City, which keeps a weather eye open for promising newcomers, had not been slow to recognize their potential. Chervil's drive and Middle East connections, Ligertwood's money and Ferrari's know-how made them a formidable combination. When they went to the public in 1982 with an issue of two billion twenty-penny shares the list was closed within thirty minutes, being so handsomely oversubscribed that the shares went to an immediate premium. Significantly, there were no speculators. It seemed that the purchasers of the shares intended, for the most part, to hold onto them.

As Fildes pointed out to Loveday, the board hadn't allowed this success to go to its head. They had rejected the offer of several steel and glass, fully air-conditioned suites of offices and had stayed in the old house in the quiet cul-de-sac behind the Minories which they shared with their accountants, Nussbaum, Lacey. The directors were discouraged from buying large cars with personalized number plates. "Can't park anything much bigger than a mini in London," said Chervil. "And the easiest way to get to the office is by underground." When they went abroad on company business they traveled economy class on short trips, first class only on longer ones. If their work could not be done in a five-day week, the weekend had to be sacrificed.

All this had been noted and was appreciated in a business community which still valued the puritan ethic of hard work.

When Hanna had finished talking and Benami had nodded agreement with his conclusions, Tom Chervil said, "Then we seem to have two options. A small issue, to supplement the government grant and pay for our immediate needs in Scotland, or an issue large enough to meet the preliminary costs of our next factory. That is, when we decide exactly where we're going to put it."

"We," in that context, thought Fildes, meant Chervil, Ligertwood and Ferrari.

Hanna said, "Why take two bites at the cherry?"

There was a murmur of agreement around the table. Chervil said, "I agree." He looked at the calendar. "There's going to be quite a bit of detail to work out. We're halfway through November now. And Christmas is a bad time for money raising. I think we'd better aim for the middle of February."

Professor Lampe, opening his mouth for the first time, said, "Why not Saint Valentine's day? Then we could decorate the offer document with hearts and arrows."

"Good idea," said Chervil. "February fourteenth."

As the meeting was breaking up, Fildes said to him, "I think you said there'd been some trouble in Italy. I've a cousin who's just joined the embassy at Rome as Trade Counselor. That's what they call him, but it isn't his real job, of course. He'd be glad to help if he could."

Chervil said, "Thank you, Frank. I'll bear it in mind. I don't think it's anything we can't handle. I'm going down this afternoon to talk to Henry about it."

When he went out of London he drove himself in his two-seater Lancia Spyder. He picked his way sedately through the traffic until he reached the M4 and then let the little car show its paces. The gatekeeper at the Laleham Sales Complex recognized it as it turned into the approach road and had the heavy steel and wire-mesh gate open by the time it arrived. In the courtyard inside there were a number of parking slots, most of them occupied. The gatekeeper said, "Mr. Pocock's away in North Africa."

Chervil said, "Thank you, Bob," and inserted his car into the space marked ADVERTISING DIRECTOR. The doorman, who had one arm and a row of campaign medals, had also seen him arrive. He had the main door open for him. Chervil said, "Good afternoon, Len. Is Mr. Ligertwood in the building?"

The doorman examined the two rows of numbered slots behind him. Some of them contained small personal bleepers. Most of them were empty.

"He's not in his office, but he's somewhere about. Will I give his secretary a ring? She'll know where to find him."

"You do that," said Chervil. "I'll go straight up."

His secretary must have moved with her accustomed speed and efficiency, because Henry Ligertwood was back in his third-floor office by the time Chervil reached it.

He was a heavy man, thick, with a suggestion that corpulence might not be far off. His face had a solemn, contemplative expression and might have belonged to a judge or a bishop. But it was not law or religion that had set the stamp on his face. He was preoccupied with money. He had been born with more money than most men acquire by the end of their lives, and he spent many of his waking hours in thinking how to protect and increase it.

He said, "Well, Tom, was it a good meeting?"

"Very fair," said Chervil. "I think we reached the right conclusion."

When he had finished, Ligertwood said, "I agree that we need new money if we're going to open a new factory. If we carry on as we are, we're in balance—just. Things aren't getting any easier. This place, for instance, cost fourteen point five percent more to run this year than it did last year."

"That's because you insist on having such a highly qualified staff."

Ligertwood accepted this as a compliment, not a criticism.

He said, "That's true. And the right sort of man is hard to get. Unless he is reasonably fluent in a couple of European languages and knows something about computers, we have to waste a year teaching him his job."

"I notice you talk about men. Have you thought about girls? They're often quicker at picking up a new technique. And some of them are frighteningly well educated."

"Girls!" said Ligertwood. "While they're in the place they make trouble. And if you happen to get a good one, what does she do? She goes off and has a baby."

"That's one of the things I came to talk to you about. Not about having a baby. About girls making trouble. I've had rather a disturbing report from Italy. I had an hour with Faldo on the telephone last night. When I explain what it's all about, you'll appreciate why it wasn't exactly the sort of thing he'd care to commit to paper."

He spoke for five minutes, making his points clearly, as though he were briefing a meeting rather than one man. Ligertwood listened almost impassively, although a close observer would have noticed the frown lines deepening between his eyes. When Chervil had finished, there was a moment of silence before Ligertwood spoke. "What's your opinion of Faldo? I think I only met him once."

"As a managing director or a man?"

"In the light of what you have just told me, I suppose we have to think of both aspects."

"As a man, I'm quite prepared to believe that he did what Paoli accuses him of. Hot-tempered, oversexed and arrogant. As a managing director, very nearly first class. Certainly the only man likely to produce the Five fifty-five as quickly as we want and at the price we want."

"If there is any delay and we lose the opening market, it will throw Italy out of balance for this year and maybe next year as well. That will be very serious for the group as a whole."

Chervil said, "Yes." Both faces were masks which concealed their thoughts.

Ligertwood said, "You met Paoli when you were in Italy

last year. Do you think he could be induced to be more reasonable?"

"Bought off, you mean?"

"Or persuaded in some way. I seem to remember that we had some success in that direction with the previous union convener. I've forgotten his name."

"Giovanni Segno. Yes. It's difficult to form an accurate judgment about a thing like that on the basis of a single meeting." He thought about it in silence for a full minute. It was the sort of decision he hated, but when it came to the crunch he was the only person who could make it.

He said, "If you want my honest opinion, Henry, I think that Paoli is made of harder stuff than Segno. And in this case there's an extra factor. His own daughter was involved. I can put it no higher than this: that I hope he will listen to reason."

"Let's both hope so," said Ligertwood. "Now, was there anything else? If not, I've got some North African sales figures I'd like to show you."

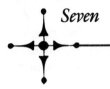

Seven

A new coil and a clean set of plugs had restored Anna's car to health, but Ermino would not let her drive in it alone. If a meeting kept him late at the factory, she waited for him and they came back together, often in convoy with Giacomo's car, for Ermino was taking no chances.

Faldo had said nothing to either of them. To anyone who inquired about the contused wound on the side of his face he had explained, briefly, that he had fallen and cut himself. The incident seemed closed.

At the farm, time began to hang heavily. The farm machinery was all in good order, and the late spell of fine weather had meant that most of the tidying up for the winter had been finished. Sometimes there was so little to do that the grandmother sent the two boys home at lunchtime.

Rather than remain idle, John now turned his attention to some of the pleas for help that reached him from neighboring farms. Walking enabled him to try out his ankle on longer and longer excursions. He visited farms as far afield as Caposele and Laviano and was made welcome everywhere. His host would usually insist on his joining the family for the evening meal and would follow this with an offer of a bed for the night. On the first occasion on which this happened, John had refused the offer, which meant he arrived back at the Paoli farm around midnight. He found that Ermino, not expecting him, had bolted and barred the door. The family slept on the far side of the house, with their bedroom windows tight shut. After ten minutes of fruitless knocking, knowing that all the ground-floor windows were barred, he had given up and spent the rest of the night in the hay barn.

His more usual plan now, while the weather remained kind, was to slip away from the farm he had been visiting in the cool dawn and watch the sun rising over the ramparts of the Apennines as he plodded back home.

Home?

It was true. More than once he had found himself expressing it in that way. He realized that the Paoli farm was becoming something very like a home to a man who had known no home of his own for twenty years.

It was going to be very difficult to tear himself away. He knew they liked having him there. Indeed, with the troubles that were brewing down at the factory his presence in the house was a comfort to all of them. Any decision about the future could be postponed until spring, but it would have to be made then.

On the last day of November he visited a farm on the other side of the valley. It belonged to a man called Otto Kurtz. Otto's father had been in the German army and his regiment had been stationed in that part of Italy and had taken part in resisting the Allied landing at Salerno in 1943. While there he had become friendly with an Italian girl and had come back after the war and married her. Otto was the only son and had inherited the farm. John and he sat up late after supper discussing these ancient battles. He wondered if his father and Otto's father had even met, but decided that it was unlikely.

Next morning he got up unusually early, packed his haversack and crept out of the house without disturbing his hosts, receiving only one friendly grumble from their guard dog. It was still dark when he reached the foot of the track that led up to the Paoli farm. The sky had clouded over during the night, and he was beginning to think that he would not see any sunrise when, as he turned the corner below the Valoris, he observed what seemed to him, for one shocking moment, to be the glow of the sun rising ahead of him.

He started to run.

As he passed the barn, Valori came hobbling out, grabbed him by the arm with surprising strength and dragged him inside.

He fought to free himself, but Valori clung to him like a limpet. He said, "Listen. Listen to me, please. Please listen."

John stopped struggling. He realized that he could not get free without hurting the old man. As his eyes grew accustomed to the darkness he noticed other things: the long form of Bruto, on a pile of hay, his legs dangling; the boy crouched over him.

Valori said, in an urgent whisper, "They came just after midnight, in two cars. When Bruto barked they broke his head with a hammer. They would have killed my boy too, only they considered him harmless and too frightened to move. They ordered him to stay in the barn. If they had not killed the dog maybe he would have obeyed them. But he summoned up the courage to follow, and he saw."

John could not have moved now, even if Valori had let him go. He knew what he was going to hear, and the realization sent shock waves through his body so sharp that they could be felt as a physical hurt.

"The boy saw it all. And he told me. They piled brushwood around the house, poured petrol on it and set fire to it. All inside must have been dead in minutes. Many hours afterward came the police. Too late, of course. They are up there now."

John could find no words. Valori had loosened his grip but still had one hand on his arm. He said, "You must go. Now. While it is still dark."

John stared at him.

"Don't you understand? Now, for a short time, while they think that you, too, were in the house, you have some safety. By the time the truth is discovered you must be far away. It is best that you go first to Genzano. He will advise you. But quickly, quickly."

"Go," said John stupidly. "How?"

"On my motorbicycle. How else? No time for talk. Come. Pray heaven we meet no one on the way down."

They met no one, either on the track or on the valley road. The dawn was coming up fast as they turned up toward the Genzano farm. The dogs had heard them and were giving tongue. It was Battista himself who swung open the gate in the palisade, gun in hand. They hurried John inside and shut the gate. A spate of hurried talk followed, of which John only heard an occasional word. Then Valori hobbled over and took him by the hand. He said, "I must be away. With luck I will be back before it is fully light. I must not be seen by anyone who will open his mouth. May God guard you and keep you."

John heard his motorcycle bucketing down the track. He stood there, listening, until the noise had died away in the distance. Genzano, who had been into the house, came out again. He said, "You are shivering. A ten-mile ride on the back of that old rattletrap will have been something of an ordeal. Come inside and warm yourself."

John was aware of his calmness and his strength and was grateful for it.

The fire in the kitchen had been rekindled. He found difficulty in walking. When he reached the fire, his knees buckled under him and he sank back into the chair beside it. Genzano went out and came back with a bottle and a full glass.

He said, "Drink this, but before you do, tell me one thing. It is very important. You spent last night at the Kurtz farm. Who were present?"

"Only Otto and his wife."

"They are both good people. They will not talk. All the same, I will get a message to them this morning. Did anyone see you going to their farm or coming away from it?"

John tried to think. He said. "I went there early in the morning, by hill paths, not by the main road. I met nobody, but I cannot tell whether I was seen or not. Coming back this morning it was dark, and I am certain no one saw me."

"Let us hope you are right. Now drink."

John gulped the fiery stuff down and felt it warming him. He had stopped shivering, and the drink and the warmth of the fire were making him so sleepy that he had difficulty in keeping his eyes open.

Genzano said, "I think it will be better if you sleep now."

When John got to his feet he was so unsteady that Genzano had to support him. He was aware that he was being taken to the bedroom he had occupied before, that his coat and his shoes were being pulled off and that he was being rolled onto the bed and covered with a blanket. He realized that there must have been something in the drink, and this was his last conscious thought as he sank down into a darkness which was first gray, then black.

When he woke and rolled over in the bed, he could see from the angle of the sun that it was late afternoon. He got out of bed. The dizziness had gone. His body was under control again, but his mind was still shaken. Sleep and the passage of time had moved the horrors of the previous night a small distance away from him. They were being edged farther away by different and colder thoughts.

First came simple thoughts of self-preservation. He realized the truth behind Genzano's words. If the least idea got about that he had not been in the farmhouse that night, they would be after him like a pack of hunting wolves.

But other thoughts were being added. Self-preservation was not an end in itself. There was, deep down in his mind, the seed of a more positive idea. He did not deceive himself into thinking that he could attack the Mafia singlehanded and obtain revenge for the obscene act of last night. Police forces and governments had tried and failed. But the Mafia, in this case, were only the hands. The brains, the people who had set them on, were in London. He might be able to attack them. If he could get there.

Genzano must have heard him moving, because he came in and seated himself on the end of the bed. He said, "I have sent word around. Mouths in this district will not be opened. But I cannot answer for people in other places. I have made a plan for you. You will have to decide whether you agree with it."

"I shall be unlikely to disagree," said John.

"It would be best if you crossed to the east coast. The Mafia is strong on the west coast. On the Adriatic side, less strong. It is to be remembered, too, that their members have ordinary occupations. They cannot, like the police, spend their time watching railways and airports. On the other hand, their intelligence system is good. Many people who are not active members will spy for them and carry messages."

59

"Then it would be safe for me to take a train when I reach the east coast?"

"Safer, yes. But not south of Termoli. In a direct line from here that is, let us say, a hundred kilometers. By the paths in the mountains which you would take, perhaps a hundred and fifty. You should be able to cover that distance in five or six days, perhaps a little more."

"Yes, I ought to be able to manage that."

"I am afraid we have seen the last of the good weather. You will need to be properly equipped." He went out and came back carrying a heavy coat with a hood. He said, "This is what our shepherds wear in the mountains. It is waterproof and it will keep you warm. Have you money?"

"That's one thing I have plenty of," said John. He had traveler's checks, as yet unused, some large-denomination Italian notes and a stock of American dollars all stowed away in his money belt.

"Good," said Genzano. "You will have to be careful about crossing main roads, in particular the autostrada between Naples and Bari. I suggest that you time your journey to reach it in the dark, in the very early morning. That would be on your second day from here."

"I do not know how I can begin to thank you for what you are doing."

"Then do not try to do so," said Genzano with an unusually human smile. "I will get some food packed up and will wake you at four o'clock tomorrow. You will then be safely up in the mountains before it is light."

The first part of the walk went according to plan. He was able to map his progress because he was following, in reverse, his journey down, and he found lodging at farms he had visited. His hosts were, as usual, too polite to ask any embarrassing questions, but the man in the second farm said something that made him think. It seemed that the police had been inquiring about foreigners walking in the mountains.

"It was the sergeant of carabinieri, from Carile," explained his host. "He is a man I should advise you to avoid."

John remembered that a similar comment had been made to him by his drinking companion at San Vito. He had not paid much attention to it at the time, but now he listened carefully.

He said, "Was the inquiry directed to any particular point? For instance, was it specifically an Englishman they were looking out for?"

The farmer was not certain. He had got the news at second hand. But he approved of John's intention of leaving very early.

"In an hour's walk," he said, "you will reach the autostrada. It will still be dark, but you will have to cross it carefully."

John promised to be very careful and managed to cross without difficulty. Thereafter he found himself in a wilder and more desolate countryside than any he had encountered before, rock and shale underfoot, a few straggling trees and a thick thorny undergrowth, like the Corsican maquis that he had met with on one of the few short walking holidays that had taken him abroad.

This desolation was an advantage in one way, since it lessened the chance of undesirable encounters, but he foresaw difficulties about his lodging for the night. To find a farm would mean descending from the high land into one of the valleys, and he was unwilling to do this for a number of reasons, the most pressing being that it would involve a climb up again on the following morning. He was beginning to realize that he would have to conserve his strength.

At the end of the third day he found shelter in a sort of cabin built by shepherds. Its walls of thatched hay and small branches might have been some protection in summer, but they were no real barrier to the wind that was now blowing steadily from the northeast.

He was woken more than once by fits of shivering and was glad to move on in the morning. He still had some of the provisions Genzano had supplied, but he had little appetite for them.

That was a difficult day. His left leg had started to ache and he decided that this was because he was going against the grain of the country, neither straight up nor straight down but along the sides of steep slopes. Countryfolk, he remembered, maintained that the legs of the badger were longer on one side than the other, and mountaineers who were forced to walk along mountainsides were described as badger-legged. He pursued the idea for some minutes and concluded that it would only help if you always went around a mountain in the same direction.

Thoughts like this were a distraction. They drove out other, darker, thoughts.

That night he found refuge in the poorest and most tumbledown farm he had yet encountered. Its occupants were an old man and an even older woman. They were, at first, unwilling to take him in and it was only after some hard talking and the promise of money that they agreed to let him stop. He spent a few unrestful hours on a sofa in their downstairs room. The old couple made up the fire before they retired to their room in the attic and this meant that he did at least start the night warm, but he was shivering again long before it was time to force his weary body to rise.

Early though it was, the old man was up too. He looked out of the door into the darkness and grunted out a single word. It sounded like a warning. John joined him and saw the thin flakes of snow drifting down.

The prospect was not encouraging. He knew that he was approaching the bleak highlands of the Monti della Daunia. Had he been fit and the weather fine, the crossing would have been nothing and he would have been down in the coastal belt by evening. In present conditions it would take him all of two days, and he would be lucky to find any shelter at all for the intervening night.

In the end it was the miserable nature of the hovel he was in and the evident anxiety of his host to get rid of him that made his mind up for him. The old man had rekindled the fire and put a saucepan of milk on it. John accepted a cupful of the lukewarm fluid, paid the stipulated price, put on his heavy coat, slung his haversack over one shoulder and hobbled out into the darkness.

At the moment the snow was falling lightly and was not settling. It was more an irritation than a hindrance, and since it was blowing straight into his face was even helpful. It was a northeast wind, and he had only to head into it to maintain the axis of his advance.

That was a day without time or space. It telescoped into one continuous ordeal, a single struggle against the snow, which thickened as the day went on; against the cold, which grew more intense as he climbed; against the pain in his left leg and left hip; against the perversity of paths that never seemed to lead in the right direction.

He knew now that he was sick. The shivering had started again, but it was alternating with moments when his face seemed to be on fire and he felt an urge to throw off his heavy coat to cool his aching body.

In a moment of clarity he realized that the shocks of the last few days must have slowed his reactions and dulled his sensibilities. If he had been thinking normally he would never have started out that morning. The old man had clearly thought that he was mad.

Perhaps he was mad. Mad or sane, it seemed likely that he would die in these inhospitable mountains, and the idea troubled him very little.

The day had brightened slightly toward noon. Now the light was fading and the snow was thickening. It was forming lumps on his chest and his thighs, lumps he could not shake off and which froze where they lay.

He wondered how much longer he could keep going and started to argue with himself about it. Ten minutes? More than that, surely. Fifteen minutes? Half an hour? Two things were helping him. He was on a path that ran through thicker woods than he had seen all day, and the trees on either side were breaking the force of the snow. Also the path was going, for once, in the right direction and was going downhill. He quickened his pace until it was near to a shambling run.

Then, suddenly, he checked.

Some way ahead of him, glimpsed through the veil of snow, something had flitted across the path. It was an animal, and he had an instant conviction that he knew what it was. It was a wolf. He had been told that wolves still existed in the remote wooded valleys between the mountain crests. Normally they were cowardly creatures, preferring to keep out of sight of man, but cold and starvation would drive them to attack. He doubted whether he could put up much of a fight, but decided that the only tactic was to put on a bold front.

He started to move forward. The great gray beast in front of him, now clearly seen, ran ahead of him. It seemed to be behaving curiously. If John stopped, the wolf stopped too and waited. When he went on, it ran ahead again. It seemed to be leading him rather than attacking him.

Perhaps it was a friend. What had old Valori said? "The blessed Saint Francis spoke to them as brothers, and they did not try to harm him."

The path underfoot had improved. It felt more like a roughly paved road, so closely wooded overhead that it was almost a tunnel. The downhill slope was increasing. As he rounded a corner he saw ahead of him the dark loom of a building. There was an open archway, and beyond it were lights.

The animal had run through the archway and was clearly expecting him to follow. He stumbled forward and found himself in a courtyard, lit by an overhead lantern. The animal, now seen to be a big gray dog with a pointed nose, gave a sharp bark. The door at the far end of the courtyard opened and a cowled figure came out, took one look at John, then turned back and shouted. Other figures appeared, seized him by the arms and led him forward down a stone-flagged passage and into a large empty room where a fire blazed on the hearth.

John knew that his senses were leaving him. He knew that he was sick. He also knew that he was safe and that tears were running down his face. He was conscious of very little more until he found himself stripped of his clothing and in bed, under a pile of blankets, with a stone hot-water bottle at his feet.

He had a last curious thought. He had come very close to death. Had he, in reality, died? Was this what death was, a coming out of darkness and cold and misery into warmth and light? It was a plausible idea. The only thing against it was that he doubted whether they had hot-water bottles in heaven.

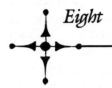

Eight

The next chapter in John's life was confused. There were more illustrations in it than words. There was a bright square of light, which dominated one aspect, and a yellow eye, which looked at him out of the darkness. And there were faces.

One of them, which seemed to come and go regularly, was a long brown whimsical face with a twisted nose leading down to a pointed chin. He had some difficulty in bringing it into focus, and often by the time he had made the effort the face had disappeared. He grew to connect its appearances with an increase of warmth, but his mind was not functioning with sufficient clarity for him to work out that it was the hot-water bottle that was being renewed.

The other face was different. It was paler and more serious. Its visits were fewer and seemed, therefore, to be important. John wished that he could have sat up in bed and engaged in conversation, but the effort was beyond him. His eyesight was improving and he contrived to view this second head from both sides. On the front there was a fringe of beard, black but going gray. On the back a round bald patch surrounded by a tonsure of hair. What troubled him was that he was not quite sure that they belonged to the same man. Perhaps there were two of them, one with a beard and one with a bald head; one whom he saw coming, the other going. How could he possibly tell?

Between these glimpses of a real world he was down, deep down, in black and suffocating night. Black, but not totally black, because in the distance a light was flickering: the light of a fire.

Such a sight should have been comforting, suggesting warmth in the cold and light in the darkness. It was none of these things. It was horrible. It was something he was forbidden to look at. Something he must on no account look at, because if he looked, the fire did not stay where it was but started to come closer until he could feel the heat of it on his face, hear the crackling of the flames and smell the rancid tang of petrol.

Then he opened his mouth to scream, but he had the illusion that no sound was coming out. Perhaps he was wrong about this, because there was a hand with a cloth that wiped away the sweat on his forehead and a voice that murmured something which was comforting and allowed the fire to die away again into the distance.

The relief, when it came to him, came as suddenly as it does to any prisoner who wakes one morning and is told that his imprisonment is over. With some difficulty he pulled himself up onto his elbows and looked around.

He was in a small square room with whitewashed walls. The only furniture was the iron bedstead, on which he was swaddled in a nest of coarse gray blankets, a bedside table and a wooden chest, on top of which he could see his haversack, his clothing and his money belt. He then realized for the first time that he was wearing a white woolen nightgown.

This amused him, for some reason, and he started to laugh but soon stopped. It brought on a pain down his left side that made laughing uncomfortable.

There was a single window in the wall opposite the foot of his bed. It was too high for him to see anything through it except the sky, which was of a blue so brilliant that it seemed to burn. This must be the square light he had seen. The yellow eye was the lamp on the bedside table.

One light by day, one by night. How many days and how many nights?

It did not seem to be a matter of great importance. There had been men who had visited him. Sooner or later one of them would come back and he could ask questions. He turned over onto his right side, carefully so as not to aggravate the pain he could feel in his left leg and hip, and fell into a deep sleep. This time it was a sleep with no dreams in it.

An indeterminate time later he was waked by the click of the door. It was the brown-faced man. He smiled when he saw that John was awake and came over and laid a hand on his forehead.

"Good," he said. "That is very good. The fever has gone. Soon you will be quite well."

"I hope so," said John. "How long have I been here?"

"Today is Friday. It was Tuesday night when Paulo brought you in out of the snow."

Three days. The long dark night could have been three weeks or three months. He said, "Who is Paulo? Is that your dog? I thought he was a wolf."

"You must not tell him so. He is a sensitive animal. He would be most upset."

"That must be avoided at all costs. Can you tell me where I am, please?"

"You are in the Monastery of Our Blessed Lady of Montagnola. We are an eremitical order, but it is our duty to care for travelers. Not only our duty," he added, with a smile which lit up his face, "but our pleasure."

"How can I thank you?"

"No thanks are needed."

"I remember your face in my dreams—nightmares, rather. You came often to visit me."

"Our Father Prior has placed you under my special care. I am Brother Bastien."

"There was another. He had a grizzled beard and a bald head. Or am I confusing two different people?"

"Two people, yes. The bald-headed one was certainly our Prior. The grizzled beard belonged to Brother Hilarion, our infirmarian. It was on his advice that we left nature to perform its own cure. He diagnosed your condition as mountain sickness. That is not a scientific term, but it is something we see much of. Also he said he could detect that your leg was troubling you."

"It's my left leg. Not long ago I slipped—"

Not long ago. As it came back to him, John was unable to continue for nearly a minute. Brother Bastien watched him sympathetically. When he was able to speak:

"I strained what they call the Achilles tendon, in my right ankle. When I was walking in the mountains I imagine that I constantly favored my right leg at the expense of my left, and in the end this put too much strain on my left hip."

"It could well be so. Our bodies are all one piece. If we cosset one part we abuse another."

There was something in Brother Bastien's voice, an emphasis on the final syllable of words, which led John to say, "Would I be wrong if I guessed that you were French? Your name, too—"

"You have guessed correctly. Like our Father Prior, I came from France. In my case, from near the Belgian border. It was a Calvinist district. When I reached the age of twenty-one I decided to take the road to Rome."

"You speak figuratively?"

"Literally and figuratively. I set out to travel to the eternal city with great faith and little money. When I reached this part of Italy, I, like you, was trapped by a snowstorm and was taken in. That was twenty years ago."

"And you went no farther?"

"There seemed small reason to do so. Many people who come here for a night remain for the rest of their lives. Our Prior, who has been here for more than forty years, will tell you of an Englishman, a prisoner of war in one of the camps in the north. After the armistice of 1943 he was making his way south to rejoin his own troops. He was given hospitality, as were many fugitives in those unhappy times. He, too, stayed here for the rest of his life. The Prior—not our present one, but his predecessor—was told his name, but to us he was Brother Ignatius. I believe he was quite a senior officer. The novices sometimes called him Brother Pugnacious."

Bastien laughed at this simple joke and John joined in, somewhat at the expense of his left side.

"But enough talk. You will be hungry. You have taken

nothing but a little water for the last three days. Brother Hilarion has prescribed broth."

"Ask him when I can get up."

"Certainly. But even if you got up you could not go very far."

"You mean because of my leg."

"Because of that. But also because it stopped snowing only this morning. All roads and tracks are two meters or more under snow. It does not trouble us. We supply our own needs."

On the following morning, when John was sitting up in bed propped by pillows and feeling much better, the Prior came. John had previously only seen the back of his head and now studied his face with interest. The forehead was broad, the eyes deep-set, the chin broad and firm without fleshiness. It was the face, he thought, of a man who devoted time to study but was also accustomed to the exercise of authority.

He said, "I understand from Brother Bastien that you speak excellent Italian but are, in fact, an Englishman."

"Not an Englishman, Father. Though long resident in that country. I come from New Zealand."

"You are a long way from home."

"Indeed," said John sadly, "and progressing away from it rather than toward it."

"I understand that you were caught in the mountains by our first snowstorm of this year. Had you not fallen in with Paulo you might have progressed into another world altogether."

He said this in the offhand manner of a man who could contemplate such a journey without great interest and with no trepidation.

"I might easily have done so," agreed John, "and I am more than grateful—"

"You need not be. As Brother Bastien will have told you, it is our pleasure to succor all travelers. You appreciate, of course, that we are an eremitical order, not a closed community."

"I'm afraid that I understand little of such matters."

"We are not perhaps as well known as the Benedictine and

Cistercian orders, but we are older than both. Our founder was Saint Pachomius. His teaching was based on the virtues of study and meditation, combined with manual labor. We see no particular value in austerity for its own sake. The cell which each brother lives in can be made as comfortable, within reason, as he desires. He has books and journals. The typewriter has replaced the quill pen. Even tape recorders are not frowned on. Much scholarly work has been done here. A work produced by two of our brothers on the sources of Dante had the honor of being translated into nine European languages and became what might be described as a scholastic best-seller. The fruits of this enterprise went to the adornment of our chapel. We do not share the Cistercian distrust of beauty, either."

"And your community lives on the money that such books earn for it?"

"We could hardly subsist on the fruits of scholarship alone. The rule of Saint Pachomius was clear on this matter. Each man works at what suits his capabilities. We have carpenters, weavers, tailors, workers in metal and stone. All good of their kind. Perhaps the product of our labors that is best known to the outside world"—the Prior here smiled for the first time—"is the Saint-Pachomius goat cheese. We make it from the milk of our own flocks. In restaurants on the east coast you will find that it rivals even Saint-Nectaire and Saint-Albray. And speaking of food, here comes your supper."

That night John lay in bed cocooned in his blankets, watching the procession of the stars and undesirous of sleep. He was wondering who the British officer might have been who had come for one night and stayed for the rest of his life. He visualized him as a brigadier with a fiery face and a regular-army mustache. Brother Pugnacious. He laughed to himself and found, this time, that he could do so without sending a twinge of pain down his left side. He was recovering fast. When the time came to go, would he too change his mind and himself ask for sanctuary? The temptation was unquestionable. It would mean abandoning certain plans, but were those plans as compulsive as he had thought? Sleep came before he could arrive at an answer.

Some hundred kilometers to the southwest of where John lay, three men were seated in the living room of a penthouse flat in a high-rise development in the Pozzuoli suburb of Naples. All of them had the black hair, brown-black eyes and olive-tinted complexions which marked them as south Italians. Two of them were small and dapper. They were Sicilians from the Trapani peninsula at the western tip of the island. The third was from Cosenza, in Calabria. He was a big man for an Italian, equal in bulk to the other two men together, not grossly fat, but large in every particular. From the way he spoke and the way he was spoken to, he was clearly the leader.

He said, "It has taken us some time to arrive at the truth, but the official report of the Naples pathologist, which I have now seen, confirms what we suspected even from the first night. There were three people only in the house: the girl, her father and her grandmother. The Englishman was not there. We encountered a strange and unusual conspiracy of silence about him. It has taken some time to penetrate."

He paused, and one of the younger men offered him a cigarette. The second lit it for him.

"We have, however, learned one significant fact. He was in the habit of visiting neighboring farms. He would stop for one night or even longer while he did mechanical work for his hosts. It therefore seems quite possible that he was away from the farmhouse when it was burned."

"And has now left the country," suggested one of the young men.

"It could be," said the big man. "If he wasted no time and took a train directly to Rome or Pisa and flew from there he could have been out of the country within twenty-four hours and we should have been no wiser. Every day after that it would have become more difficult. We had by that time a name and a passable description. There are, as you know, people who watch for us at airports and other points of departure. The word went around very fast."

He had got up from his seat at the table. The room had been designed as a studio and had a single window which filled most of the northern wall of the room. From it you could see across the flat coastal strip, where the Volturno River snakes its way out to sea right up to the foothills of the Apennines dominated by the peak of Monte Maggiore. The big man stared out for a long minute at the rolling line of snow-covered mountains etched against the blue of the sky. "I feel it," he said, softly. "I am sure of it. He is somewhere out there."

When he was allowed to leave his bed, John set about getting his body back into order. It irked him that he should have been unable to stand up to five or six days of walking over country that, if not easy, had certainly not been difficult in any sense in which a mountaineer would have understood the term.

He thought back to the days when he had been preparing for the inter-university sports. He had devised for himself a system of eurhythmics, based on the standard Mullers exercises, but with variations and improvements designed particularly for strengthening the leg muscles. He now started them cautiously and by the end of the first week was putting in an hour every morning. He was glad to find that the tendons in his right heel had suffered no permanent damage, while the muscles of his left leg soon came back into line.

On one occasion Brother Bastien came in and found him flat on his face on the floor. John said, "It's all right. I'm not having a fit. Just exercising."

"I am glad to hear it. I have a message for you from our Prior. He hopes that now that you are active you will consider yourself free to use his study whenever you wish."

John drew his legs under him, raising his torso into a horizontal position without support, and said, "It is very good of him. I shall be delighted to take him at his word." Clasping his arms behind his back, he lowered his head several times toward the ground. "This is good for the thigh muscles and the stomach." Bastien watched him with interest.

"Truly," he observed, "every man says his prayers in his own way."

The eremitical regime of the monastery, though relaxed in some respects from the strict rule of Saint Pachomius, did mean that the brothers spent most of the day shut away in their own rooms. They emerged for the midday and evening meals, which were taken in silence, and for the various services in the chapel. There was no form of common room or communal apartment. John was therefore very grateful to the Prior for his concession, particularly since, in the mornings and in the early part of the afternoons, the Prior was busy about his administrative duties and this gave him the uninterrupted use of a room that was part study and part library. He spent some time dipping into the books which filled the shelves on three sides of the room.

He discovered that there were more books in French and German than in Italian. He mentioned this in the course of the evening discussion with the Prior which had become an agreeable part of his daily program.

"Like Brother Bastien," said the Prior, "I am not a native of this country. I was born and brought up in a small village in the southern Ardennes, what we called the Forest of the Argonne. My family was Catholic, as were all our friends. Long ago though it was, I still retain vivid memories of our daily life. The social part of it centered around the evening meal and the coffee drinking."

"Coffee drinking?"

"With our people it was a ceremonial. You might almost have described it as a ritual. During the course of the evening ten cups were drunk. Each one had its particular name. The first was simply Café. Then came Gloria, Pousse-café, Goutte, Regoutte, Surgoutte, Rincette, Rerincette and finally, before bed, the Coup de l'Etrier."

John, who had been keeping a tally, said, "That's only nine."

The Prior looked worried. His lips moved as he repeated the names to himself. Then he said, "Did I mention Surrincette?"

"No, I don't think you did."

The Prior was relieved. "Then that makes ten. I should not like to think my memory was failing. The brain, like the body, will only retain its powers if it is kept active. You agree with that, I am sure. Brother Bastien tells me that you exercise ferociously."

"I should like to do something a little more constructive as well. I am told that each of the brothers pursues his own special bent. But they wouldn't want any assistance from me, I'm sure."

"You are right," said the Prior, "but since you will not, I hope, be thinking of leaving us for some time, why should you not undertake a project of your own? I notice that your French is almost as good as your Italian. Is there not some particular branch of study"—he indicated the rows of books around them—"which you would care to pursue?"

"I'm afraid that the only thing I really know anything about is the theory and practice of computers."

"It is interesting you should say that." The Prior rose to his feet and after some research brought down a book with yellowing leaves strapped and bound in boards. It was in French and turned out to be a collection of essays by a group who called themselves La Confrérie des Étudiants de la Philosophie et de la Mathématique.

"Published in Paris," said the Prior, "not dated, but of the early eighteenth century, I would judge." He was turning the pages as he spoke. "That is the one I had in mind. It is a study of the Hisab Hindi, the best-known work of the Arabian mathematician Al-Huwarizmi. It is clear that he understood the theory of binary mathematics, and he constructed a machine—there is the picture of it—by which calculations could be made and information retrieved."

"Good heavens!" said John. "The great-great-grandfather of all computers. Fascinating. I shall commence my studies tomorrow."

Next morning he discovered a more practical use for his skills. As he was leaving his room, on his way to the Prior's study, he heard a sound which was unusual in that placid place, the sound of a voice raised in reproof. John went out into the courtyard to see what was happening. Here he found the gatekeeper, a surly lay brother, speaking his mind to a nervous-looking youth whom John took to be one of the novices. Brother Bastien was attempting to pour oil on the troubled waters.

"You call yourself an expert mechanic, a chauffeur, a man with a knowledge of motorcars and now it appears—hah!—that you cannot even start this useful vehicle."

The useful vehicle was standing in a part of the courtyard that had been cleared of snow. It was a nice old Morris 1000 Traveller, perhaps fifteen years old, which had been maintained in spotless condition. The novice, whose ewe lamb it evidently was, was almost in tears.

"Of what use," continued the gatekeeper, throwing his arms in the air, "to tell us that the key is somewhere. Perhaps you dropped it! Then perhaps you will remove all the rest of the snow in the courtyard and discover it again."

"The good Lord will remove the snow in due course," said Brother Bastien. "Then, no doubt, the key will come to light."

"No doubt," said the gatekeeper. "And suppose, as is most possible, that our Father Prior requires the use of the car *before* all the snow is gone? Perhaps"—he turned to the novice—"if you prayed hard enough, the good Lord would provide a spare key, which is something you should certainly have had."

"Excuse me for interrupting," said John, "but do I gather that all that is needed is a method of starting the car?"

"If it could be started," said the novice, "I could drive it to Termoli. The garage there could certainly provide or cut a key for me."

"If that's all," said John, "your problem is easily solved." He went to his room and came back with the haversack which had accompanied all his wanderings.

"If you will open the bonnet. All that is required is this useful length of flex, bared at both ends, which I keep handy for such contingencies. I will now show you how unscrupulous persons help themselves to other people's cars. Particularly older cars, which have no steering lock."

He prodded one of the ends of the flex into the hole in the live terminal of the battery and fastened the other to the coil. Then he took out a small screwdriver and laid the metal shaft across the terminals of the solenoid. The engine sprang to life and remained ticking over happily when the screwdriver was removed.

John listened to the engine and then said, "Clearly a very well-maintained machine."

The young novice blushed, the gatekeeper looked provoked and Brother Bastien said, "You have performed a miracle."

That evening the Prior said, "Your fame is established. Although I am not certain whether it is fame as a mender or a stealer of cars."

"Brother Furacious," suggested John. "Do you realize that I might in fact be a car thief on the run, that I might be anything at all? No one has expressed the slightest interest in what I was doing wandering in the Molise mountains in the dead of winter."

"It was none of our business."

"Nevertheless, Father, with your permission I will try to tell you. It will be a comfort to me if I can manage to do so."

"If it will be a comfort to you."

Having made the offer, John wondered if he could go through with it. To make it easier, he started at the very beginning, with his arrival in Italy, his wanderings in the mountains—so long ago that they seemed to be almost a matter of prehistory—his arrival at the Paoli farm and what had happened there. He repeated what he had learned about the troubles at MBA and the activities of Sergio Faldo. He did not omit Anna's estimate of Sergio as an unpleasant man but the only one likely to put through their production program. He was quite frank about his feelings for Anna. When he had finished there was a long silence. He wondered what the Prior would say. When he did speak, it was a surprise.

He said, "How many people work in this factory?"

"I'm not sure. I think I was told about six hundred. Two thirds of them girls and women."

When the Prior had absorbed this information, he said, "Three foreign enterprises have been set up recently in this part of Italy. Two of them were concerned with the recovery of methane and propane gas. One of them manufactured a new type of plastic. All three had one thing in common. They all failed. With a loss of several hundred promised jobs."

John said, trying to keep the anger out of his voice, "Are you trying to tell me, Father, that what Faldo did was justified if it secured the continuing prosperity of the factory?"

The Prior smiled. "I had thought that your scientific training would have made such a question unnecessary. All coins have two sides. I was seeking to examine the other side of this particular coin. No, I do not hold to the philosophy that the end justifies the means. Evil can only, in the long run, produce evil. But, I emphasize, in the long run. The immediate results may appear to be good. You may have to wait for a very long time indeed before the evil flowers and the poisoned fruits appear."

"But they appear in the end?"

"Certainly. The patience of God always outlasts the impatience of man."

John could think of nothing to say to that. It was the Prior who broke the silence. He said, "What do you propose to do?"

What *did* he propose to do? When all the thinking and the talking was done, when right had been weighed against wrong and both had been weighed against expediency, it still left unanswered the only question that mattered.

"Whatever you do, I trust that you will not yourself go outside the law. That would not only be morally wrong, it would be worse. It would be stupid."

John said, speaking slowly to allow his words to catch up with his thoughts, "I shall go to the headquarters in London and do my best to get Faldo removed and punished."

"And if you find that the management in London approves of what he did? May even have arranged it themselves?"

"Then I shall have to tackle the management. It will not be easy. But I have one advantage. I know a good deal about their company."

"And you think you can attack them—legally?"

"I shall have to move very carefully. First, I will have to find out more about them."

"The first thing you will have to do," said the Prior soberly, "is to get out of Italy."

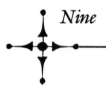

Nine

This was the subject matter of many evening meetings in front of the log fire in the Prior's study. Outside the monastery walls, further snowstorms swept across the Molise mountains, blocking roads and deepening drifts, until at last, with the arrival of March, the snow started to disappear and spring began, cautiously, to work its old magic.

"Like a man getting out of bed," said John. "He pokes his nose out from the blankets, decides it's too cold and disappears under the bedclothes again."

"By the end of March," said the Prior, "I would anticipate that most of the snow will be gone. April is a lovely month in these mountains. A warm wind comes up from the south, bringing with it the first whisper of summer. Before the end of April, I fear you will have to make your mind up."

They had come to know each other so well that John had no need to ask him what he meant.

"It is true," he said. "I had thought of staying. But a task has been given to me. I cannot shirk it."

"Perhaps you will come back here, when you have done what you have to do. For the moment, let us be practical. I have been giving thought to your problem. Ideally you should leave the country as unobtrusively as you came into it. If you had the equipment and the skill it might be better to cross the Alpine barrier and make for Switzerland or Austria. But this would mean avoiding the known passes and taking a mountaineer's route."

"I have done a little rock climbing, but I've no real experience of snow and ice."

"As I feared. Then it will be necessary to make for France. The first part of the journey will be simple enough. You follow the backbone of the mountain range, first northward, then to the west as you approach the plain of Lombardy and the valley of the Po. It would be better to stay always a little way down on the eastern side of the highest parts. You will find no lack of small hill farms that will give you a night's lodging. And in one particular I can help you. There is a companion house of our order above the Borgo Val di Taro. I will give you letters to Prior Paul which will assure you of a welcome, also of discretion, which will be very important, since you will be approaching the most difficult stage in your journey."

The Prior's own map underlined the point. The Apennine range, that safe corridor for fugitives, started to swing to the west at Ancona and was running due west by the time it reached Piacenza. After Asti it turned to the south and became steeper and narrower.

"At that point," said the Prior, "you enter the Alpi Marittime. You will be approaching the French frontier, and you will have to proceed with the greatest possible care. You will observe how the run of the mountains drives you down toward the sea."

It was all too clear. The coastal plain, which clung to the foot of the mountains, was here little more than a mile wide, and it was along this narrow strip that the great roads and the railway ran to Monaco and Nice and the resorts of the French Riviera. It was at this point that the opposition, if it was still looking for him, would be concentrated. It was the mouth of the trap.

"To keep clear of the coastal strip," said John, "I shall have to do some scrambling."

"I admire your choice of words," said the Prior. "But a cross-country route at this point will involve more than scrambling. It is true that there is nothing there to match the giants of the Swiss Alps, but the Costa Rossa and the Cima d'Argentara are considerable peaks and will still be snow-covered. It would be wise not to go too far north."

"I think," said John with a smile, "that it will be, as the lawyers say, a matter of *solvitur ambulando*."

He left the monastery on the first day of May. All his efforts to get the monks to accept payment for their hospitality had been met with a placid refusal. He reflected that he could always send them an anonymous gift. They might suspect that it came from him but could hardly return it since, by that time, they would have no notion where he would be. Come to think of it, he had only the vaguest notion himself.

For the first fortnight of his travels he drove himself hard, covering greater and greater distances each day, along the mountain trails and footpaths of the high Apennines. Partly this was from anxiety to reach the frontier, but there was another reason for forcing the pace, a reason he hardly admitted to himself.

During the last part of his stay at Montagnola he had started dreaming about Anna. He wondered whether his talks with the Prior might have brought this about by unlocking certain inhibitions. Whatever the cause, he wished it had not happened. Sometimes he saw her as she had first appeared to him, in the freshness of a Renaissance dawn; at other times more prosaically, around the farm or driving in the car. But always he was aware that he must keep away from her. He half realized that it was a dream, but he knew, too, that if he dreamed too long something unimaginably horrible was going to happen and he would be forced to witness it. So far, the thought of this had been sufficient to wrench him back to consciousness at the moment of crisis, with his heart thudding and the sweat pouring down his face. It was for this reason that he sought to tire himself out, hoping that physical fatigue would bring the oblivion he wanted. Often he was successful, but not always.

Daytime was agreeable. He was moving along a clearly defined watershed. So much so that on one occasion he found himself within less than a mile of the headwaters of the Ronco, which ran down to the Adriatic, and of the Arno, which reached the Mediterranean at Pisa. The sun shone, the air of May was fresh and he took pleasure in his renewed strength and the almost unfailing kindness he received from his hosts each evening.

On the evening of the sixteenth day, he reached the monastery above Borgo Val di Taro. When Prior Paul had digested the letter which John handed to him, he pursed his lips.

He said, "I am bidden not to inquire why you wish to pass into France by an unusual route but am assured that your motives for doing so are personal to you and not improper. I have to warn you that your route will not be a simple one. From this point onward you will be walking, as it were, on a tightrope. One thing you will not be troubled by is river crossings. The rivers here, for the most part, run northward into the Lombardy valley. But if you desire to avoid attention you will have to be very careful when crossing roads. Three, in particular. There is the A Seven, which is the main Genova–Milano highway, and the A Twenty-six, which runs north, through the mountains, to Alessandria and Aosta. A short distance after that there is the A Six from Savona to Torino. All these will need great care."

"It would be better to cross them after dark, you think?"

"Certainly. I should perhaps have advised you to make the whole of the last part of your approach to the frontier during the night, were it not for the fact that you will be in a part of the Alpi Marittime where the going is very difficult and the ground so irregular that to attempt it in the dark would be asking for a broken leg or worse."

Prior Paul added, with a smile, "To look at me now you might hardly believe it, but in my youth I was an enthusiastic mountaineer. I have traversed the country I am describing many times, and I still carry the stigmata of my passage." He ran one finger down a long white cicatrice which John had noticed on the side of his face. "That was when I was climbing on Monte Mongione. A sizable piece of rock became detached and struck me. Fortunately it was a glancing blow, but I lost consciousness and a lot of blood. Since I had committed the crowning folly of climbing alone I might have left my bones on the mountainside, had not a shepherd, in the valley, observed what happened. In those parts they are of necessity mountaineers as well as shepherds. He carried me to safety. One of his sons is with us in the monastery today."

"I can clearly see," said John gratefully, "that I am speaking to an expert."

He spent much of the next day studying a map that Prior Paul had found for him. It was many years old and John guessed, from its creased and battered condition, that it was one the Prior had carried with him on the mountaineering expeditions of his youth. It was in no sense a tourists' map, nor was it up-to-date, and the Prior had had to pencil in the new autostradas and many of the minor roads, but it had corresponding advantages. The mountains and valleys were not vague washes of color but were denoted by firm contour lines and spot heights.

"A soldier's map," said the Prior. "A relic perhaps of the campaigns of 1917. There have been many changes since that time in roads and railways and buildings, but the hills do not change."

"It will be absolutely invaluable," said John. "And I promise to return it as soon as I reach France. How long, do you think?"

"Two days to reach Torriglia. That will be the easiest part. Time yourself to cross the first two main roads after dark and lie up in the hills above Arenzano. Cross the A Six *very* early in the morning and make what progress you can during the third and fourth days. From that point it will be inadvisable to seek shelter in farmhouses. Most of the farmers are paid by the police to watch out for smugglers. However, you can carry four days' food with you. By the fourth evening you should be within distance of the frontier. It will be for you to choose whether you can risk a crossing by night."

John listened to this advice gratefully and followed it precisely. He chose the loneliest paths and moved only when he was certain that the way ahead was clear. He met sheep and rabbits, and on one occasion a startled roebuck bolted down the hill ahead of him. The fowls of the air observed him from above, suspicious of his maneuvers. He had, he thought, avoided being seen by any human eyes.

He crossed the first two autostradas at last light on the second day, encountering only a boy on a motor scooter who had looked at him incuriously. The A6, which crawled up the massif from Savona, twisting like a wounded snake, had proved a more difficult obstacle.

The Prior had suggested crossing it in the very early morning, and this had been his intention. Unfortunately he had slept too well and the sun was up by the time he reached it. The traffic was not yet thick, but every time he had thought there was an opportunity to slip across, another car or lorry had appeared. The day was wearing on, and he realized that the traffic would soon be continuous. He had resigned himself to waiting until evening when it occurred to him that if he could not go over the six-lane highway he might contrive to go under it. There were a number of culverts under the roadway. He chose the largest and driest and wriggled his way along it on knees and elbows, hearing the magnified thunder of the traffic passing overhead. When at last he emerged into daylight it was a pleasant thought that the last of the major obstacles was behind him.

The next two days he had spent much of his time on his knees or flat on his stomach. He had met only one man late on the fourth day, and this encounter had been unavoidable. He had slid downhill out of a patch of scrub onto a path and had almost trodden on an old man who was asleep in the ditch beside it. He seemed to be some sort of peddler, and when he had got over his fright, he had been disposed to talk. He was evidently curious about John. He asked no direct questions but discussed the difficulties of travel in the mountains. His accent was a mixture of north Italian and Savoyard patois which made it difficult for John to follow all that he was saying.

He seemed to be warning him particularly about the *frana*. From the gestures he made with his hands, John thought he might be talking about the sudden fierce gusts of wind which came from the sea and blew up with amazing force between funnellike crevices in the mountains.

Later that day he discovered what the *frana* was. Had he not been behind a firm outcrop of rock, which acted as an anchor, it could have been the last discovery in his life.

Quite suddenly and with no warning the earth in front of him started to shift. He thought it was an illusion, until he saw bushes and small pieces of rock sailing past him, heard the growing roar and saw the dust clouds rolling up from the valley below.

He clung for five minutes to the friendly rock while the slide continued. When he ventured out, he saw that he was standing at the top of a raw slice that had been planed off the side of the hill, exposing the underlay of red clay. He crawled up until he was clear of the top of the slide and then tiptoed forward, wondering at every moment whether the ground would hold firm.

He knew now that he was within striking distance of the frontier. For some time he had been following the Arroscia stream, one of the few that ran south to the sea. On the map it had looked an excellent guide, since its springs were within a short distance from the source of the Tanaro stream, which ran northward. By keeping to one until he reached the other he would be sure of his position.

At first he had tried moving up the bed of the stream itself, but this was so deeply cut into the rocks that it had not been practicable; and when he had nearly suffered the same fate as Prior Paul by bringing down a lump of loose rock when negotiating a waterfall, he had kept above the stream and followed its general course.

After four hours of careful ascent, the leveling of the ground showed him that he was approaching the headwater and a glimpse of the peak of Monte Mongione gave him a cross bearing. By this time it was past eight and the sun had almost disappeared, throwing long shadows toward the east. The question which had to be decided was whether to try the frontier crossing at once or lay up where he was until first light.

His reading of the stories of two world wars had taught him that many escaping prisoners, after long treks across enemy country, had reached the frontier line in rags and starving and had made the mistake of rushing headlong at the last hurdle, instead of taking their time and tackling it sensibly.

He had no intention of making this mistake. He was hungry, but he was not starving. Prior Paul had supplied him with adequate food for four days and, by careful management, he still had enough for at least a further day. True, his trousers had suffered in the last forty-eight hours, but he still had the shepherd's coat that Battista Genzano had given him, and this invaluable garment, which doubled as a coat by day and a sleeping bag by night, covered most of his deficiencies.

Two further considerations influenced him.

First, there was the chance of becoming involved in a further landslide. By daylight, avoiding action might possibly be taken; certainly not in the dark. Second, by close study of the contour lines on the map and a calculation of intervisibility factors (a mathematical exercise he enjoyed) he had succeeded in working out a route to the frontier by which he would only be in view of an observer on the very summit of one or other of the neighboring peaks, and it seemed to him most unlikely that any such observers would be about at five o'clock on a May morning. This route involved taking regular and precise compass bearings.

John weighed these factors with all the care he had formerly given his business problems. He had found a comfortable crevice in the rocks, which had the advantage of facing due east, so that the first lightening of the morning sky would wake him. On balance, he thought that the arguments for staying where he was were marginally stronger than the arguments for pushing on.

John wriggled down into the crevice, swallowed a mouthful from his water bottle, put his haversack under his head and slept.

Ten

Next morning there was no mist, and the peaks stood out with a clarity which suggested that the fine weather was over and rain was coming.

A calculation he had made the night before had shown him that he was not more than five miles from the frontier. When he had covered perhaps half this distance, following his planned line of advance with frequent pauses to check his position, he saw something unexpected on the skyline on the right. It seemed to be a construction of iron girders. It looked like a scaffold.

John sank down into a fold in the ground and examined it. It was certainly not marked on his map. He wondered if it might be a watchtower; but if it were, surely it would have been constructed on the crest of the ridge, not on the far side with only its top showing.

As he watched, a speck of light appeared, twinkled and was gone. The first rays of the rising sun had been reflected from something on the iron structure. It might have been glass, it could have been bright metal. John watched patiently, but it did not reappear. Whatever it was, it was not going to stop him. He marched steadily forward on his chosen track. An hour later he thought that he must be on French soil. True, there had been no physical border line, but elaborate fences existed only in wartime. In peacetime the official controls moved down into the valleys. He had kept his eyes open for the concrete triangulation pillars with benchmarks cut into them which the surveyors would have set up when they marked the frontier line, but he had not been surprised to miss them. They must be somewhere there, hidden in the long grass and the scrub.

The ground now began to slope steeply. His progress became a mixture of walking, crawling and sliding. When he emerged suddenly onto a main road he realized, with a catch of his breath, that it must be the one that ran up from Ventimiglia to Tende, paralleling the border but on the French side.

He felt that the moment called for a celebration. Unfortunately he had nothing to celebrate with. A bottle of champagne would have been nice. He had to make do by taking a drink of the dregs of water left in his water bottle. That done, he laid out a compass course due east.

He was heading for the mountain village of Roquebillière. Twenty miles of rugged country lay between it and him.

Toni Gallopi was an Italian Swiss. He was expert in the construction and maintenance of ski lifts, of which there were a number in the small ski resorts that lie on either side of the Italian-French border.

Being head and patron of the maintenance team, he had developed certain privileges for himself. When the skiing season finished and the maintenance period began, he would rig himself up a personal and private sleeping apartment, often in the canteen at the head of the ski lift. This had two advantages. First it meant that, unlike the rest of the team, he would not be faced with an uphill trudge to the scene of operations in the morning. The second, which was even more important, was that it gave him the opportunity to carry out certain irregular activities, for which he was paid almost as well as for his regular duties.

The speck of light John had seen had been the rays of the rising sun reflected from the Zeiss 7 × 50 binoculars that Gallopi was using. He had spotted John when he was three miles from the frontier and had observed his cautious movements and his craftily selected line of advance. Not an innocent walker. Probably a smuggler. Possibly even someone for whom he had been told to keep a special lookout? At that distance the face could not be observed, but the general description fitted.

Gallopi reached for the telephone and suffered the first disappointment of a frustrating day. The line was a private one, which was carried down the ski lift and was connected with the exchange in the valley at Ponte di Nova. He could hear the telephone ringing at the other end, but there was no reply. The idle pigs who should have manned the exchange were still snoring in their beds. Gallopi abandoned the telephone and filled in an hour by completing his interrupted toilet and making and consuming a jug of coffee. Then he tried again.

This time there was an answer, but it was not an encouraging one. Signor Gallopi could not be connected with the main telephone exchange at Savona, because a section of the line between Albenga and Ponte di Nova was under repair. The damage had been caused by a landslide the day before. There was every hope that it would be mended before long.

"Call me as soon as the line is open," said Gallopi. "It is most urgent."

It was midday before the call came through. Gallopi asked for a Naples number, but when, after further delay, he was connected, he was told that the man he wanted had left his office for a business luncheon. If the matter was urgent, he could be contacted and would ring back.

Gallopi, who was beginning to wonder if the matter was as urgent as it had seemed in the early hours of the morning, gave his own number and said he would wait for an answer. This came at a little after two o'clock. The man at the other end listened to what Gallopi had to say, agreed that he was right to report the matter, thanked him and rang off. He said to one of the two young men who seemed to accompany him everywhere, "This could be our man. The timing is approximately right. If he holed up in the mountains until the snow had gone and then made his way into France, he would be crossing at about this time."

The young man agreed. It was his place to agree. He said, "Did our informant obtain any idea of the direction in which this man was proceeding?"

"Unfortunately, no. He lost sight of him before he reached the frontier. However, it would take him more than a day on foot to reach the coast. We will alert our friends in Marseille, and they should be able to intercept him. See to it, please."

The young man moved off to set the necessary wheels in motion. His own view was that Mr. Gabriel, if it was indeed Mr. Gabriel, had left Italy months before and was, by this time, back in England—or even in New Zealand, which some said was his country. It would have been a breach of etiquette to have disagreed with his capo, but he did not feel that the matter was one of the highest urgency. It was six o'clock before he succeeded in contacting the man he wanted in Marseille.

John reached Roquebillière at six o'clock that same evening and made for the Hotel Commerce. He realized that his appearance was against him. He had not shaved for nearly a week. There were holes in the knees of his trousers and the sole of one of his boots had come adrift. The rain, starting in the afternoon and continuing for four hours, had added the final touches to his appearance. It was only after he had undertaken payment in advance that he was allowed to enter. The proprietor then relented to the extent of offering him a pair of trousers that had been left at the hotel the year before by an American visitor. They were too wide in the waist for John's trim figure and a bit gaudy for his taste, but he accepted them gratefully.

Soap and hot water removed a lot of his surface grime. He decided to keep the beard. He was becoming attached to it and thought that it added a needed touch of dignity to his appearance. He ate a large supper and slept for ten hours.

The next morning found him ambling down the road toward the coast. He was in holiday mood. The crossing of the frontier seemed to have put a barrier between him and the unseen forces that had been menacing him. The rain had stopped and the warm Mediterranean sun had reappeared.

One of the first things he did was to post back Prior Paul's map to him with a warm letter of thanks. He was now reduced to a small guide to the Côte d'Or. This showed him that there were two roads he could take. One of them led to Monaco and the other to Nice. He had no immediate intention of visiting either of these resorts. What he was looking for was a pied-àterre in the foothills that overlooked the coastal strip. He badly needed an interval for rest and refitting.

He found what he wanted on the outskirts of Aspremont. La Caravelle was a medium-sized hotel, new but not offensively new. It was separated by a paved courtyard from a side-road that ran downhill past the village to a junction with the main road. The proprietor, Monsieur Brazier, received him kindly and accepted his story of a walking tour in the hills. He did not even ask for money in advance. John felt that his beard must already be beginning to pull its weight.

He explained that he planned to be there for a week or two and would like a quiet room, it did not matter how simple. The proprietor said that he understood perfectly. Monsieur was an artist, or possibly a writer? John decided that his appearance fitted an artistic background. He admitted that he painted a little.

This conversation took place in the lift, which trundled them up to the fourth floor. The room the proprietor showed him into was tucked away under the tiles, at the back of the hotel, looking out on a *jardin fleuri*. There was a stream at the far end of the garden. Behind it the hills rose steeply. It seemed to John to be exactly what he wanted.

When the proprietor had left him, he padded around the upper landing, in the way that a cat circles before settling into a new resting place. There were two other bedrooms, which seemed to be unoccupied. There was a small bathroom with a curious bath, three feet long and three feet deep. Bathing in it would be an experience. Being apprehensive about fire risks, he was pleased to note that there were two staircases. The main one ran down to one side of the lift. The back one, which he explored on his way down to dinner, gave directly onto the garden.

Before he set out next morning on a shopping expedition, Monsieur Brazier produced the hotel register, which John signed in the name of Michaels, giving his address as Otago Province, New Zealand. He explained that his passport had been in his second knapsack and had been lost when he was involved in a landslide some days before. It was his intention to visit the nearest New Zealand consulate and get hold of a temporary travel document. Monsieur Brazier readily accepted this explanation. He had himself, he said, experienced a landslide in the mountains. They were a terrible danger to walkers. If there was not a New Zealand consul in Nice, certainly there would be one in Monte Carlo.

John decided that his reequipment should take place by steps. As he approached civilization he would become progressively more civilized. First he located a shoe shop in Aspremont and bought a pair of walking shoes, presenting the remains of his boots to the proprietor. Then he caught the bus for Nice and got off in the outskirts of the town, where he made several purchases at different shops: a pair of gray worsted trousers with a pinstripe, a set of workman's overalls, a light raincoat and a grip to hold his purchases.

His next stop was at a barbershop, where he had his hair washed and cut. The barber admired his beard. He advised that, in a week or two, when it had developed its full potential, it should be curled. Many men, said the barber, grew beards to conceal a certain weakness of the chin. In the present case no such subterfuge was necessary. His client had an excellent chin. The beard, in his opinion, added a real touch of distinction.

Feeling in every sense a new man, John strolled down the long tree-shaded Avenue Gallieni which led to the center of the town. Here he changed a traveler's check at the bank and did some further shopping. He observed that the popular wear for men was linen trousers, brightly colored open-necked sports shirts and sandals or espadrilles. These were added to his purchases, along with a number of more ordinary shirts, socks and underclothes. He then deposited his grip, which was becoming heavy, at the Central Station and walked down toward the sea.

It was not yet the high season, but the fine weather had attracted a fair number of strollers. He ate his luncheon under an awning in a garden named for King Albert the First and over coffee arrived at a decision.

He would allow himself a fortnight's holiday in this delightful place before moving on. He would have to keep an eye on his money, but he reckoned he had quite enough to finance fifteen days of idle pleasure. The balance would buy him tickets for his onward journey. This would be by train. For the moment he had had enough, and more than enough, of walking.

It was on the morning of the third day, which was a Friday, that his plans were modified.

He was in the Rue Victor Hugo staring into a shop window and trying to resist the temptation to treat himself to a pigskin belt with a silver buckle when he saw a woman, reflected in the glass, approaching him along the pavement. He had five seconds to record his impressions before she came up. She was in her late twenties or early thirties. She carried herself with the assurance of someone who knows she is good-looking and well dressed; but if her clothes were French, her face was unquestionably English.

None of this was guesswork. John knew her very well indeed. For the last four years of his business life, Monica St. Aubyn had been his secretary.

As she came up with him, he half turned, bringing the two of them face to face.

Monica looked at him, incuriously for a moment. Then a look of surprise was followed, instantly, by incredulity and something close to horror.

She said, "Oh!" and then, "No, it can't be. I'm very sorry. I thought for a moment—"

"What did you think, Monica?"

Her reaction to this simple question was to go white and start to keel over. He caught her as she fell and held her up. He said, "What's the matter, Monica? Come and sit down." There was a café next to the shop. He supported her to it and sat her down in a chair. By this time she had started to recover.

He said, "I seem to remember that you had a weakness for Dubonnet with ice. Is that still your tipple? Or would you like something stronger? A cognac?"

Monica nodded and, assuming this to be agreement with his second suggestion, he ordered two café cognacs. As the waiter departed, John said, "What was it? A touch of the sun, perhaps? Or was it surprise at suddenly running into me?"

Monica, who seemed to be recovering, said, "For God's sake! Of course it was a surprise. You're dead."

"Come again?"

"You died nearly a year ago. In a Tristar crash in the desert. You were one of the best-known people on board, so you got the headlines."

"Do you know, I never trusted that damned plane. And how right I was. I got off at Rome. I suppose they were so disorganized they didn't notice I wasn't still there." A further thought struck him. "Was no attempt made to identify the bodies?"

"They identified some of them. Not all."

"I see."

John was slowly absorbing the news that he was dead. It seemed to him that in his present position it might have considerable advantages.

Monica said, "Do you mean to say you didn't know?"

"I was out of touch with any newspapers for a couple of months. Later I did see an occasional Italian paper, but by that time the crash must have faded out of the press."

"But what have you been doing, for God's sake?"

"It's a long story. Finish your coffee, and we'll find ourselves something to eat."

Over the meal John recounted some, but not all, of his more recent adventures. While he was doing so he was changing his mind about Monica. When she had been his secretary she had been someone he dictated letters to, who hired cars, booked airplane tickets, reserved rooms in hotels and made all the complex arrangements of his business life.

He had been too busy to realize that as well as being an excellent secretary, she was a very attractive woman. Also, in the intervening year, she had grown up a lot.

He said, "Enough about me. Tell me about yourself."

"When you sold up and departed, most of us were taken on by MBA. In fact, any of us who wanted jobs were offered them."

"That's right. It was part of the deal I made."

"I went straight to Laleham. It's the MBA sales complex. The fact that I spoke French and knew the ropes got me a good place there. I worked chiefly for a chap called Mike Collins. He was a friendly sort of person."

"*Very* friendly?"

Monica laughed. She said, "That's a lovely way of putting it. Yes, very friendly. But not as friendly as he would have liked to have been, if you follow me."

"I follow you perfectly," said John. "What happened next?"

"After a couple of months I was shifted to France. My job is liaison with London. Our factory here is on what was wasteland behind Anthéor and Agay. You ought to see it. It's quite a place."

"I'd like to, but I reckon I'd better keep clear. Tell me more about Laleham."

"It's what I said, a sales organization. We didn't have anything to do with the scientific research and that sort of stuff. That was a separate outfit, at Teddington, under a brain called Ferrari. Parties of us were sometimes taken on conducted tours. I imagine the idea was to impress us, so that we could impress customers. It's a huge place. Had been a television studio that went bust. It was full of people doing things I didn't begin to understand, although I expect you would have."

"I know all about James Ferrari. He's a genius in his own line. And he's put together a remarkable team. Some of them he bought from his competitors. Others he's grown himself. He has a knack of picking the best young mathematicians from the universities. I noticed they'd got a couple of tame dons on the board to help them."

"They may be geniuses," said Monica. "From what I saw of them, most of them looked as if they wouldn't have known how to come in out of the rain."

John said, "I didn't have a lot to do with Ferrari personally, though I've read all his published works. My personal dealings were with the accountant, Arnold Lacey, and the merchant bankers, Harriman, Hanna. As I'm sure you remember, since you had to write all the letters. I was never allowed near the sales side. I'd like to hear more about that. But I can see the waiter thinks we've sat here long enough. What are your plans for this afternoon? Are you on holiday?"

"I've got a long weekend off. Actually, I've got a date this afternoon to go sailing."

"What about this evening?"

"Well . . ."

"You've got a car, I expect. Then why don't you drive out and have dinner at my place? It's La Caravelle at Aspremont. If the weather stays fine we eat out at the back, overlooking a very lovely flower garden."

"It sounds attractive," said Monica. She was looking thoughtfully at John as she said it. She seemed to come to some conclusion. "All right. I'll be there at half past seven. Is it the sort of place where one has to dress up?"

"You can wear practically anything or practically nothing," said John happily.

The other guests who were dining that evening on the terrace at La Caravelle may have debated among themselves what the precise relationship was between the couple at the corner table. The man, in his early forties, with the weather-beaten skin of someone who lived his life in the open, was said to be an artist. Quite a distinguished face, with the small pointed beard and the hair with the suggestion of gray in it. The men, had their opinion been asked, would simply have said that the woman with him looked attractive. The women would have analyzed her more closely. Not French, though wearing French clothes and wearing them well. Very little makeup. A cool, rather businesslike appearance. A modern type.

Had they been able to listen to the conversation at the corner table, they would have found that it was entirely about business. John seemed to have an insatiable curiosity about the organization of MBA.

Monica described to him what she could remember about her time at Laleham. It was not much. "It's an ordinary business office," she said. "Almost all our letters were to people in France and Italy and Corsica. A few of them were to the new factory that had just been set up in the Lowlands of Scotland. It's in a backwards area south of Glasgow and needs a good deal of nursing along. A lot of the business I was involved in was the result of the sudden decision they made to shift all the requirements of the fighting services away from the works here and up to the new outfit in Scotland."

"Tell me about that."

"I can't explain the technical side of it, but I know it caused one hell of an upset out here. It meant cutting down staff, and work is so hard to find that this was bound to cause ructions. I was told that one of the workmen actually organized a strike committee to try to stop the redundancies. It didn't get off the ground, because he fell under a train. There was a rumor that it wasn't an accident, but a put-up job organized by the Union. What's wrong?"

She noticed that John had gone white. He put his wineglass, which he had been lifting, back onto the table very carefully, as if he was afraid of spilling it. When he got it there, he seemed to have some difficulty in loosing his fingers from it.

After a long moment he said, "What union?"

"The Union Corse. It seems that we are, to a certain extent, under their protection. It's not public knowledge. I only happen to know about it because I work directly under a man called Emile Lytaudy. His official title is Assistant Personnel Manager, but actually he's our troubleshooter. He keeps in touch with his opposite number in Italy, Ronconi, who deals with the Mafia."

Monica was talking to allow John to recover from whatever it was had upset him. He had picked up his glass again, and she saw that his hand was now quite steady. He said, "Are you telling me that the Union Corse are blood brothers of the Mafia?"

"I don't know about blood brothers. I think they respect each other's spheres of operation. The ordinary people don't talk about them much. There's no reason for them to have anything to do with either organization. I don't think Emile enjoys that side of his work. He talks about it to me occasionally, when he's in a very unbuttoned mood."

Given a woman who was attractive *and* sympathetic, men would very quickly become unbuttoned. The thought, expressed in that way, amused John. Monica was relieved when she saw him smile. She said, "Something upset you just now. Was it something I said?"

John hesitated. Now that more time had elapsed, he was able to view the past more dispassionately. He was beginning to be able to relate it as though it were a story, something which had happened to other people. The time, the place and the listener invited confidences. But there was another reason for embarking on the narrative at that moment. He wanted to keep Monica with him as long as possible. He was almost entirely inexperienced in the ways of women, but he had a feeling that she would not object to certain plans he had formed.

The story took time to tell. John modified it in one particular. He said nothing about his feelings for Anna. He reduced her to a secondary character, an inhabitant of the farm, who had perished with the other two. It was easier to tell it that way.

By the time it was finished, the other diners had long departed, the tables had been cleared and they were alone in their candle-lit corner. The proprietor, who was taking a benevolent interest in his curious guests, would have let them sit as long as they wanted. It was the hotel porter, a swarthy creature called Marco, who came out and started to close and bar the shutters. He banged them shut in a manner which indicated that, in his view, it was time for guests to be thinking of retiring and not keeping poor menials out of bed until all hours.

They got up and moved into the salon. There was no one else there. John said, "I'd no idea it was so late. If I had a word with Monsieur Brazier, I'm sure he'd find you a room. That would save you a drive down these hill roads in the dark."

"That's quite an idea," said Monica with a tiny smile.

Monsieur Brazier was amenable. It seemed to him to be a natural and desirable development. He pointed out that the only empty rooms were, at the moment, on the fourth floor. One of these could quickly be made available.

Later that night his wife said to him, "If you continue in this way, you will acquire the reputation of being no better than a ponce, a procurer of women."

"I have done nothing," said her husband. "Nothing but facilitate a development which was bound to have taken place. One cannot stand in the way of human nature."

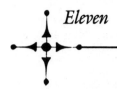

Eleven

Monica had come into his room and into his bed with no false modesty and no fuss. They had found each other entirely satisfying. She was more experienced in lovemaking than he was, and to start with he had let her take the lead. Later, she had put up a token resistance, which had given him additional pleasure. After that had come deep sleep.

When they woke they lay beside each other in the light of the early morning sun and talked.

"Tell me about Anna," said Monica.

"Anna?"

"Do you imagine I was deceived? Your voice went up two semitones every time you mentioned her name."

"You're exaggerating."

"Did you sleep with her?"

"Certainly not. She was only a child. Well, a bit more than that perhaps. I don't say that if she'd been a bit older, or I'd been a bit younger—"

"Was she very beautiful?"

John said simply, "She was the most beautiful creature I've ever set eyes on."

"If things hadn't happened the way they did—I mean, if you'd been there a bit longer—would you have asked her to marry you?"

"That's not a question I can answer."

"No, I'm sorry. It was stupid of me. It's not something you'd want to talk about."

But, curiously, he didn't mind talking about it. He said, "I used to dream about her. Not dreams. Nightmares that ended in the flames of hell. Not any more now. That doesn't mean that I've forgotten or forgiven what was done to her. I'm going after the men who were responsible—really responsible—the men in London who make the decisions."

"How will you do it? When you say the men in London, you mean the board?"

"Not the board as a whole. They may call themselves directors, but I soon realized they were only subordinates. There are just three people who matter in that outfit: your boss at Laleham, Henry Ligertwood; the technical head, James Ferrari; and the chairman and managing director, Sir Thomas Chervil. I know quite a lot about all of them. I had them investigated in depth when I was planning to do business with their company."

"I never met Chervil. Everyone calls him Sir Tom. People seem to like him."

John lay back in bed, with his hands under his head, and thought about the head of MBA. He said, "I met him three times. Once socially and twice in the way of business. Of course, he's charming. His charm's one of his many weapons. Eton, Oxford, the Guards. Then a spell in the Middle East, in various diplomatic posts. And he must have been a success there, because a lot of the money behind MBA comes from high-ups in the Gulf."

Monica said, looking at him out of the corner of her eyes, "It sounds to me as though you're jealous of him."

"I don't know him well enough to be jealous of him."

"He's coming out here next week."

"Is he, though," said John. "He wouldn't leave London unless it was something important. What's up?"

"It could be about the redundancies."

"I should have thought that was the sort of thing he'd leave to the local man. Enough about business. What are we going to do today?"

"The first thing I'm going to do today is go back to my place and get some clothes and things. Do you realize that all I've got with me at the moment is one bottle of Blue Grass?"

"That sounds deliciously depraved. What are your ideas about the rest of the day?"

"We could bathe. There are still one or two little beaches that are not too crowded."

"And tomorrow?"

"On Sundays the beaches are impossible."

"Then we'll go for a picnic in the hills."

"You realize that I shall have to be back at work early on Monday."

"Monday's a long way ahead," said John.

One of the good things about Monica was that things did not have to be explained to her. This made conversation easy and agreeable. As they lay on the hillside above Aspremont in the Sunday-afternoon sunshine digesting the picnic Monsieur Brazier had put up for them, their talk switched easily from the past to the present and from the present to the future.

John said, "If I stay more than two weeks, I shall have to start thinking about money. There are complications."

He still had his passport, which identified him as John Gabriel Benedict from London. This had to be produced when he cashed one of his traveler's checks. To the rest of the world, including the hotel, he was Mr. Michaels from Otago, New Zealand.

"But you have money in London. What will have happened about that?"

"I've got an extremely cautious solicitor who looks after all my affairs in England. In the absence of definite and irrefutable proof of my death, Jonas Pickett will have been very slow to start distributing my estate."

"Then you can get money from him?"

"Yes. But I shall have to do it personally. It's no good ringing him up and saying I'm not dead after all. He'd assume I was either an impostor or a lunatic. Anyway, I want to go to London to attend to some unfinished business."

Monica said, "When I asked you what you were going to do, you sidestepped the question. What *are* you going to do?"

"The Prior at Montagnola asked me the same question. I can only give you the answer that I gave him. I shall try to get Faldo punished for what he did. If his bosses won't act, I shall have to see what I can do about them."

"What can you do?"

"I shall have to find that out when I get to London. I already know quite a lot about the activities of their Italian branch. It's the sort of dirty linen they won't want to have washed in public."

He told her about the voyage of the S.S. *Lucania*. Monica said, "I think it's true, particularly in the early days when they were getting off the ground; they did cut a few corners, though they try to give the impression now that they're whiter than white. But there was one thing I heard about when I was at Laleham. Mike Collins mentioned it, as a sort of joke, when we were out one evening. It's about a factory in Copenhagen that wasn't really a factory at all."

"A ghost factory?"

"Something of the sort. I didn't understand it, and when I mentioned it later I got the impression he was sorry he'd told me. But what I was going to say was that if you wanted to find things out, why don't you get yourself a job at Laleham?"

"Get myself a job?"

"You could do it easily. They're always advertising for people, but since one has to be bilingual or trilingual *and* know about computers they don't get a lot of applicants."

John sat up and thought about it. He said, "Do you know, that's quite an idea. I don't think I ran into any of the people on the sales side. I was dealing with the head office types. What about our own people who joined MBA on the amalgamation? I'd have to steer clear of them."

"The only ones who knew you well were Ron Layfield—he's gone to the Scottish plant to help them set it up—and Ransome and Monroe, both in the laboratory at Teddington. Some of the junior staff might still be about, but I think most of them took their redundancy pay and left."

"I wish we didn't have to waste so much time talking about the future," said John. "It makes it all seem so much nearer." He slid one arm under Monica and moved it about until he had worked her shirt clear and could feel her bare body. "It's not very far away," said Monica. "If you're going at the end of the week, it looks as if we've only got one evening. I can get away on Wednesday and be up here by eight o'clock. Even that won't be easy."

"You must be working for slave drivers."

"They like to keep an eye on what their senior staff are up to. I had to tell Emile about you."

"Why?"

"He'd have found out anyway."

"What did you tell him?"

"I said I'd been picked up by a lecherous New Zealander who was on a walking tour."

"You said that, did you? Would you care to be spanked?"

"Not now. There's a sheep looking at us."

"Poor creature," said John. "I expect he has a very dull life. Let's give him something to be shocked about. . . ."

Later they spent an agreeable half hour discussing what they were going to eat and drink on Wednesday evening.

But the meal was not destined to take place.

On Wednesday evening John had two telephone calls. The first came just before eight and was from a man who said that he was speaking on behalf of Mademoiselle St. Aubyn. Business commitments would unfortunately prevent her from being with him that evening. He rang off before John could question him.

The second call came at half past nine when John, puzzled and unhappy, was on the point of making his way up to his room. This time it was Monica herself, though he had some difficulty in recognizing her voice.

She said, "Don't say anything, John. Let me do the talking. You've got to get away. As quickly as possible."

"But, Monica, darling—"

"Please don't talk. Please. I have just heard from Emile and I know that he is speaking the truth. He risked his own life by telling me and I may be risking mine by telling you. Can you understand that? *You must go.*"

"I can't go without knowing why."

There was a short pause. When Monica spoke it sounded as though the words were being forced out of her mouth by some internal pressure she was unable to resist. She said, "Two men are coming to kill you. The porter at your hotel, Marco, has given you away. One of the men is Paul Rocca. Emile knows him. He is a professional killer. Do you understand? Emile told me to protect me from getting hurt. You must not try to do anything stupid. Promise me you will go now. Promise, promise. They will be with you very soon."

The despair in her voice moved him more than the words. While he was thinking what to say, the line went dead.

John stood for a long moment with his hand clenched around the receiver. His overmastering feeling at that moment was not fear, but rage.

It was not what Monica had said. That was not important. What was important was the inescapable fact behind her message. The faceless people, whose presence he had long suspected, had now emerged. They had come out into the open. And they were coming to punish him. For what? His only crime was that he had not been burned to death six months before. And he was expected to take to his heels. He was forbidden to fight them. He was not even to be allowed to see their faces. Though they could see his back, while he ran away.

The idea made him so angry that he found he was shaking. He took three deep, slow, deliberate breaths and started to consider his position more coldly.

First he had to secure a line of retreat.

He found Monsieur Brazier in his office and explained that an unexpected development had forced him to depart at a very early hour on the following morning. He would be going on foot and would like to leave his other pieces of luggage for later collection.

Monsieur Brazier was desolated. He had noticed the non-appearance of Monica at dinner and the telephone calls and suspected a rupture in the romance he had done so much to propagate. Yes, he would have the account made out at once. And yes, he would certainly look after anything which Mr. Michaels wished to leave behind.

Having settled his account, John returned to his room, stowed away everything he did not need in his grip, put his haversack handy and sat down on the bed to think.

If he had to move, he decided that he would wear the workman's overalls. They were inconspicuous and gave him freedom of action. He would carry only the haversack and the raincoat.

Then he considered a more immediate problem. Monica had said two men. They would arrive by car. If they both entered the hotel, he would take himself off at once down the back staircase. Odds of two to one were not acceptable in an encounter of this sort.

On the other hand, if the second man stayed in the car and the killer—what was his name? Paul Rocca—came in alone, the odds would be shortened and he proposed to accept them. He did not intend to kill Rocca. His rage had cooled and had turned into something more calculating and more dangerous.

He intended to hit him, hard enough to render him unconscious for a long time; possibly to disable him.

If he could pull this off, it would greatly strengthen his own position. For consider: When Rocca was found, the proprietor would inform the local police. An intruder, armed, lying unconscious on his premises. And it would be the Aspremont gendarmerie who would be summoned. The Union Corse might have some arrangement with the police at headquarters in Nice to keep them conveniently out of the way. But such an arrangement would hardly extend to the local gendarmerie.

Now think about the second man.

When Rocca failed to reappear he would know that something had gone wrong. He might stay in the car for a time and await developments. When the police arrived he would want to push off inconspicuously. *But he would be embarrassed by not knowing what had happened to Rocca.* The opposition would be unable to take any positive steps until the position was clearer—probably not before the following day. This would give him a very valuable start. If he simply ran away, the men would be on the telephone at once, and on his heels.

John realized that these were plausible arguments in favor

of the course he had mapped out. But an inner honesty told him that they were not the clinching reasons. The true position was much simpler. He wanted to hit someone.

He had a useful weapon, a stick he had bought, with a heavy head, and there were ready-made spots for him to lie in wait.

For instance, if Rocca came up by the main staircase, the door of the bathroom could be left open and he would be well placed if he stood just inside it. If Rocca used the back staircase, even better. It emerged through a narrow opening beside the window embrasure, where he would not be seen at all by someone coming up until he had stepped out into the open.

Moreover, he was well placed to see which staircase was used. The lift, when not employed, stood at the bottom of the shaft. If he leaned forward and looked down the shaft, the glass front of a showcase gave him a view of the hallway. So far, so good. The hardest part remained.

That was the waiting.

Twice in the next hour the arrival of cars took him to the window at the far end of the passage. Two false alarms. Guests that he recognized, returning. The third arrival was different. This was a Peugeot, driving on side lights only. It passed the front of the hotel and went out of his sight. Then it must have turned, for it came back with its lights out and its engine cut and slid onto the verge at the other side of the road, pointing downhill toward the village.

After that, for some minutes, nothing happened. Then the off-side door opened and a man got out, crossed the road and the paved courtyard and entered the hotel. John could see him quite clearly in the lights of the portico. He was a stocky man, dressed in a respectable dark suit, the double-breasted coat buttoned rather tightly across his chest. He walked with a peculiarly deliberate gait, placing one foot carefully in front of the other, as though intent, all the time, on preserving a perfect balance.

As he disappeared into the hotel, John raced back to the lift shaft. He saw the newcomer pausing for a moment opposite the main staircase. Then he seemed to change his mind. So, it was to be the back stairs after all? Wrong again. The man opened the grid and stepped into the lift.

For a moment John's brain refused to function. Then it started to work at twice its normal speed.

There was no cover near the exit from the lift. No question of an easy ambush. But he had been offered an alternative.

As an engineer he had, of course, studied the simple mechanism of the lift. It embodied certain safety devices. For instance, no door on any landing could be opened until the lift was exactly opposite to it. This was achieved by a short spring-loaded arm, which stuck out and was pushed up by the lift cage as it rose. When the arm was exactly vertical, the door could be opened. The other device was a spring under the floor of the cage. When you were inside, your weight on the floor depressed it, ensuring that no one outside could operate the lift.

John did not have to work these things out. He knew them already. By the time the lift was passing the first floor landing he had arrived at the right answer. Standing on tiptoe he could reach and raise the spring-loaded arm. This enabled him to open the gate. Some way below him he heard the lift stop with a jerk.

Peering down, John estimated that it had stopped roughly halfway between the second and third floor landings, possibly rather closer to the third floor. As long as he kept his gate open, Rocca was stuck. He went down on his knees, folded up an ample piece of the corridor carpet and wedged it in the gap between the gate and the frame.

Below him he heard the door of the cage clashing open. Much good that would do. Rocca could open the cage door, but the landing door would remain tightly shut. And not only was the lift immobilized, but since Rocca was inside and standing on the floor, no one else could use it. This seemed to John to be a perfect solution. He picked up his stick, shouldered his haversack and raincoat and descended the back stairs. As he reached the second floor he heard a further clashing from the lift. If Rocca went on like that he would probably upset the works. Then he would be stuck permanently. Sooner or later he would have to shout for help. He would have some awkward explanations to give.

John made his way out into the garden and along the covered passageway that ran along the far side of the hotel.

He had won the first round, but he had no intention of abandoning the field of battle.

The second man, John told himself, was probably not a professional killer like Rocca. If he had been, he would hardly have waited tamely in the car. He was just a chauffeur, a person of no great account. If he got tired of waiting and came to investigate, there was a convenient patch of shadow at the end of the wall—

John had reached this point when a second car drove up.

Reinforcements? No. It was only Monsieur Patou, a stout and talkative lawyer, holidaying at the hotel with his wife. They had evidently been spending a sociable evening in Nice and had hired a car to bring them back. They got out, the car drove away and they entered the hotel.

This new development was going to precipitate matters. Monsieur Patou was the last man to wish to climb three flights of stairs to his bedroom. When he discovered that the lift was out of order he would summon the porter or the proprietor.

Then the scream came.

It was a horrible sound, starting in terror, sharpening into agony and cut off as suddenly as it had begun.

The man in the car heard it, flung open the car door and ran toward the hotel. John waited until he was through the front door, then vaulted the low wall and made for the car. The car door was hanging open, but the driver, hurried though he was, had not forgotten to remove the keys.

This mattered little. The car had been left pointing downhill. John released the parking brake, giving a push with his leg as he got in, and the car started to roll.

He had two immediate problems. The first was to steer the car around the corner. The second, and more urgent, was to stop himself from being sick.

For he knew what had happened to Rocca. Imprisoned in the lift, it had not taken him long to see that there *was* a possible way of escape. If he could reach the spring-loaded arm above the third-floor gate and lift it, that gate could be opened. To do this he would have to hoist himself up, with a knee on the edge of the landing.

But he had forgotten one thing.

As soon as he took his weight off the floor, he put the lift back into commission. At a moment when he was partly inside but mostly outside the lift, Monsieur Patou, on the ground floor, had pressed the button. The descending cage would have almost cut Rocca in half.

He was a killer, John told himself, and he deserved to die. It was a horrible death. But stop thinking about it. Think about more immediate things. You can't coast through the village. You must start the engine.

He rounded the bend, pulled the car into the side of the road and got out his knapsack, but his hands were shaking so much that it took him several minutes to carry out the simple drill. Then he got back into the car, with the engine ticking over, and sat while his breathing steadied and his heart stopped bumping.

Which way should he turn when he reached the main road? Left would take him back to the hills and to a choice of very bad roads that might eventually get him to Briançon. Right went straight down to Nice, where he could pick up the coast road to Cannes and the N 85 to Digne, Serres and the center of France.

This involved risks, but he would go farther and faster by main roads than by mountain roads. His mind was made up before he reached the end of the village street. He swung to the right.

Then there was the problem of petrol. The gauge indicated a little above the quarter mark, and he was going to need full tanks for a night's run. He had money. But there was a practical difficulty. One did not normally leave one's engine running when refueling. By the time he had thought this out he was running down toward Nice. At the first traffic light a police car drew abreast but showed no interest in him. He drove with increased confidence, through the emptying streets and out along the Corniche road, through Antibes to Cannes.

In the northern outskirts of Cannes, at the point where the Avenue Franklin Roosevelt joined the N 85, he found what he wanted: an all-night petrol station with no other cars there. A bell invited him to SONNEZ and brought out a sleepy youth whose first suggestion, as he had anticipated, was that he should switch off his engine.

"Unfortunately," said John, "I cannot do so. I have lost the keys."

The youth said that regulations in the matter were strict. John observed that, in emergencies, regulations had sometimes to be broken. He added that he realized that, in the circumstances, it would be appropriate to pay rather more for the petrol. Say, twice the regulation price. This seemed to the youth to be entirely appropriate, and he filled the tank without further demur.

John reflected, as he drove away, that the youth would pocket the difference and would therefore be unlikely to make any mention of the transaction. It was with a lighter heart that he headed for Digne as the clock of Notre Dame de Bon Voyage struck the hour of one.

At six o'clock he was threading his way through the streets of Lyon. They were already beginning to fill up with traffic.

In five hours he had come nearly four hundred and fifty kilometers. An experienced driver would have made light of such a journey, but there was a difference between being walking-fit and driving-fit. He was very tired, but he knew that Lyon was not the place to stop.

Thirty kilometers farther on, at Villefranche, he found something more suitable. The town was the right size and had a railway station with a big car park. This was almost empty when he drove into it but would soon be full of the cars of workers going south to work in Lyon or north toward the vineyards of Macon.

By the time he had parked the car and walked back into the town, the early cafés were filling up. He breakfasted at the busiest, taking some time over it to allow the shops to open, so that he could buy a map.

He reckoned that he was twelve hours ahead of any hue and cry and decided that his next moves could safely be by rail.

He would catch a train at about nine o'clock when there would be plenty of people about and leave it when he reached Macon, which seemed to be some sort of junction. Here he could take a train to Chalon, change again and take another to Seurre. He was glad to see that immediately beyond Seurre lay the Forêt de Citeaux, a promising expanse of light green on his map.

From that point he would abandon the railway and proceed on foot, taking such lifts as were offered, sleeping out and getting his meals in small cafés. His general idea was to keep east of Paris and head for the coast.

Twenty-four hours later he was strolling along a small road south of Dijon. He had breakfasted at one of the Relais Routiers and was feeling at peace with the world. As he turned the corner he spotted a lorry. It was a very large lorry, really a moving van, and it was in a curious position, half on and half off the verge at an angle to the high grass-covered bank.

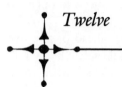

Twelve

As he came up with the lorry, the driver's door opened and a man hopped down. John wondered, for a moment, whether it was in contrast to the height and bulk of the vehicle that the man looked so small but then realized that, though not a dwarf, he was well below average height. The moment he opened his mouth John realized something else. Here, in the heart of France, was a London sparrow.

"'Ullo, 'ullo," he said. "Would you by any chance be a garden angel?"

"I'm not sure," said John cautiously. "What does it involve?"

"A garden angel'd wave his bleedin' wand and this bleedin' mechanical monster'd start to perform."

"What's wrong with it?"

"That I dunno. It's got what you might call a fit of the sulks. Mind you, it's bin actin' up all morning. On that long hill outside Deejong I thought, 'ullo, it's going to 'and in its cards altogether, but no, some'ow we got to the top and then, seein' as we was on this nice flat stretch, I think: Time for lunch. So I pull the old bitch into the side of the road, and when I've finished my five-star re-past and start up again it gives a fart and a coupler sneezes and that's its idea of a good day's work."

By the time he stopped for breath, John had got around behind the vehicle. On the doors at the back, the legend W. ROSSALL AND SON REMOVERS had been put on by a slapdash sign painter. He bent down to examine the exhaust pipe which stuck out under the tailboard.

The driver came around to watch him.

John opened his haversack and extracted a knife. He said, "All proper scout's knives have an implement on them designed for extracting stones from horses' hooves. There, now. Try her again."

The driver started to say something, thought better of it and climbed back into the lorry. At the second try the engine fired. Leaving it running, he climbed down again, walked around and said, "Just as I thought. A number-one top-class garden angel. What was wrong with the old cow?"

John showed him the thick pellet of dried mud he was still holding in his hand. "When you backed into the side you ran the end of your exhaust pipe into a soft bit of the bank and blocked it. Cars are like humans. They can't function unless they're open at both ends."

"Well, ta. Simple when you know, I suppose."

"All the same, if you've got a long way to go, I think something ought to be done about that engine." He was listening critically. "It might only be dirty plugs, but I think it's missing on at least one cylinder. If you're not in a tearing hurry to catch a boat or something, half an hour now might save you a lot of trouble later."

"She's all yours and welcome. We'll run her up the track where she'll be out of the road. By the way, the name's Rossall, Albert Rossall. My friends call me Midge, bein', as you might guess, short for midget."

Midge might not know much about engines, but he knew how to drive. He backed the monster neatly up the track and John got to work. It took nearly an hour, but when he had finished the engine had been restored to a state of purring contentment.

"Wunnerful," said Midge. "Now, what about something to eat, or have you had lunch already?"

"Actually, no."

"Come into the 'otel Splendeed."

There was a side door behind the driver's compartment, and John saw that the interior was divided into two parts. The larger part, at the back, was for the cargo and was separated by a partition from the front section, which had been fitted up as a combined living room, bedroom and kitchen.

"Snug, innit?"

"You seem to have made yourself very comfortable," agreed John, watching while Midge let down a folding flap, which served as a table, and set out lunch for John on it.

"We manage to survive," said Midge, "without undoo 'ardship. That bench what you're sittin' on makes another bed. Should suit you."

"Well—"

"Unless you've got other plans, that is. What I'm doin' is headin' back for England home and beauty. The beauty bein' my girl Lois. At the rate this old cow goes it'll take us two days, best part of."

"That would suit me very well," said John slowly. "The only thing is, when we get to the port, there may be some trouble about my papers."

"There's ways round most things if you know 'ow to look for 'em. We'll be goin' out through Belgium. I got friends in Ostend."

"What's your cargo on this trip?"

"My cargo? Well, it's what you might call special. 'Ave a dekko."

Midge switched on another light. John knelt on the bench and looked over the top of the partition at the stuff that filled the rear of the lorry. As far as he could see from the wrappings, it was furniture, carefully stowed and in some cases boxed in protective frameworks of wood.

John said, "It certainly looks like top-class stuff."

"Should be," said Midge complacently. "Came from a castle. And when I say castle, I don't mean a shatto. A real castle, with battlements and dungeons and every modern convenience."

John could make out that there were a dozen pictures in heavy gilt frames, a number of chairs and a chaise longue with an elaborately carved back and sides.

"Bit knobbly for relaxing on, I'd have thought," said Midge, "but pitcheresk, you must agree."

One item that caught John's eye was a beautiful chest. Its

walnut panels were inlaid with lighter wood, forming illustrations of what seemed to be hunting scenes. It had been so carefully fixed into a protective wooden frame that he judged it must be exceptionally valuable.

Midge said, "That's one of our 'eadaches. It's 'istorical."

"I should imagine you have to take particular care of a piece like that."

"It's not just looking after it." Midge sounded embarrassed. "It's what I was tellin' you. Why we got to exit through Belgium. They're not so fussy as the French."

"Do you mean—?"

"Now don't get me wrong. You was thinking maybe this lot had been nicked, wasn't you?"

"I did wonder why you were adding another hundred miles to your route."

"Well, it wasn't a crook deal. It was a fair sale. Price agreed and money down, on the nail, or I wooden 'ave touched it. No. The trouble is like I was tellin' you. Some of these items are 'istorical. There's a crowd of geezers up in Paris, call themselves the Bo Zart. You may 'ave 'eard of 'em."

John, who had succeeded in translating Bo Zart into French, said he supposed they were people who kept an eye on national treasures.

"That's right. They're hot on anythink with 'istorical associations, like it might be the bed the Pompydoor slept in when she was having it off with the Dolphin: that sort of thing. You follow me?"

"Perfectly."

"With a thing like that, you gotter get a certificate saying it's O.K. to export it, and if it's particularly 'istorical they won't give you one. On the other 'and, there's a lotter money to be made if you do get it out. Americans are dead nuts on history. You offer 'em a table. They're not interested. Then you tell 'em it's the one King John signed Magna Carta on and the sky's the limit."

"But if the item is important enough and the French authorities hear about it, I imagine they'd make trouble."

"*If* they hear about it, likely they would. But what the eye doesn't see, the 'eart don't grieve after. In any event, all *I've* got to do is get the stuff back to England. If there's trouble afterwards, that's something for other people to sort out. I aim to stay clear of it."

All that afternoon they drove north. They used secondary roads. Midge never consulted a map and took little notice of signposts. He seemed to set his course with the instinct of a homing pigeon.

At four o'clock when they were crossing the main road between Nancy and Paris they ran into a police patrol, two black-suited motorcyclists of the Gendarmerie Mobile. They examined Midge's logbook and driver's record, took a quick look at the load and then turned their attention to John.

"He's my co-driver," Midge explained. "My oppo."

"*Votre copain?*"

"That's right. What I said. My oppo."

The gendarme was either prepared to accept this explanation or was unwilling to spend more time disentangling the linguistics. Already two cars and another lorry were queuing behind them. He made a note in his book and waved them on.

By eight o'clock, with the light beginning to fade, they left the secondary roads for smaller ones and finished by driving through the main street of a village that was hardly wide enough to admit the lorry and up a track into the Bois d'Ery.

After supper, since it was a fine night, John arranged his mattress and blankets in the lee of the truck and Midge and he sat smoking as the last of the light went out of the sky.

"Calls itself a forest," said Midge. "I've seen more trees in a London park."

John said, "The Scots call a thing a deer forest when there are no trees in it at all."

The rolling, scrub-covered hills at their feet were not unlike Dartmoor, the wilder parts of which John had come to know in a number of his snatched holidays. A few lights were visible in scattered farmhouses. He wondered if they were still drinking the ten ritual cups of coffee the Prior had told him about. As he rolled himself up in his blankets he found he could

116

only remember Rincette, Surrincette and Rerincette. He was asleep before this could worry him.

The next morning they crossed the frontier into Belgium. It was a small border post and there seemed to be few formalities. The French official took a cursory look at Midge's driving record, noted from a stamp in the margin that it had been examined the day before and lost interest in him. The Belgian customs officer waved them through.

"I always use the same place," said Midge. "Then they get to know you and there's no trouble."

All the same, he sounded relieved. John began to suspect that maybe there *was* something rather special in the back of the lorry.

When they reached Ostend, Midge did not drive directly into the embarkation area. He parked outside and went in on foot, through an entrance that said STAFF ONLY. He was gone for some time. When he came back he said, "The man I want won't be on for another hour. He's on his lunch break. Two hours they get. What a lovely country. Give us time to snatch a bite ourselves."

They had lunch at a café on the dockside, which announced, in English, that it was prepared to serve hamburgers and chips or bacon and eggs. Feeling hungry, they had both. After lunch they returned to the dock and drove into the lorry park, queuing behind half a dozen monsters carrying the logo of the Transport International Routier. When their turn came they moved forward into a covered area. There were three men on duty. One of them waved to Midge, who drove up to him and hopped down and accompanied him into the office.

Ten minutes later he emerged. The bar in front of them was raised, and they drove up the ramp into the bowels of the ship. Midge locked all the doors of the lorry, front, back and side, before they climbed up onto the deck and found a sheltered spot in the lee of the bridge.

As the boat cleared the end of the mole and lifted to the slow swell of the English Channel, Midge said, "Shoot me down if I'm speaking out of turn, but what you said, about you might 'ave trouble with your papers and one or two other things like the way you didn't look at those motorcycle goons, or the customs people—"

"Was it as obvious as that?"

"Yers. Well, you can always tell. Like I said, it's not my business, but it did seem to me you might 'ave 'ad a bit of trouble and wasn't too anxious to push yourself forrard into the public eye."

"That's very well put," said John. "I have had quite a lot of trouble in the past few months. I didn't tell you—"

"And I didn't ask," said Midge quickly. "It wasn't none of my business."

"You're a good chap and I'd have told you the whole story, willingly, only a lot of it's past history and what I'm thinking about right now isn't the past, it's the future. The immediate future. The fact is, I've got a job to do in England, and it's the sort of job that will be a lot easier to do if I can manage to keep out of the public eye. All I can tell you is that it's not criminal, but it's tricky."

"You wooden be one of those what's-its? Spooks. Men what moves in a mysterious way be'ind the scenes of 'istory."

"No. I'm sorry. I'm not in the Secret Service. I wish I was, because then I might have a lot of ready-made aliases to slip into."

"'Tisn't only the Secret Service who have aliases. I remember Dad telling me a friend of his 'ad six different names. It was when they'd got rationing and identity cards and all that caper. What 'e did, so my dad told me, 'e wrote to the people concerned prompt on the first of January and said, This year my name's going to be Smith—or Taylor, or whatever 'e fancied."

"And they couldn't do anything about it?"

"'Ow could they? 'E'd changed his name. That was it."

"It sounds too easy," said John. "There must be a snag somewhere. What about documents? I'll need a new passport and I'll have to open a bank account. And I'll want a driving license, and that'll mean an insurance policy. Everything's so tied up in paper these days. When I find somewhere to live that'll mean a tenancy agreement and rates and a telephone and maybe a television license—"

"And a dog license," said Midge, grinning. "Take it easy, lad. One thing at a time is the motter. Lay the foundations before you start to e-rect the building. What you need fust is something like say a passport and a drivin' license. Any bank will accept them. Specially, that is, if you're paying money in. When you've got your bank account, you use that as your reference for the other bits and pieces. Right?"

"How do I get a passport and a driving license?"

"You pay for 'em. Passport'll cost you five hundred smackers for a good one. Driving license might be fifty."

"Could you get them for me?"

"If you've got the money, no difficulty. Any idea about names? I only ask because a friend of mine 'oo works in that line was tellin' me the other day that he could lay hold of a nice one in the name of Naylor. About your age. They'd 'ave to fix the photograph, because Mr. Naylor 'ad a squint and two chins."

"Naylor," said John thoughtfully. "Yes. I like it. I think it sounds businesslike."

"I might be able to get that one for a bit less than five hundred. Favor to me. 'E owes me one."

"If you can get it for less, the balance is your commission."

"I call that 'andsome." Midge watched a seagull, which was following the boat and keeping up with it with insolent ease. He said, "You was talkin' about findin' somewhere to live. Might take some time. Where are you going to stay whilst you're fixing it?"

"No idea."

"What I thought was—but say no if the idea doesn't appeal—I've got a spare room in my 'ome from 'ome. It's in Barnard Street and that's in Soho, which some people reckon isn't the most salubrious part of London—"

"I've always enjoyed it when I've been there."

"Ah, but that'd be to eat a meal, not to live in. When you live there you meet some very dicey characters."

"It's a terrific offer," said John sincerely. "And if you feel you can put up with me for a week or so, I say yes to it at once."

"The bed's a bit 'ard."

119

"Compared with some places I've slept in lately it could be a rockery and I wouldn't notice the difference."

"You're a glutton for punishment," said Midge. "I can see that."

By this time the coastline of Belgium was out of sight.

"Midge tells us that you've been having ever such a lot of adventures lately," said Lois.

"Then I'm afraid he was exaggerating," said John politely. He took particular care to be polite, because his first impressions of Lois had been almost entirely unfavorable. He guessed that she was barely out of her teens, but she must have been an exceptionally early developer, because she had already reached a point where the most descriptive word that occurred to him was lush. It was clear from the care with which she spoke that she considered herself a cut above her husband and father-in-law.

"Not that he told us very much. We were hoping that you'd do that. All that walking. Pass him the cheese, Dad. I'm sure it must have given him an appetite."

Bill Rossall, whom John had identified as the W. Rossall on the back of the lorry, grunted, cut himself a large slice of the English Cheddar and pushed the dish across to John. He said that speaking for himself he never took more exercise than a daily walk to the Blue Posts public house at the corner of Barnard Street, but he had an excellent appetite.

John said, "It wasn't really anything much. I retired last year, and I thought I'd try something I'd always wanted to do. I went by air to Naples, then by train down to Reggio di Calabria—that's right at the bottom of Italy—and started to walk back to Calais."

"Goodness," said Lois. "You must have got very tired."

"Actually, I took it pretty easily, stopping at various places which appealed to me. I wore out two pairs of boots."

"Should 'ave worn army boots," said Bill Rossall. "Mine lasted me the whole war."

"We want to hear about Mr. Naylor's walk, not about your war, Dad."

"Well, by the time I'd got halfway up France and met

120

Midge, I decided I'd had enough. I was getting to the northeast corner, you see, which isn't particularly attractive. More like Liverpool and Manchester."

"Nothing wrong with Manchester. I was born there."

"Dad!"

"All right, all right." Mr. Rossall refilled his mouth with cheese.

"Bein' as he's so modest," said Midge, "what John 'asn't told you is that he did me a bloody good turn. The old lorry had gorn on strike. What I'd done, I'd backed into the bank and stuffed its arse up with mud."

"There's no need to be coarse," said Lois. She turned the lamps of her eyes on John. "The language he picks up from those lorry driver friends of his, you wouldn't credit it."

"Some of the language I heard in the army—"

"Dad!"

John said, "I can tell you one thing that walking does for you. It makes you very sleepy. Since I don't want to disgrace myself on my first night here by falling asleep at table, I think I'll make for my bed."

"I hope you'll find it to your liking," said Lois. "I turned the mattress when I heard you was coming."

"From what I can remember of that mattress," said Midge, "both sides are as 'ard as each other."

Settling himself cautiously down on it, John was inclined to agree with Midge. He wondered about the curious household he had landed up in. There was no lack of the obvious luxuries—wall-to-wall carpeting, a modern television set with a cassette attachment, a liquor cabinet that played a tune when you opened the door and which contained, among other items, the largest bottle of gin he had ever seen. Could it be right to refer to a magnum or even a jeroboam of gin? He wondered where the money came from. Old Mr. Rossall would be contributing something to the household expenses from the profits of the bookshop that occupied the ground floor of the house, but he suspected that he didn't entirely approve of his daughter-in-law and would be unlikely to present her with television sets. Midge must be earning good money on his continental trips—above the normal fee if he was helping his employers to sidestep the French controls—but this meant that he had to spend a lot of his time abroad, and Lois looked the sort of girl who would not be happy without attentive male company. Was someone else filling in the gaps?

And was it any business of his? He realized that it was only bothering him because he had become fond of Midge. It did not bother him enough to keep him awake.

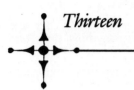

Thirteen

Next morning he found Midge drinking tea and eating toast at an otherwise deserted breakfast table. Midge poured out a cup for John and put a slice of bread for him into an outsize electric toaster cleverly designed as an imitation of the Taj Mahal.

"I look after myself at breakfast," he said. "Lois likes to lie in, and Dad don't open the shop till eleven. The sort of books 'e sells, people need to think a bit before they buy 'em."

A quick glance through the window on the previous evening had shown John that the Modern Bookshop dealt almost exclusively in pornography, with a sideline in sado-masochism. He agreed that thought would be necessary before making a purchase.

"Gotter get busy on your little problem," said Midge. "Might take all day. Depends if the man I want's attorne. If the old Bill are looking for him, he may be on the move."

"Then I'd better be seeing about the money," said John.

When he had set up his first tiny office in Highgate, and had been offered a very one-sided tenancy agreement for it, he had walked around the corner to take advice from Jonas Pickett, Solicitor and Commissioner for Oaths. Jonas had sorted out the landlord and, from that moment, had dealt with all his legal affairs. When John's business expanded and finance had to be arranged in the City, his colleagues had sometimes suggested that they go to a larger firm in central London, but John refused to shift. He had found Jonas perfectly satisfactory and had kept him not only as solicitor to the Company but as his personal solicitor as well. He had two sterling qualities. The first was that he was clearly and absolutely trustworthy. The second was that he had never appeared to be surprised by anything that John did.

John felt that he might be going to try him pretty hard that morning.

When he telephoned him from a callbox, he recognized the voice of Jonas's secretary, a nice girl called Claire. She said, "Mr. Naylor? I'm not sure. Could you tell me what it's about?"

"I'm afraid it's rather confidential. But if Mr. Pickett's there I could explain it to him quite quickly."

There had been an odd note in Claire's voice. She had known him well, and he wondered if she had recognized him. After a moment's hesitation, she said, "He's very busy this morning, but I'll find out. You said the name was Naylor?"

"That's what I said. And don't be too long, because I'm speaking from a callbox and a queue is already forming. Two girls, both impatient types from the look of them."

A few minutes later Jonas Pickett's voice said, "Mr. Naylor?"

"That's my pen name. The real name's Benedict. John Gabriel of that family."

There was a very short pause and Jonas said, "It's the wrong time of day for jokes, and I'm a very busy man."

"It's the wrong time of day for using this callbox," said John. "When I was talking to Claire it was only two girls waiting. Now there's also a West Indian and a nasty-looking type carrying a hammer. So let's be brief. Could we meet in Waterlow Park."

"Waterlow Park?"

"Don't tell me you've forgotten where it is. I remember you saying that when you were first starting up and were comparatively poverty-stricken, your lunch sometimes consisted of a couple of watercress sandwiches in Waterlow Park."

There was a long pause while John bet with himself that Jonas would say either "Then you aren't dead" or "Weren't you in that aircraft?" He would have lost. What Jonas said was, "How long will it take you to get there?"

"Half an hour. One of the seats by the bandstand."

"So that's the story," said John.

How many times had he told it, in different versions? To the Prior, to Monica, to Midge. This was the fullest and the longest.

At the end of it, Jonas said, "What are you going to do about it?"

"What I'd like to do is to smash the Mafia and the Union Corse singlehanded and have the governing directors of MBA hanged, drawn and quartered and their heads exposed on Tower Bridge. That being impracticable, I have had to modify my plan somewhat. The Prior at Montagnola gave me some sound advice. He said—I can't remember the exact words—that when you are dealing with people who have gone outside the law, it's good tactics to stay within the law yourself."

"Excellent advice."

"He also said that I should look for success, not victory. So what I had in mind was a modest piece of satisfaction. As well as MBA's use of strong-arm tactics, there's at least one instance— the case of the good ship *Lucania*—where they clearly acted illegally."

"Where it's alleged that they acted illegally."

"All right. Be a cautious old lawyer. It's alleged that they acted illegally. But I've got a feeling that MBA is the sort of outfit who were prepared to cut corners when they were starting. So when I've unearthed as much dirt as I can, I propose to write a short thesis on the *Lucania* and other similar matters. "The Birth of a Giant" might be an appropriate title for it, don't you think? It will show—all right, most of it may be allegations rather than legally provable facts—how MBA has grown in ten years at such a phenomenal pace and become the power in the land that it undoubtedly is now."

"And then?"

"I shall send a copy to Sir Tom Chervil with my compliments. I shall say that if he cuts all connections with the Mafia and the Union Corse and any other illegal strong-arm bodies, and kicks Faldo out without compensation of any sort, I will refrain from publicizing my thesis."

"Suppose they say yes. How will you know whether they keep their word?"

"I can find out, quite easily, through Monica."

Jonas thought about it. He said, "I've a feeling that the top brass of MBA would be pretty tough characters."

"I agree," said John with a smile. "And that's why I shall deposit a second copy of my thesis in your strong room, just in case *I* happen to fall under a train. And I'd like you to find out for me just where they stand. I mean, how much do they need the confidence of the City and the Government right now and how sensitive is this going to make them to anything I could do? But be careful. I don't want you to get into the line of fire."

"I shall look after my own safety with great care," said Jonas. "As a matter of fact, I believe I could manage it without appearing in the matter at all. My office, as you will remember, is immediately opposite Highgate School, and over the years I've acquired a number of the masters as clients. Boys nowadays are all crazy about computers. I will get them to set up an investigation into the leading computer companies. They'd love to do it, and it should give you most of what you want."

"Could they handle it?"

"An earnest schoolboy, particularly if he happens to be wearing glasses, can ask anyone any questions he likes. They did a study on pets that involved questioning everyone from television stars to cabinet ministers. They got some remarkable answers."

"All right. I believe you. But tell them to be careful. I don't want to alert anyone to what's going on." He watched a pigeon annexing a piece of bread which two sparrows had thought belonged to them. It put him in mind of something. He said, "I imagine my reappearance from the dead will upset Uncle Frank and my two cousins. They'll have to return anything they've had out of the estate."

"They won't have to return anything, because they haven't had anything."

"Why not? They're the only next-of-kin I've got."

"You must imagine," said Jonas, "that the law moves with great speed. Since you had been thoughtless enough to die intestate, we had to obtain Letters of Administration. That takes time, even in a normal case. Yours was by no means normal, since we had to apply to the High Court for leave to presume your death. Now I think of it, the application comes in front of one of the Masters next week. I must remember to cancel it." He took out his diary and made a note. "There was a further complication. Your Uncle Frank was to have been the administrator. He died last month."

"I'm sorry," said John. "He was the only one I really got on with. He was Father's youngest brother. The two in between were both killed in the war. I suppose Frank was getting on."

"He was sixty-five and fit as a fiddle. He died when a tractor overturned and broke his back."

John thought about his Uncle Frank, a true Benedict, a farmer and a fighter. Neither of his sons had been much use. Ronald had gone into a bank. Tim, he understood, had taken up professional photography, the last refuge of the idler. He said, "So what's happened to the farm?"

"When your uncle died it was offered to Ronald and Tim. They both declined it."

"I suppose they didn't want to get their hands dirty. What did you do? Sell it?"

"I arranged for a manager to take it over temporarily."

"This is all going to come as a bit of a shock to them."

"No doubt. I should think they've already spent your fortune in their imaginations."

John was unworried about the feelings of Ronald and Tim. He said, "That means that all my money's still available here."

"Certainly. I can reopen your account at Hoares Bank."

"No. A different bank, I think. And a different name."

"What name?"

"It will probably be Naylor. I'll let you know as soon as I can. John Naylor, I hope. I wouldn't want to have to get used to a new Christian name. Will there be any difficulty about it?"

"None at all. You can have any name you like."

"When Midge told me, I didn't believe it. I thought you had to have something called a deed poll *and* lodge it in court."

"A common fallacy. You change your name by deciding to change it. A deed poll is simply formal evidence of what you have done. Some people like to insist on it. The passport office can be very difficult, and some of the insurance companies. But banks are more broad-minded. I opened an account for a lady the other day in the name of Pussy's Friend."

"You mean," said John fascinated, "that that's how she signs the checks?"

"Certainly. And they've got pictures of cats all over them."

John thought about this. It would be fun to have a personal checkbook with pictures on it. He felt, however, that in his case prudence was called for. He said, "Let's make it the London and Home Counties. They're a respectable outfit. Their West End branch. Meanwhile, I'll need some cash."

"How much?"

"About seven hundred pounds to be going on with. In fives and tens."

"Sit tight and I'll send Claire down with it."

"Then you'll have to tell her about me."

"She'll find out as soon as I start writing to New Zealand. She's perfectly reliable."

"I'm sure she is," said John. "But you do realize that for the next few months I shall be playing with fire. And I don't want anyone else to get burned."

He could say a thing like that, now, without any noticeable reaction, he found. But the wound was still there. It would always be there. The effect of the passage of time was that the surface area was no longer raw.

After Jonas had gone he sat on, in the sunlight. He noticed that a lot more people were arriving. Three more had sat down on the seat beside him, and the other seats were filling up. Turning his head he saw that a band concert was about to begin. Soldiers in dress uniform were climbing onto the bandstand. A notice announced that it was the band of the Irish Guards.

Sir Tom Chervil, he remembered, and Henry Ligertwood

had both been subalterns with short service commissions in that regiment.

When John got back to Barnard Street that evening, Midge was still out, presumably hunting for his friend in the passport business. Bill Rossall, who was shutting up shop, suggested a visit to the Blue Posts—a suggestion which John agreed to willingly. A pint or two of beer would slip down nicely, and there were one or two questions he wanted to ask.

There was no old-fashioned segregation of drinkers at the Blue Posts into public and private and saloon bars, just one large room with a horseshoe bar in it. At that hour of the evening there were only a few steady performers present, with one foot on the brass rail and one elbow on the mahogany.

"Real beer," said Mr. Rossall. "Not the thin muck you get in Yurrup."

John sampled, with appreciation, the dark brown bitter brew, full of hops and stamina. He had almost forgotten the taste.

"Mindjew," said Mr. Rossall, "I've nothing against Yurrup—as a place, that is. In the old days I used to drive up and down it, doing jobs for anyone who wanted 'em done. I'd a lot of friends in the same line. That's one thing about driving lorries in Yurrup. Not a lot of people go in for it, so we're what you might call a cleek. Mostly we knew what sort of racket the other chap was in and we'd swop tips."

Mr. Rossall paused to drink and added, "When I say racket, you've gotter appreciate that I don't mean nothing dishonest. That's not something I approve of, dishonesty."

"Certainly not," said John. "This is very good beer. Let me get a refill."

When John got back to their table, Mr. Rossall's mind still seemed to be running on dishonesty. He said, "Tell you the truth, I'm a bit worried about Midge. The people he's working for now are hot. Very hot. If there was real trouble he might get involved. Also, it takes him away a lot. It was different with me.

129

My old lady was killed by a flying bomb, almost the last one of the war."

John had not thought about Midge's age before. If his mother had died in 1945, he must be into his forties. And Lois, he thought, hardly in her twenties. He said, "I did wonder about Lois. Are they—I mean—"

"Married," said Mr. Rossall judgmatically. "Yes and no. She's what you might call his common-law wife."

Since he said this as though it explained everything, John hardly liked to pursue the matter.

Mr. Rossall said, "I'm not denying there's a difference in age. June and December."

"Isn't that a bit hard on Midge? April and July would be nearer the mark."

"Well, I suppose twenty years isn't too much. And Midge has got what she wants. Which is plenty of money. Too much, to my way of thinking, and it brings the bad types round her like wasps round a jam jar. And then, people sometimes laugh at her, on account of Midge being so much shorter than she is. That's the sort of thing that upsets a girl. There's one or two loudmouths round here—"

Mr. Rossall broke off what he was saying and swung his chair around so that he presented his back to the room. He said, "And here's the worst of 'em."

There were two doors leading into the bar from the street, one at each end of the horseshoe bar. The far one had now swung open and a man had stalked in.

"Looks as if he owns the whole bloody place, dunnee?" said Mr. Rossall.

"Who is he?"

"Name of Frankie Simmons."

John studied Frankie across the far end of the bar. He was a good figure of a man—could have been a boxer once, thought John—but going to seed now. He had a flat, pale face, which looked paler against the black hair and the dark eyebrows. The hand that came up to the counter had rings on three of the fingers, but apart from that there was nothing unduly flashy in the getup. But for the warning signal of the face he might have been a businessman dropping in for a drink on the way back from the office.

"Is that the one who hangs round Lois?"

"When Midge is away, you might say he almost lives there. And sometimes when Midge is there, too. He'd like to turn him out, but no one doesn't want to start a free-for-all in his own home, do they? And between you and me, I can't see why Frankie bothers about Lois at all."

"She's an attractive girl."

"I'm not denying it, but girls aren't Frankie's scene. Everyone knows he's a poof."

"He only does it to annoy, because he knows it teases," suggested John.

"Something like that. Is there anyone with him?"

"He's buying two drinks, so there must be. Yes. I can see him. It's a youngster. Fair hair. Looks a bit soft."

"Right. That's Gareth. He's the current boyfriend. No one else?"

"Not that I can see. Should there be?"

"He usually ponces round with his brother, Morrie. One's as bad as the other."

In trying to get a clear view, John had half risen in his chair. The movement seemed to catch Frankie's eye. He strolled across in their direction, carrying his drink in his heavily ringed right hand, his left hand in his pocket.

As self-conscious in his movements as in his getup, thought John.

"If it isn't old Bill himself," said Frankie. "How's the lovely daughter-in-law? Devoting herself to her ever-loving husband this evening, is she?"

Mr. Rossall turned half around in his chair, looked at Frankie with distaste and said, "Why ask me?"

Frankie was not discouraged. He seated himself on the corner of the table and said to the beautiful Gareth, who had now joined them, "Bill seems to be in a bad mood tonight. Porno book trade falling off, perhaps. Clean you and your shop up."

This was for the benefit of Gareth, who rewarded it with a

131

titter. Mr. Rossall swung his chair again so that he presented an uncompromising back to Frankie and said, "Time for another, John?"

John said, "Just about," and shifted his own chair back a bit. At close quarters Frankie stank of hair oil, aftershave lotion and sweat.

"Friend of yours?" said Frankie. "You haven't introduced us. Not very polite. Or—wait a moment." A smile revealed a handsome set of dentures. "Do you think he's being tactful, Gareth? P'raps he doesn't want to tell me. But I've guessed. It must be Lois's latest boyfriend."

"I'll get the drinks," said John. In view of possible developments, he thought it would be better if he was on his feet.

Frankie gave him a look that was half appraisal and half insolence. He said, "He's a better size than Midge. More up to it, I should say."

"I've two things to say to you," said John. He had started to pick up the glasses, but now returned them to the table. "The first is that no one with any manners would talk about a girl like that. The second is that I suggest you should stick to your boyfriends and leave girls alone altogether."

Frankie's face was no longer white. The blood that had rushed up into it seemed to have invaded his eyes. He put down the glass he was holding and moved a step toward John. He said, in a voice which had gone treacly, "I think this is a boy who needs a lesson in manners, Gareth. What do you think?"

Gareth said, "Yes, Frankie. He does." His face was bright and eager.

Mr. Rossall said, "Lay off."

John took no notice of either of them. He was watching Frankie's right hand. That was where the blow would come. The rings would be calculated to hurt. And though the man was grossly out of condition, he was now sure that he had once been a boxer. He'll feint with his left, thought John, and then bring up that right. He may only have one good punch in him, but you'd better see it doesn't connect. He was as poised as though getting ready to jump for the high bar. When the feint came he swayed to avoid it but didn't move his feet. As the right hand came up he jumped back, clear of the blow.

The result was more than he had dared hope.

The upward swing of his arm failing to connect with anything but air took Frankie forward in a wild stagger. He might have recovered his balance if Mr. Rossall, still seated, had not stuck out his foot. This completed Frankie's downfall. He went onto his knees, hitting his head against the next table and upsetting four pints of beer.

This did not stop him. He climbed back onto his feet, blood pouring down his face, stood swaying for a moment and then came headlong at John, arms outstretched to grab. John sidestepped. Frankie's rush carried him as far as the end of the bar.

By this time the landlord and his assistant had come out from behind the counter. They grabbed Frankie expertly, taking an arm each. The struggle that followed was short, vicious and decisive. In the course of it Frankie put his elbow onto the assistant's face and the two of them banged Frankie's head against the bar.

"'S all right. I can hold 'im now," said the barman. "Fetch the law."

The assistant shot out into the street.

At this point it must have occurred to Gareth that he had not played a very heroic part. He moved irresolutely toward the end of the bar where the barman stood, having twisted one of Frankie's arms behind his back, using his own arm to throttle him. Gareth said, "Let him go, you beast, you're hurting him."

"Fuck off," said the barman.

Gareth seemed determined to rescue his patron, and the barman had no hand to spare. John decided that the next move was up to him. He stepped forward, took Gareth by the arm, steered him to a chair and sat him down in it. Gareth made an attempt to get up, but it was not a very convincing one.

At this point the street door burst open and the assistant reappeared with a police constable. Seeing him, the barman released Frankie, who made a rush for the door and became entangled with the policeman. To John it seemed that his real object was not to fight the policeman but to get out into the street. After two cracks on the head he probably wanted to be sick.

On the following afternoon, John learned the score from Midge, who had been at Marlborough Street Magistrates Court that morning. "They all turned up," he said. "Old Cobbett, the landlord and young Bert—he had a beautiful black eye where Frankie had put the elbow in. The police laid it on with a trowel. Assault causing actual damage, resisting arrest, criminal damage to property: to wit, one table and four glasses. They didn't leave nothing out. I'd guess they've been wanting a chance to nail Frankie, so they grabbed it with both hands. Frankie had that solicitor, the one they call Niggly Nix, telling the story. To listen to him you'd have thought Frankie was just a big boy scout. He said how much he regretted the whole thing and he was prepared to pay for any damage he'd done."

"You mean he pleaded guilty?"

"That's right. Nix told him to. Good advice. If he'd started to argue, he'd have got six months. When Nix had finished spooning out the soft soap and saying how it was his client's first offense and how all the damage was going to be paid for handsome, the beak cooled down a bit and redooced it to fourteen days."

"Without the option."

"That's right. Nix tried 'ard to make it a fine and costs, but the beak wasn't having any. It was assaultin' the pleece that did 'im. Gotter stand up for the boys in blue."

"As a matter of fact," said John, "I don't believe he meant to assault the policeman at all. He just had the bad luck to run into him."

"Don't you start feeling sorry for him," said Midge. "I wooden say this if Lois was here, because she seems to think he's all right, but between you and me he isn't all right, he's all wrong. He's nasty. There's people round here I could name who've got across him and come home with their bottom jaw in two bits and not many teeth left neither. And his brother Mor-

134

rie's just as bad. And the boyfriend, Gareth. He's said to be eppy-lectic. Goes quite mad sometimes. That's why it'd be a good thing, all in all, if you could fix yourself up with a nice quiet pad somewhere else, the further off the better. You've got fourteen days to do it. They won't start nothing till Frankie comes out."

"I had a word with my solicitor on the phone this morning. He thinks he's found something for me. I've no objection to making what the army calls a tactical withdrawal. What I don't like is leaving Bill and you on the spot."

Midge looked surprised. "'E's got nothing against me, and from what I 'eard Dad didn't take any real part in the punch-up. It's you 'e's going to be gunning for. You did the one thing no one musn't do."

"What's that?"

"Laid hands on Gareth."

"Laid one hand," said John. "And persuaded him to sit down in a chair. Which he was very happy to do."

"That's not the way he's telling the story. In *Gareth's* account of this thrilling drammer, he was rushing to Frankie's aid when you caught hold of his hair, twisted his arm, punched him in the stomach and several other little items. He adds one each time he tells it. By the time Frankie gets out you'll have kicked him on the kneecap and cracked a couple of his ribs."

"I see," said John thoughtfully. "Then you may be right. Perhaps it's time I did move on."

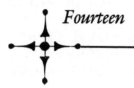

Fourteen

"Then we're agreed," said Chervil. "Our next factory goes up in Ireland."

"It's the best offer at the moment," said Ligertwood. "Fifteen years' freedom from tax on export profits, a fifty percent contribution to the cost of the site, an interest-free loan of all money spent on building and machinery and an assisted training scheme thrown in if we want it."

Ferrari nodded. Financial matters meant little to him. His mind was already turning on the magna-integrated circuits necessary to create the next generation of microchips.

The three men were sitting in the library of Crowninshield Court, which was the Hertfordshire home of Sir Tom Chervil and had been the home of his father and his grandfather before him. The evening sunlight slanted across the flagstones of the courtyard and lit up the meadow beyond, where a dozen Aberdeen Angus heifers were grazing and trying to ignore the flies.

There was a tray of drinks on the library table but no papers, except for a scribbling pad with a few words on it in front of Chervil. When conferences took place at this level, no minutes were taken and no records were kept.

"I meant to tell you," said Ligertwood. "I was waylaid yesterday. By a schoolboy. He wanted to know how MBA was doing. My first reaction was to tell him to push off."

"I hope you did it politely."

"In fact, I changed my mind. It occurred to me that it might be a newspaper stunt, so I told him we were doing very well and hoped to do even better next year. It seemed to be something his school was doing as a project. Have they been on to you?"

"Not yet," said Tom, "but one of them managed to penetrate Mike Hanna's sanctum. He brought a list of questions with him. When Mike asked him why he was particularly interested in MBA, the boy said that naturally he was concentrating on us because we were the most important company in the computing world."

"Tact would seem to be one of the things being taught at his school."

"Mike was so taken with him that he not only answered all his questions, he nearly offered him a job on the spot. What about you, Jim?"

"They haven't tackled me yet," said Ferrari, "and if they did, I'm afraid they wouldn't understand much of what I said."

"Don't you believe it," said Chervil. "All schoolboys talk computerese. They write letters to each other in Basic and answer them in Pascal." He looked at the pad in front of him. It seemed to remind him of something. He said, "When I was in France last week I got the beginning, but not the end, of an odd story. It seems there was a contract out on a mysterious stranger, a man called Michaels, who had walked into France from Italy and was stopping in a hotel above Nice."

"My dear Tom," said Ferrari, "you complain about computerese. What you're talking is gangsterese. Please explain yourself."

"I meant," said Chervil patiently, "that the Mafia had been paid to kill him. When he moved out of their territory, the job was subcontracted to the Union Corse. It went wrong. One of the agents of the Union was killed and the man got away."

Ligertwood said, "Is this anything to do with us?"

Before Chervil could answer, Ferrari looked up from some scribbles he had made on a piece of paper and said, "You're worried, Tom. Why?"

A cat was crossing the courtyard. Chervil followed it with his eyes until it had disappeared over the far wall. Then he said, "I don't know. It may be nothing. You remember that farmhouse in Italy that caught on fire."

"Vaguely. Wasn't it something to do with a petrol store?"

"It was thought at first that the only people living in the house were the farmer, his mother and his daughter. And they were certainly the three people who were killed. But now it seems there was another man staying there. A New Zealander, who'd been on a walking tour. A man called Gabriel."

As Chervil said this, a very faint recollection of something in the past flickered across his mind, as faint as the blip on a radar screen and disappearing as quickly. It did not seem important.

"And—" said Ferrari.

"It's clear that he wasn't in the house that night. But there was no record of his leaving the country. He just disappeared. When the police examined the register in the hotel above Nice they found that the stranger had given his name as Michaels and his address as Otago Province, New Zealand. He said that his passport had been lost in a landslide."

"So it might have been," said Ligertwood. "Is there any real reason to suppose it was the same man? There must be hundreds of New Zealanders wandering round Italy at any one time."

"Of course you're right," said Chervil briskly. He appeared to put the matter out of his mind. But Ferrari, who understood him better than Ligertwood, knew that he was still worried.

"I hope you like it," said Jonas, "because they aren't easy to get hold of. The rent's low and the location is agreeable. I only got it because the landlord is one of my oldest clients."

"It's exactly what I wanted," said John, "and I'm most grateful."

The flat was on the fourth story of one of the dozen blocks that made up the Holly Lodge Estate on Highgate Hill. It was a bachelor's pad—living room, bedroom, bathroom, kitchen— and it was furnished with a soothing lack of taste. There was a small balcony leading from the living room; standing on it, the two men had a view across the smoke and glitter of London to the hills of Kent in the blue distance.

"Worth it for the view alone," said John.

"No garage, I'm afraid."

"I wasn't thinking of buying a car, although I've acquired a perfectly good driving license, also a passport. Both in the name of John Naylor."

"I must remember that when I write to you."

"And when you send me your bill. Don't forget that."

"Like tax inspectors and the angel of death," said Jonas, "solicitors always present their bills in the end."

They moved back into the living room, leaving the balcony window open. It was the beginning of August, and the sun had a lot of strength in it.

"I've got the outlines of what you want," said Jonas. "And no need to thank the boys. They much enjoyed buttonholing tycoons. First things first. I don't need to tell you that England is the only European country which is in the top league in the field of information processing. America, of course, is top in the world ranking. IBM have got an unchallengeable position in the States, and at one time they had a big part of the market here too. But by 1975, the British ICL was treading on their heels. Then along came MBA. It was a totally new conception. It didn't start nationally and develop into a multinational. It was multinational from the word go. Headquarters in England and *all* manufacture abroad. It took guts and money to set that up."

"No shortage of either commodity at MBA," said John. "All the same, it's odd when you come to think of it that ICL only hit the big time when they took over English Electric Computers—*and* were helped to do so by a kindly handout of seventeen million pounds of government money. *And* that this happened in 1968 when Benn was Minister of Technology!"

"Which demonstrates an important truth," said Jonas. "It has become a non-party article of faith that we must keep up with the U.S.A. Look at the Alvey Report and the promise of even more money. Two hundred and fifty million this time. So when MBA crowned their excellent start with a highly successful public issue in 1982, the City guessed they had an implied guarantee behind them. Nothing in writing, of course. All done over discreet little parties in private rooms in City lunch clubs. But the promise was plain enough. If and when MBA reached level pegging with their only real rival, ICL, the government would step in once again and force the sort of merger they underwrote in 1968. It would be a shotgun wedding, the gun being a substantial share of the two hundred and fifty million that would be available to the taker-over. By which they meant, of course, whichever was the more successful of ICL and MBA. *And now the money boys are betting that the winner will be MBA.* You realize that the joint enterprise would be very big indeed. It couldn't touch IBM on their own ground, but it could outsell them here and maybe in the international field too. MBA are strong there. They've got the best international sales and after-sales organization of the three."

While Jonas had been talking, John had been lying back in the armchair in front of the open window, relaxed and still. His mind was moving on two different planes. He was taking in what Jonas was saying, but at the same time he was thinking back to his own struggles and the deal he had eventually made with MBA, which had enabled him to retire. It was a short time ago, as measured on the calendar, but so much had happened that thinking back was almost like opening an old photograph album and being surprised to recognize faces in it.

He said, "Then it looks as though this is a moment when MBA would not want to be publicly reminded of spots in their murky past."

"That's a considerable understatement. They want every scrap of public approval and confidence they can get. Rock the boat hard enough now, and you might rock them right overboard."

"You've given me a lot to think about," said John. He was remembering what the Prior had told him about the loss of work in areas of Italy that needed work so desperately. He said, "By the way, did I tell you that I was getting a job at Laleham?"

"You said you'd applied."

"I've got an interview there on Monday. I'll see what I can unearth there before I make up my mind."

When Jonas had left, John walked out again onto the balcony to look down over London. A thought had occurred to him. The date was August second. It was on August second, a year before, that he had set out for Heathrow Airport on the way to New Zealand. He was now a mile or two farther back than when he had started. An odd result for a year of travel.

On the next day, which was a Friday, John bought a new Yamaha motorcycle and tried it out. It was the sort of machine that had taken him on his holidays to Dartmoor and the Lakes. On such occasions, if the short time available to him was not to be wasted, he had had to cover long distances as quickly as possible. He was pleased to find that his old skill had not deserted him.

On Saturday he used the machine to carry out a plan which had been in his mind ever since he got back to England. He set out at about eleven o'clock and rode north. By half past eleven he had cleared the London traffic and by one o'clock was tucking the Yamaha away in the crowded car park of a roadhouse between Aylesbury and Bicester. Here he ordered the most expensive luncheon the place could offer and further endeared himself to the management by topping it off with a large brandy. Then he tackled the manager. He had an important and rather confidential call to make to a business contact in the south of France. He would probably have to wait for some time for the reply. Was there a telephone he could use?

"Use the one in my office," said the manager. "Then you can wait in the lounge and my girl will tell you when the return call comes through."

John thanked him and telephoned the home number in Cannes which Monica had given him. He realized he would have been more likely to find her at home if he had telephoned early in the day, but it would have been more difficult to set things up the way he wanted.

He could hear the telephone ringing at the other end. Four times. Eight times. Twelve times. At sixteen he would give up. She would be out swimming or sailing.

Then she answered. John said, "It's me, Monica. John. Listen. This is an English number. Don't talk. Just write it down. Then go to your nearest public telephone box and ring me back."

141

There was a moment's pause, before Monica said, "All right," and rang off. He had only to wait ten minutes before her call came through. She said, "Now perhaps you'll tell me what it's all about."

"I'm getting security minded," said John.

"Do you think my telephone's tapped?"

"I thought it might be."

"If anyone was listening won't they be able to trace you through the number you gave me?"

"It would do them no good if they could. I'm in a hotel miles from anywhere special. It's the first time I've been here, and it's going to be the last."

"I can't tell you what a surprise it was when I heard your voice."

"Oh, why?"

"Why? Because when you upset people like the Mafia and the Union Corse it is always a surprise to hear that you're alive and well. A nice surprise, of course."

"I'm glad you're glad. Did they trace the car?"

"Eventually. It had been stolen in Cannes that evening. The Union were able to use their pull with the local police to get a country-wide search organized next morning, but it doesn't seem to have been very efficiently carried out, because it was days before they located the car in a station car park north of Lyon."

"Hold it," said John. "This could be important. You said days. How many?"

"Emile said at least two. It might have been more. Why?"

"Because," said John slowly, "the only contact I had with the French police was at about four o'clock in the afternoon on the Friday. If there had been a general alert, which included a description of me, I presume they'd have held me. As it was I sailed through without any trouble, thanks to a splendid little man called Rossall. A real Good Samaritan."

"You sound very cheerful. Have you been having a good time in England?"

"I've just had a very nice meal."

"With a very nice girl?"

142

"I lunched alone. Who do you think I am, Casanova?"

"I admired your technique. Very smooth, I thought."

"Technique?" John was starting to splutter when he realized that his leg was being pulled. He said, "As a matter of fact, I did meet a girl when I was staying in Soho. Her name was Lois."

"She sounds terrific."

"She was. Measured in any direction." He heard Monica laugh and added, "I'm ringing you because there's something I want to find out. Do the people in the Italian factory *know* what happened at the Paoli farm?"

"They know there was a fire."

"But nothing else."

"It was given out that it was accidental."

"I see. Mightn't it be a good idea if someone let them know the true story?"

Monica had to think about this. She said, "It could be done. It would take a little time."

"I'll ring you back at exactly the same time next week. I'll say, in my best French, 'This is number so-and-so. I regret to say that your hairdressing appointment has had to be postponed until Wednesday.' You can express your displeasure, ring off, get to the nearest call box and dial that number, which will be a hotel in quite a different part of the country."

"You're being very cautious."

"I'm learning," said John.

Sam Cox, who interviewed John at Laleham, looked like a wire-haired fox terrier. The same ruffled brown hair sticking up rebelliously, the same shrewd brown eyes.

He started in English and switched smoothly, first into competent French and then into adequate, but rather schoolboy, Italian. John followed him without difficulty.

Cox said, "Your Italian's very good. In fact you lost *me* once or twice. Some of those slang expressions. How did you pick it up?"

"An Italian girlfriend," said John. For a moment he was

143

back in front of the fire at the Paoli farm swapping collo-quialisms with Anna.

"Very useful when you have to chat up customers. Of course, when it comes to letter writing you need the commercial jargon too. I see from your application that you've had some experience in computers. Could you tell me about that?"

"I worked for nearly three years for a firm called Tolcom."

Cox looked puzzled. "I thought I knew most of them, but that's a new one to me."

"It was a one-man outfit, run by a chap called Tolhurst. It made parts for matrix printers. They went out of fashion when the daisy wheel came in. We could all see that Tolcom was only just keeping going. Then one morning Tolhurst didn't turn up at the office. The hospital telephoned later. He'd had a massive heart attack. Died that evening."

"Overwork," suggested Cox sympathetically. "One-man firm. Yes. I can see that really would have caused difficulties for everyone."

"A normally conducted outfit might have survived. This was the sort of firm where the boss knew where everything was and no one else knew anything. The records were in a mess. I believe the liquidator was happy to sell it, lock, stock and barrel, for what he could get. I'd gone by then, of course."

John knew that most of this was true. He had himself bought Tolcom for a modest sum. All he had wanted was their stock of components. Their records had been in such chaos that he had scrapped the lot and opened new books.

"So what did you do next?"

"Had a holiday. My people come from New Zealand. I went out to see them. I'd some idea of starting up on my own there, but I soon gave it up. It's a wonderful country. Three million people and three hundred million sheep. But a limited outlook for someone from outside wanting to set up a new industry."

"I've heard that they're a bit parochial."

"Parochial. They're late-Victorian. The only thing that's up-to-date is their rugby football."

"You picked up just a hint of the accent. I noticed it when

144

you started to speak. I thought, Australian or New Zealand." Cox seemed pleased with his detective ability. Then, without any change of tone, he said, "What do you think of gas discharge display?"

It took John a moment to gather his wits. Then he said, "You mean, as an alternative to the cathode ray tube apparatus?"

"Right."

"Well, there are good and bad points. If you use G.D.D. you don't need an electron gun, and that means a flatter and more compact unit. Some people say the display clearer, too. Less flickering. The real drawback is the price. I shouldn't think there's much future in it now that LEO display is being developed."

"All right, all right," said Cox with a grin. "I just wanted to find out. You'd be surprised the number of people who come along looking for jobs and say they know all about computers. When you ask a few simple questions, you find that all they've got is a home computer for the kids to play Star Wars on. If you'd like to come along now, I'll show you the setup."

He led the way from the annex in which they'd been sitting into the main building. Here John was introduced to one or two people who grinned politely and whose names he forgot as soon as they moved on to the next one. They had a cup of coffee in the canteen, which was presided over by a smiling West Indian woman. When they had finished their tour and were back in the annex, Cox said, "Well, you've seen us. What do you think?"

"I think I could do a good job here," said John.

He felt oddly treacherous as he said it.

"Then we'd better discuss money." Cox mentioned a sum that seemed to John to be adequate. He said, "I suppose you haven't got the cards you had with Tolcom?"

"Cards?" said John. "I suppose there was someone who looked after that sort of thing. I just felt happy if I got my monthly check. You'd have to ask the liquidator about that."

"I expect we can sort it out," said Cox. "You mentioned two references in your application. A bank and a solicitor, wasn't it?"

145

"The solicitor will be more use to you. He's known me a lot longer."

"Fine. Then subject to these references, which I'm sure will be O.K., when can you start?"

"The sooner the better," said John. "Next Monday if you like."

"Excellent."

"And if you want to get in touch with me, I suggest you do it through my solicitor. I'm on the move at the moment. I'll let you know as soon as I've got a permanent address."

Thinking it over afterward, he was unsure why he had withheld his Holly Lodge address. Caution, or a sort of overcaution which was becoming a bad habit? Difficult to say.

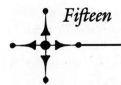

Fifteen

When John arrived at the office on the following Monday, he was pleased to find that he was to share a room with Mike Collins. Monica had said he was an agreeable person, and John found him so.

Mike said, "It'll take you a bit of time to learn the ropes. There's more to this outfit than meets the eye. But rather than start by giving you a long spiel, most of which you'll forget, I've got hold of a head office memorandum which shows the lines we run on. When you've mastered that, I can fill in some of the gaps. We could do it over lunch."

"Fine," said John. "Let's do that."

It was a comprehensive document. It dealt first with the factories in Italy, France, Corsica and Scotland and went on to describe the particular sales areas allotted to each. Italy, he found, sold to Switzerland, Austria, southwest Germany, Yugoslavia, Greece and Turkey. France covered northwest Germany, the Benelux countries and Denmark. Corsica dealt with Spain, Portugal and the states along the northern seaboard of Africa, from Morocco through to Egypt.

(Here John paused for a moment. Surely Paoli had told him that their factory sold to Tunisia? Perhaps they changed about from time to time.)

Finally there was Scotland, which was the newest. It had been allotted Norway, Sweden, Finland and the North Sea oil rigs. They had also, he remembered, taken over the defense sales from France.

As he got more deeply into the memorandum, analyzing

the facts and figures, he realized that MBA was a formidably constructed outfit, the product of a few hard and clear-thinking minds. It not only controlled manufacture in the four centers, and direct sales into more than twenty states, but acted as middleman in a number of other transactions. He was interested to see that they bought keyboards, desk units and card readers in Britain and sold them to Vinercasta, a Milan firm he had often dealt with himself.

By lunchtime he had covered two sheets of paper with queries.

"The point you have to grasp," said Collins, "is that we're unique. Other companies have become multinational when they got big enough to locate some of their production abroad. In our case that was the plan from the word go. But it did mean that we had to find the money out of our own pockets to run everything in this country: the office here, the laboratory at Teddington, the headquarters in the City. To say nothing of the sale and service organizations abroad."

He said "out of our own pockets," thought John, as though it was, in fact, out of *his* pocket that the money had come. He had already noted the communal pride which animated the whole outfit.

"You'll appreciate that expenditure on that scale couldn't go on for long. The foreign producers simply *had* to generate profit, and pretty quickly, or we should have been sunk. And they had to get the cash back here. That was another of our problems."

"You mean Exchange Control?"

"Yes. Well, that sort of thing. Italy is the real stinker. They can't prevent money going out for actual expenses, but they draw a rigid line at exporting capital."

"So what do you do?"

Mike paused for a moment, then said, "Well, one of the things, obviously, is to make as little profit in Italy as possible. We've set up an outfit in Denmark to buy everything that Italy makes. It buys it at a low price and invoices it on to the actual customers. The whole thing's a paper transaction. The goods never actually go into Denmark at all, but it's the Danish company that makes the profit."

"Which it has to pay tax on."

"Certainly. But no skin off their nose, because Danish tax rates are the lowest in Europe and there's no bar to their feeding the profits back to us."

John thought about it. Evidently this was the shadow factory in Denmark that Monica had talked about. Equally evidently, although a bit slim, it was legal, or Mike wouldn't have discussed it so openly. What interested him more was that Mike had called it "one of the things we do." That sounded as though there might be other, less reputable, methods of getting cash out of Italy.

Don't press it. Change the subject.

He said, "What's the significance of the letter X, in red, on every page of the memorandum?"

"Part of our security system. X is the lowest rating. It only means you're not supposed to take it out of the office. If a paper is marked Y you have to keep it under lock and key. Z papers are collected every evening by Loveridge."

"Loveridge?"

"At the table by the window."

John saw a middle-aged man with black hair, which he thought might be dyed. The hair had a suspiciously regular wave in it and this, with the trim mustache, gave him the look of a twenties star of the silent films.

"Is he your security officer?"

"Officially he's Assistant Personnel Manager."

John very nearly said, Like Emile Lytaudy, and stopped himself just in time.

There were two men sitting at the table with Loveridge.

"I suppose those are his assistants."

"Retired police officers. Yes."

"You take security pretty seriously here."

"Certainly. We all try to plant spies on each other. It's part of the game."

149

A rough game, thought John, looking at the trio at the window table.

In the course of the next few days he worked his way into the job, which was not too difficult except when it came to translating complex technicalities into a foreign language. However, he found Mike's bookcase well stocked with specialized dictionaries and handbooks. It was while he was looking for one of these that he spotted, tucked away on the bottom shelf, a collection which seemed out of place: half a dozen small books, well produced, each dealing with one of the lesser-known Catholic saints and the lessons to be derived from a study of their lives. They had been published by the Catholic Texts Translation Society, which had an address in Brocklehurst Terrace. Each book carried on its title page the personal endorsement of Cardinal Gandolfo, head of the Religious Education Department in the Vatican.

John was studying the life of Saint Paulinus, one of whose teachings was that all men should go bareheaded and barefooted as a sign of humility, when Mike came back. He spotted the book and said, "I bought those because I thought they might amuse the children."

"Not a very practical guideline for children," said John. "Bad for their feet, not wearing shoes, so I'm told."

"And unpopular with hatters and shoemakers," said Mike. "Look, I've got a letter here that Ligertwood wants to go out this evening without fail."

"He's the boss," said John. He pushed the book back into the shelf.

When he got there on the following morning he was interested to see that the little books had disappeared.

Getting to the office in the morning was rather easier than getting away in the evening against the outflow of London traffic. In the end John found it better to put in an hour at the Dolphin public house down the road. It had an additional attraction. He was able to talk on easy terms with members of the staff he would not otherwise have met socially.

There was Bob, who kept the gate, and one-armed Len,

the doorman. Len was cool at first, but thawed when he found that John's father had been with the New Zealand Division. "A great crowd," he said. "I was with Sixth Armored. Wounded at Cassino."

They fought old battles together in the public bar of the Dolphin, joined from time to time by other members of the staff. John gathered that Sir Tom, who seemed popular, still gave preference where possible to ex-servicemen.

One thing puzzled him, and toward the end of the week, when he knew them better, he raised it. He said to Bob, "I should have thought you and Len would be the very last to get away. Seeing people off and doing all the locking up."

"Not our job," said Bob. "Loverboy sees to all that. Him and his two goons. Go round all the rooms seeing no one's left papers lying about which they shouldn't."

"Better watch it, John," said Len. "Get your balls chewed off if you do."

John promised to watch it.

On one occasion he saw two people he knew, through the partition, in the saloon bar. They had both worked for him in the old days. One, he remembered, was called Pym. He had been a junior cashier. The other had been a typist. She had come just before he sold out to MBA. He couldn't remember her name.

John placed himself where they could hardly fail to see him. Neither of them took the slightest notice of him. His beard, his suntan and a pair of steel-rimmed, plain-lens glasses which he had taken to wearing at the office were no doubt an adequate disguise. But he realized that the main reason for previous acquaintances not recognizing him was that they all thought he was dead.

On Friday, which was payday, the party in the public bar was larger and more uninhibited than usual. The floor was held by a character variously known as Rob Roy, Red Rob or the Scottish Rebel. He worked in the packing department and held strong views which three or four pints of beer made even stronger. He was not really a rabble-rouser, thought John. More a licensed buffoon.

"I've nae doot," he said, "that you've haird of the Scottish Nationalist Party."

"Every Friday," said one of the audience.

"They're a daft crowd o' sump'ns and their heads are full o' whigmaleeries, but our people up there find a use for them."

"They're no bloody use to anyone, Rob. Least of all to themselves."

"Aye, but they are. 'Gin one of the boys suggests perhaps the management might conseeder raising wages, he finds the Nationalists calling him a stooge o' the Yanks. In that part of Scotland the anti-American drum makes a lot of noise."

"Like you, Rob."

"Ye ken what Burns said."

It seemed that everyone knew what Burns had said, because this set off a male-voice plainsong choir:

> *"We labour soon, we labour late*
> *To feed the titled knave, man,*
> *And a' the comfort we're to get—*
> (All together, now!)
> *Is that a yon't the grave, man."*

This effort was received with a round of applause. But at this moment, when the party seemed to John to be getting nicely under way, it started to tail off. His next-door neighbor whispered something to Rob Roy, who looked aggrieved but fell silent. One or two of the men finished their beer and made for the door.

Glancing across the bar, John saw that Loveridge and one of his men had come in. He finished his own beer thoughtfully and made his way out to his motorcycle.

By this time the traffic had diminished a lot. It could have been because he had to pay less attention to cars approaching him that he happened to notice the dark blue Volvo behind him. It looked like a fast car, but when he slowed down it made no attempt to pass him. When he put on speed it had no difficulty in keeping up with him.

John thought of various devices by which a man on a motorcycle could throw off a car but abandoned them. He decided to play the hand quietly. When he reached the Holly Lodge Estate the Volvo had fallen back. He tucked away his machine in the yard, walked across to the restaurant on the other side of the road and ordered his normal evening meal.

The Volvo was now parked at the end of the road. When he came out, it had gone. He saw the porter standing in the entrance to the yard and said, "Was someone asking for me?"

The porter looked at him curiously. He said, "There was a man, Mr. Naylor. He looked like a policeman. I hope you're not in some sort of trouble."

"Not that I know of," said John. "What did he want?"

"He said he just wanted to check your address. Was I wrong to give it to him?"

"Of course not. When you've nothing to conceal, why bother to conceal it?"

The porter agreed with him but still looked worried.

First thing on Monday morning John went into the annex to have a word with Cox.

He said, "I told you I hadn't got a permanent address. Well, that's all fixed now. I signed the agreement last week. One-four-one Makepeace Mansions, Holly Lodge Estate, N Six."

Cox said, "Thanks. I'll make a note of it." He got out his personnel files.

As he was doing this, John spotted a name on one of the lists. He said, "I didn't know Mike's wife worked here."

"Mrs. Collins? That's not Mike's wife. Different person altogether. A canteen cleaner. Anyway, Mike isn't married. One of the secretaries made a good shot at it, at the firm's Christmas dance, but he sidestepped."

"Odd," said John. "I thought he said something about his children. Must have been talking about other people's children."

"I've had Naylor looked into," said Loveridge. "He seems O.K. to me. He's got a little furnished flat up in Highgate. Rather a nice part of London, actually. The porter said his solicitor wangled it for him."

Ligertwood grunted. The sound might have indicated

153

agreement or skepticism. His face, in repose, was dull and heavy. Only the eyes were alive.

"Collins says he's a good worker. Picking up the job fast. And he seems to get along all right with the chaps. Likes a pint of beer in the evening."

Ligertwood grunted again. Loveridge said, his tone sharpening a little, "Was there some particular reason you wanted him checked, sir?"

"No particular reason," said Ligertwood. "Call it instinct, if you like." He picked out a paper from the folder on his desk. "He seemed a bit too good to be true. A sound technical knowledge and two European languages. One of them good, one very good. And we're paying him little more than a top secretary."

"That is odd," agreed Loveridge. "Those boys don't often underprice themselves."

"I'm not happy about him. He turns up here with a story that he was employed by Tolcom. It seems the Tolcom records are unavailable. Either they're with the liquidator or the Benedict people took them over."

"Benedict? Isn't that the company we bought last year?"

"That's a thought." Ligertwood picked up the intercom and spoke to Cox. He said, "Come up, would you. And bring the records of any staff we took over from Benedict Engineering."

When he arrived and the papers had been sorted out, it seemed that only six people had actually transferred. Ligertwood fastened on one of them.

"Layfield," he said. "He came to Benedict's from Tolcom. That's the man we want. Get hold of him."

"He's up in Scotland, sir."

"Then bring him down."

"I think, sir, that he's due here on Friday anyway. For a sales managers' conference at Teddington."

"Get him over here before the conference starts. I'll have a word with him myself."

On the Saturday of his second week, John again took his motorcycle out of London, going east this time, into the farmlands of Kent. He found the sort of roadhouse he wanted, between Canterbury and Dover, and repeated his tactics.

Monica sounded worried. She said, "There *is* something wrong with my telephone. I don't think it's just my imagination. A sort of echo when I talk. If you hadn't suggested it I wouldn't have noticed it, but now I'm beginning to believe it has been tapped. Why should anyone have done a thing like that?"

"It was perfectly logical," said John. "The police and the Union are interested in a Mr. Michaels who was staying at the Hotel Caravelle and has been tactless enough to vanish. His only known connection is a girl he got friendly with while he was staying there."

"I like it when you say 'girl.' It makes me feel ten years younger."

"That's just how I think of you."

"Don't fluff. I want to know about my telephone."

"Police logic. Sooner or later Mr. Michaels will ring the girl up. Then we shall be able to trace him."

"Why on earth should they bother? You hadn't done anything. Rocca's death was accidental."

"Don't forget that I made off with a stolen car."

"One that had been stolen already. And was recovered undamaged two or three days later. Surely that's not worth a lot of effort to trace you. I don't believe it's the police at all."

"I know," said John. "Don't tell me. You think it's the Union Corse. Well, let me tell you this: I don't give a brass button for the Mafia or the Union. They may be big boys in their own countries, but they don't cut a lot of ice here. And even if they knew both numbers I've phoned from and could trace them, it wouldn't get them a yard further. I chose roadhouses with big car parks, always crowded at weekends, and I've stowed my machine well away at the back where it won't be noticed. So let's stop worrying about me and think about something important. Did you do what I suggested?"

"Let the Italian factory know the truth about what happened to the Paolis? Yes. I got the news to them."

"What were their reactions?"

"They were very angry. But they wanted proof. I told

Giacomo that if he had a word with Valori or Genzano he'd hear the truth. If he could get them to talk."

"I don't think old Valori will dare to open his mouth, and I don't blame him. But I think Genzano might. He's a man with very strong principles. But it would depend."

"Depend on what?"

"It would depend," said John slowly, "on whether he thought the men were going to do anything about it."

"I told you they were angry. Paoli was a well-liked man. And his daughter had a lot of friends. But they're frightened, too. They remember what happened when Faldo was kidnapped. How the Mafia looked after him. They think that anyone who lays a hand on him will incur the displeasure of his protectors."

"And that's the way it goes," said John bitterly. "Something needs doing, but no one will do it in case something happens to them. The only way that anything worthwhile ever gets done is when someone is prepared to say, 'Damn the consequences' and push right ahead."

"I don't like it when you're in that mood," said Monica. "I don't like it, and I don't trust you."

"I'm sorry about not liking me," said John mildly. "But you're quite right not to trust me. I don't often get angry, but when I do, it brings out my great-grandfather. I'll tell you about him some day." He thought for a moment. "Things are coming to a head here more quickly than I'd thought. Could you be at home every evening this week between eight and nine o'clock?"

"It'll murder my social life," said Monica. "But I'll do it."

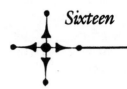

Sixteen

When Sam Cox got to his office on Monday morning he was surprised to find Henry Ligertwood already there. A surreptitious glance at his own watch assured him that he was not late. Ligertwood seemed to have been examining a number of files he had taken out of Cox's filing cabinet. He said, "Good morning, Sam," and perched himself on the corner of the desk.

Like a bloody raven, Cox thought. Ready to peck out some poor animal's eyes. However, his tone sounded reasonably genial.

He said, "I've been thinking about that new man, Naylor. Didn't it seem a bit odd when he couldn't produce any national insurance cards or P.A.Y.E. records or anything like that?"

"He did explain about the firm he was with before—"

"Yes. Tolcom." Ligertwood had the file open in front of him.

"That's right, sir. Apparently the records were in a mess. Naylor didn't need his cards, as he was planning to go out to New Zealand and maybe stay there permanently, so he just pushed off without bothering about them."

"I understand that. But it isn't very satisfactory from our point of view, is it? What are we doing about our records?"

"I've written to the local branch of the Employment Ministry and explained the position."

"A letter which they will sit on for six months and then write back apologizing for losing it."

"Judged on their past performance, I think that's not unlikely."

"Tell me, have you ever had a situation like this before?"

"We've had people coming here directly from school or university. Then we set up the paperwork ourselves."

"Certainly. But can you remember anyone who had been employed before, coming along without any papers at all?"

"Now you mention it, I don't think I can."

"It's the tax side I was thinking about. If you start off on the wrong foot with the P.A.Y.E. records, you can get into a mess."

"That's true," said Cox. He thought the old man was making a real meal out of a routine morsel.

"What I'd like you to do is get in touch with our legal people. Ramage would be best. Get him to put in an inquiry with the Official Receiver's Office. I want to find out what did happen to its papers when Tolcom folded. Ramage could probably do it, if you made a point of getting him to handle it himself."

Ramage was one of the senior partners in the City firm who handled MBA's legal business. It seemed odd to ask him to carry out personally an assignment that would normally have gone to a junior assistant. However, his not to reason why.

As soon as Mr. Ligertwood had heaved himself off the desk and departed, Cox picked up the telephone.

That evening John spoke on the telephone to his own solicitor. He said, "I want you to find out something for me."

"More about the computer industry?" said Jonas.

"Something else, this time. Are some of your friends and clients papists?"

"Members of the English Roman Catholic community. Yes."

"And there are papers people like that read?"

"You make it sound as though they were a secret society. There are a number of well-known Catholic periodicals. Do you want their names?"

"No. What I want you to do is to find out the name of someone fairly high up in one of them."

"Just the name?"

"That's all. Christian name and surname if possible."

"If that's all you want, I can give it to you now. I know Bernard Martindale quite well. He's assistant editor of the *Catholic Times* and will be editor as soon as the existing chap checks out."

"That's just the sort of man I wanted."

"If you're planning to see Bernard, you might give him my kind regards."

"I wasn't actually planning to see him."

"Are you up to something?"

"I'm laying down a few lines," said John. "Things are moving. I may have to trespass further on your kindness some evening this week."

"You know where to find me. I'm very rarely away from the office before seven."

On Tuesday evening Cox went up to Mr. Ligertwood's office. He was rather pleased with himself for the speed with which he'd carried out his instructions. He expected a pat on the back.

This expectation vanished when he saw Mr. Ligertwood's face. He was in what the office called one of his bilious moods.

Cox said, "About Naylor, sir. I got onto Mr. Ramage and explained the position. It was very fortunate that he happened to know the Official Receiver personally. They'd been on a Law Society Inquiry together."

Ligertwood grunted. He did not waste time explaining that this was why he had suggested Ramage.

"He got a quick answer to your inquiry. The Tolcom liquidation *was* rather an unusual one. The company wasn't in a particularly bad way financially. It was just that Tolhurst handled everything himself—"

"I know all that. Get to the point."

"Well, the only big creditor was the firm that did the printing and advertising for them. They had an outstanding account of about nine hundred pounds, and since no one seemed able to write them a check they petitioned for liquidation. Then, before any real steps could be taken, Benedict Engineering came along

159

with an offer for the company. They paid fifteen hundred pounds and took it over lock, stock and barrel."

"Then?"

"The printers were paid off and the liquidation was stayed by agreement."

Mr. Ligertwood was making some calculations. He said, "Nine hundred to the printers, and they'd have had to pay their legal costs and the liquidator's fees as well. There can't have been much left out of fifteen hundred pounds."

"Actually, I believe there were only two or three other trade creditors. Very small amounts indeed."

"Then there's something I don't understand. If the tax records were in a mess, as Naylor told us, why wasn't there a substantial claim by the Revenue?"

"Well, yes—I suppose there would have been."

"Of course there would have been. I'm surprised you didn't think of it."

Ligertwood picked up a letter and started to read it. The interview appeared to be over. Cox retired with his tail between his legs.

After he had gone, Ligertwood put down the letter and sat for some minutes, staring out of the window. People who live in countries which are subject to earthquakes sometimes maintain that they can feel advance tremors before the seismograph starts to flicker. Any threat, however distant, however indistinct, to the complex machine into which he had put so much labor and so much money affected Henry Ligertwood in the same way. He knew that the next few weeks—maybe the next few days— were vital. They would make the difference between MBA's mounting to the top of the ladder or slipping down, rung by rung, to an undistinguished second or third position. He shook his massive head angrily. The intercom on his desk purred. His secretary said, "It's the Chairman, sir. He's on his way up."

By the time Chervil arrived, Ligertwood had recovered some of his equanimity. He said, "They only told me fifteen minutes ago, Tom, that you were honoring us with a visit. I didn't have time to get the red carpet rolled out."

Chervil dumped himself down in one chair, hurled his

briefcase onto another and said, "I'm exhausted. I have just sustained an hour's talk with a gentleman called Lambert Mather. And I mean sustained. It was a monologue most of the way. And who is Lambert Mather? How dare you ask such a question? He is a *most* important man. At least that is the impression he likes to give you. He is the Junior Minister of State in the Department of Industry."

"That sounds promising," said Ligertwood. "If he talked to you for an hour, he must be taking us seriously."

"Oh, he's a serious man. When I heard that he wanted to see me I looked up his record. He's been chairman of two companies, both in the field of plastics. Under his inspired leadership, one of them folded up altogether and the other was taken over by its main competitor. That's what's known as 'having a background in industry.'"

"I hope," said Ligertwood, with a note of reproof in his voice, "that you didn't let your unfavorable opinion of him appear too clearly."

"My dear Henry, credit me with some sense. In any event, I was hardly allowed to speak. I was content to listen. One thing is quite clear. At this moment, we are their favorite sons. Mr. Mather said, and I quote, that although I must understand that he could not make any definite promises, he could say, off the record, that if nothing happened to upset currently held views, it looked fairly certain that we should be considered to have achieved a position of authority and integrity in the field of information processing sufficient to place us at the head of the queue for government subvention."

"But that's excellent, Tom. If a civil servant is prepared to commit himself as far as that, it must mean they've made their minds up."

"Civil servants pick their words carefully. You notice he said '*if* nothing happened to upset' them. And then again, the use of the word 'integrity.'"

"What are you getting at?"

"I wondered if one of our competitors might have whispered in his ear that our record wasn't entirely clean."

"Clean? For God's sake! Surely our political bosses are realists. They must know that any successful outfit has episodes in its past which they'd prefer to forget. I could name two leading oil companies that wouldn't care to be reminded of how they secured their first drilling concessions. But after a few years of virtuous and profitable operation, these things get forgotten."

"Unless people's noses are rubbed in them. Whitehall has been a bit sensitive since the Can-Tag revelations last year."

"Had you anything specific in mind?"

"Well, I'm not worried about our arrangements with Denmark. The Revenue knows all about them and has tried to challenge them and failed. No. Our two weakest spots are the Catholic Texts and our understandings with the Mafia in Italy and the Union Corse in France."

"I never really approved of that," said Ligertwood gloomily. "I've told you often enough."

You've started to say it recently, thought Chervil. But you voted for it readily enough when it was first suggested. He refrained from putting this into words. It was a difficult moment, and it would be made no easier by disagreement at the top. He contented himself with saying, "There were arguments for and against it. I may have been unduly influenced by the men on the spot. The thing now is not to blame ourselves for past misjudgments but to consider how to rectify them."

"We can stop the Catholic Text operation easily enough. It was important when we needed funds direct from Italy, but our reserves are now large enough to make all payments from London. And they'll be even larger if we get this government money."

"Right. Then we tell them—let me think—that with these new developments and increased public participation, we have to be careful not to appear to favor one religious group above others. Many apologies and a handsome parting present."

"A golden handshake for the Pope," suggested Ligertwood. He sounded happier. Then a further thought occurred to him. "Do you think it's possible that the opposition might actually have tried to insert someone into our organization simply to scratch around for dirt?"

"It's what I should have done in their position. Why?"

"It makes sense of something that was puzzling me. There's a man just joined us here who doesn't quite add up."

He told him about Naylor.

"You could be right," said Chervil. "But why should it worry you? If you've the slightest suspicion, throw him out. Pay him to the end of the week and tell him not to come back. He hasn't been here long enough to take us to a Tribunal."

"He could sue us for wrongful dismissal."

"He could, but I'd guess he won't."

"Suppose he simply refuses to go?"

"Then you can give Loveridge and his boys a free hand. If they get a little rough, that's his lookout. After Friday he'll be a trespasser here. Trespassers sometimes get hurt. I only wish all our problems were as easy to solve. I'd like to treat the Mafia and the Union in the same way as our Catholic friends. Thank them very warmly for their past help, explain that we're now quite big enough to stand on our own feet and kiss them good-bye."

"Why don't we do just that? After all, there's nothing in writing between us. No binding agreement. If we gave them a quiet hint—"

"You're talking about them as though they were insurance companies. Of course there's nothing in writing. You don't write letters to the Mafia. *Dear Sirs: We would like to commission your organization—*"

"All right, all right." Ligertwood was getting angry again. "I told you I didn't understand these things. How was it fixed?"

"Person-to-person, at top level. Through a man called Ronconi in Italy and through Emile Lytaudy in France. And if it's to be unfixed, they'll have to do it the same way. Unfortunately it's a bad moment for fixing anything. They're on the verge of war."

"Over what?"

"Over a man called Michaels."

"The one you told us about?"

"Yes."

"Why would they be fighting over him?"

"Lytaudy explained it to me. It's an unwritten rule. If one

organization asks for help from the other and the helper gets killed, generous compensation is payable to his family. In this case the Mafia—not unreasonably, I think—objected to paying. They said that Rocca, the man who was sent by the Union to do the job, had bungled it. Had behaved, in fact, with unbelievable stupidity. They didn't feel inclined to pay anything."

"What sort of money were they talking about?"

"A hundred million lire."

"Fifty thousand pounds." Ligertwood thought about it. He had a very precise idea of the weight and effectiveness of money. He said, "That's the sort of sum we'd give to a senior departmental head if we had to get rid of him."

"It's not a great deal of money in the budget of either organization, I agree. But that's not the point. Something more important than money is now at stake. Prestige. Positions have been taken up. Hard words have been spoken. There was an incident last week at the border post at Ventimiglia. Bloodshed was avoided on that occasion. Next time it may not be."

Ligertwood said nothing for some moments. His mouth was working as though he would have liked to chew up both organizations and spit them out. He said, "Is this anything to do with us?"

Chervil said, in the tones of a professor stating an axiom, "If Michaels is not Gabriel, it does not concern us at all. If Michaels is Gabriel, it concerns us very much indeed."

There was a silence which Ligertwood seemed unwilling to break. He was not a stupid man. He understood quite clearly the implications of what he had heard. When, at last, he said, "What *did* happen at that farm, Tom?" he sounded like a man who feels compelled to ask his doctor a question but is afraid to listen to the answer.

"I've seen the official report. They kept a reserve store of fuel for the tractors in a shed outside the house. The firemen and the police both noted a smell of petrol. Their idea is that the fire started, somehow, in this shed and spread to the house. Most Italians sleep with their windows tight shut. The fire could have been well under way before they noticed it. The downstairs windows were barred and the doors elaborately locked and bolted.

The theory is that the family tried to get out but were overcome before they could do so. This was borne out by the fact that the body of the man was found actually in the downstairs room and the girl on the staircase. The old lady was still in her bed."

"Do you believe that?"

"I'd like to believe it, but no, I can't."

"Why not?"

"You understand as well as I do, Henry. Don't try to dodge it." There was a hard edge to Chervil's voice. Harder than Ligertwood had heard for many years. Since that night in the Irish Guards mess. . . . "Think," said Chervil. "Gabriel had been lucky enough to be away that night. But if Michael *is* Gabriel, it appears that, instead of congratulating him on his good fortune, the Mafia has been following him for the last six months with the intention of shutting his mouth. Why?"

"You're telling me," said Ligertwood, speaking as though he could hardly get the words out, "that they set the house on fire. That the doors were barred *on the outside*. That the three people in the house were deliberately burned to death. And this was done on your instructions."

"I gave no such instructions. A message was conveyed, through a number of intermediaries, that Paoli was to be stopped from making trouble. It was the same sort of message that was sent when we suspected that the Americans had planted spies in our factory. You were not dissatisfied with the result in that case, I seem to remember."

"That was quite different. Industrial spies must expect hard treatment. But a girl—and an old woman—who had nothing to do with the matter."

Chervil was not moved by the accusation. He said, in his normal level voice, "I don't know about the old woman, but the girl had, I understand, a great deal to do with it."

Ligertwood was hardly listening. He had slipped back more than twenty yards. A subaltern, new to the regiment, had been playing poker in the mess after dinner. He had been stupid enough to accuse Chervil of cheating. With the full approval of all the young officers present, the room had been cleared. Chervil and the newcomer had taken their coats off and had fought

165

with bare fists. Chervil was sober and a very competent boxer. His opponent was no boxer and must have been slightly drunk or he would not have made the accusation. Chervil had cut him to pieces. He was removed to the Regimental Aid Post and, subsequently, to hospital. The only explanation given was that there had been the sort of horseplay which, with tacit approval, often took place on dinner nights when the senior officers had retired, and that on this night it had been somewhat rougher than usual. The young man kept his mouth shut. But he did not rejoin the battalion. What Ligertwood remembered most about the incident was Chervil's reaction to it. When the tables had been replaced, the game had continued. At the end of it Chervil, who had won a fair amount of money, had said, "On the whole, rather a good evening."

Ligertwood had been afraid of him then, and he was afraid of him now.

He brought his mind back, with an effort, to the present. He said, "You realize that this theory of yours all depends on one point. That Gabriel and Michaels are the same man."

"Certainly. If they aren't, there could have been any number of other reasons for Michaels' incurring the Mafia's displeasure. Nothing to do with the fire at all."

"And we've no proof one way or the other."

"No real proof. There was the fact that both of them were New Zealanders and roughly the same size and age. Michaels seems to have been starting a beard, which might have been a sensible bit of camouflage."

"But nothing, really, to go on."

The relief in Ligertwood's voice gave him away. He was too anxious to convince himself.

"It was a possibility, no more. Recently it has become a little more probable. It's a small thing, but we're dealing with guesses. Our friends in the Police Judiciaire at Nice have made some progress in tracing the movements of Michaels. He appropriated the car which Rocca had come in and, incidentally, seems to have started it without a key. Clever chap. He drove it through the night. It was noticed two days later, in the parking lot at Villefranche station. It seems to have been standing there since early Thursday morning. So what would Mr. Michaels have planned to do then? He might have decided to make a little distance by rail, but he's a cautious character. If he used public transport he wouldn't have stayed on it for long. Well, the next piece in the puzzle is a sunburnt and bearded character riding shotgun on an International Transport lorry. He was noted at a police check on Friday afternoon, near Bar-le-Duc, between Nancy and Paris. What interested the police was that he didn't talk."

"Was that suspicious?"

"Unusual. When they stop an English lorry, their experience is that the driver and his mate relish a bit of back chat. This man seemed anxious to avoid attention."

"Still a bit thin."

"Oh, certainly. We are pursuing shadows. However, the details of the lorry were noted. It crossed into Belgium at Givet, south of Charleroi, at about ten o'clock and was in Ostend at midday. One of our friends spoke to the customs official, who always dealt with that particular lorry. He knew the driver quite well. A man called Albert Rossall. He was curious about the fact that he had a co-driver. Normally he operated alone. Rossall explained that the man was a stranger he'd picked up. He was under some obligation to him for repairing his lorry. An expert mechanic, he said. Now we know that Mr. Gabriel was famous through the countryside as a doctor of all sorts of mechanical transport. The ends seemed to be joining up."

Ligertwood said, "I still don't think it's convincing, but if you're right, and I hope to God that you're wrong, what are we going to do about this man?"

"First, we're going to find him. Loveridge has got contacts in the police?"

"Both his assistants were sergeants in the C.I.D. Abbot was at Vine Street. Corkery was at West End Central."

"Then it shouldn't be too difficult. The lorry seems to have been owned by a firm of cowboy transporters called W. Rossall and Son. Albert, I imagine, is the son. Some of his trips were probably on the windy side of the law. Once they get hold of him they won't have much difficulty in extracting enough details about his passenger to lead us to him."

"And when we find him, what are we going to do?"

Chervil did not answer this immediately. Then he said, "What we're not going to do is jump the gun. Some steps have got to be taken immediately. First, we sign off the Catholics. Loveridge can handle that. He needn't be given any explanation. Just tell him what to do. Then I think you must go to Nice, Henry, and try to straighten matters out there."

"Why me?"

"Because there's a more important job. If Mr. Gabriel-Michaels has come back here asking for trouble, I'd like to make sure he finds it. And I'd like to attend to that myself. Unless you'd prefer to do it."

"No," said Ligertwood. "No. I think you must handle that."

"I think so too," said Chervil.

"So what's the story, Corky?"

"I don't exactly know the story," said ex-Detective Sergeant Corkery. "All I know is that we want a bit of help. We want it fast, and the old man's prepared to put the money on the table."

"Fair enough," said Detective Sergeant Thomassen. "I suppose it's straight."

"Straight as a Chinaman's prick. Why, we're that respectable these days you'd hardly credit it. Drive on the left of the road, don't park on double yellow lines, pay our taxes."

They were in the private bar of the Eagle and Child public house, which is so handy for the personnel of West End Central Police Station that they have come to regard it as private territory and discourage outsiders.

"Who are these characters?"

"One character is Albert Rossall. His father runs a porno bookshop in Barnard Street."

"Midge Rossall. Is that the one you mean? So-called because he's not much bigger'n a pisspot."

"I wouldn't know what size he is, never having had the

pleasure of meeting him. But if he's a chap who drives a lorry on the Continent, he's the one we're looking for."

"That's Midge, all right. What's he up to?"

"It's not what he's up to. It's what he did on his last trip. Picked up a man, somewhere in the middle of France, and gave him a lift back here. Seems they got friendly, on account of he put Midge's lorry right when it broke down. From what we've heard he wangled him through the Customs at Ostend without any papers, pretending he was his co-driver."

Thomassen looked at him shrewdly and took the top off his beer before saying, "It's not Midge you're really interested in, is it, Corky? It's the other bod you're after."

"Ten out of ten."

"And you think we can get his address by shaking down Midge."

"You wouldn't have to get too rough. Not with a little fellow like that."

"Don't bet on it," said Thomassen. "The small ones are sometimes the toughest. Give you a ring this evening."

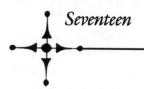

Seventeen

When the Great West Road was built, Brocklehurst Terrace was blocked at one end, transforming what had been a busy thoroughfare into an agreeable backwater. The offices of the Catholic Texts Translation Society were at the closed end of the terrace. It was half past two on Wednesday afternoon when John parked his Yamaha against the curb. He had told Mike Collins that he had an appointment with his dentist, which was true. What he had not told him was that the appointment was for five o'clock. He had other plans for the earlier parts of the afternoon.

John rang the bell. The sound tinkled away into the interior of the house and died. Then came the slap of sandals on stone, and the door was opened by a mild-looking, middle-aged bespectacled man dressed in clerical black. John said, "You must excuse this intrusion. My name is Claxton. Roger Claxton. I'm afraid I haven't the pleasure—"

"Crowley. I am Father Crowley. Won't you come in."

He hobbled ahead into the front room of the house. This had started with some pretension of being an office but now looked more like the sitting room of an untidy author. There were books and papers everywhere. A lonely filing cabinet seemed lost in the clutter.

"I'm afraid we don't have many visitors. I advise against that chair, Mr. Claxton. It suffers, as I do, from a weakness in one leg. Try the one by the fireplace. That's right. Now, what can I do for you?"

"Does the name Bernard Martindale mean anything to you?"

"Martindale? I'm not sure—"

"*Catholic Times*."

"Of course. He's the editor, isn't he?"

"The subeditor actually. He was very interested in the work you're doing here. He wanted to do a piece on it."

Father Crowley looked startled. He said, "Are you sure he meant us? We're not a large organization."

"Size is not always the criterion of importance."

"I suppose that's true."

"He'll want some more detailed notes from you eventually, but I thought that if, for the moment, you could just give me a general idea of how you operate. I've seen some of the little books you produce. Do you print them here?"

"Good gracious, no." Father Crowley was quite alarmed at the idea of being a printing works. "My job is to arrange the translations. I can do the German and Greek texts myself. I can't manage the Yugoslavian and Turkish, but I have friends who help. A firm that specializes in color transparencies does the pictures, and the books are printed in Florence."

"I thought the ones I saw were excellent. If the printing is done in Florence, I suppose the packing and shipping is done from there too."

As he said this, a vague idea of the truth was already forming in his mind.

"That's correct. The books are packed in cartons and go directly to six centers: Berne, Klagenfurt, Munich, Banja Luka, Thessalonica and Izmir. Those are the ones we are concerned with. I have always supposed that there are other offices that deal with other centers."

"You say that you are concerned with those particular centers. Could you expand a bit on that?"

"We organize the transport and the finance. You understand that these books are never sold. We donate them to schools and seminaries and other Catholic institutions."

Another bad mark, Mike. Didn't you say you *bought* the

books? "Tell me about the transport. If the books are printed in Florence, wouldn't it have been simpler to arrange the transport from there?"

"On the face of it, I suppose that's right. I think the answer is that since almost all our money comes from English sources, it was thought fair that English transporters should reap what profit there was."

"Yes. That's another thing I wanted to ask you about. Where *does* the money come from?"

It was clear that Father Crowley was embarrassed. He took off his spectacles and polished them. He said, "Some of it, small amounts, come from schools and charitable organizations in this country who have had our books and feel they ought to make some return. But the greater part—really the only substantial contribution—comes from a large firm who would wish, I think, to remain anonymous. Or that is certainly the impression I got."

"Perhaps I can save you some embarrassment," said John smoothly. "Other sources have indicated to us that the firm in question might be Multinational Business Aids."

"If you knew it already, then of course that's different. But I think, when you are writing your article, it might be better to describe them as a large firm without actually naming them."

John promised that he would do this. All he wanted to do now was get away and think about what he had found out. For the sake of appearances he had to stop for ten minutes more and ask a few more questions before he left. Father Crowley watched his departure with relief. He was looking forward to a quiet afternoon devoted to correspondence with enthusiasts in other parts of the world on the subject of Catholic systematology. He had just received an interesting letter from a priest in Arkansas. Hardly had he taken up his pen when the doorbell rang again. He sighed mildly and hobbled once more to the front door.

Ten minutes later he was sighing in earnest.

"I hope you understand our position in the matter," said Loveridge. He was not a tactful performer. He thought that Crowley was a scruffy old man who had no notion of efficiency

172

and business methods, and he had often wondered why they wasted money on him.

"I appreciate what you have told me, Mr. Loveridge. It is only that the withdrawal of your support will make it very difficult for us to function. Indeed, unless we can secure another sponsor, it will be more than difficult. It will be impossible."

He looked wistfully around the comfortable, untidy room.

"I hope this will go some way toward making things easier for you." Loveridge slapped down on the desk a check for £1,000. Money down the drain in his view. "You understand that it's for you, personally. Recognition of past services, and so on and so on."

Father Crowley had not looked at the check. It was not money that was at stake. It was a way of life.

"If there's nothing else then—" Loveridge got up thankfully.

"There was one other thing. In the circumstances, perhaps rather unfortunate. I had a reporter here, earlier this afternoon."

Loveridge sat down again. He said, "What's that?"

"He was from the *Catholic Times*. They are planning to do a piece on our work."

Loveridge said, without much pretense of civility, "You didn't leak our name to him, did you?"

"There was no need. He appeared to know already that you were so kindly assisting us. It seems so inopportune that just when we were getting this publicity—"

"Inopportune? I should have called it—well, never mind. When this reporter was talking to you, did he produce any credentials?"

"Credentials?"

"I mean," said Loveridge controlling himself with an effort, "how did he show that he was from the *Catholic Times?*"

"Oh, I think he was. He mentioned the name of the sub-editor, Bernard Martindale. Besides, he struck me as a responsible sort of man. Really, I mean—" Father Crowley was trying to think of a tactful way of saying that he had thought him of a

173

higher class than Loveridge, but he was interrupted before getting further entangled.

"What did he look like?"

"He was somewhat sunburnt and had a short pointed beard, which I believe is sometimes described as a Van Dyke."

"Anything else?" Loveridge was on his feet by now.

"There was a faint suggestion—nothing obtrusive, you know—that he might have lived in the Antipodes, either Australia or New Zealand. I couldn't be certain—"

Before he had finished the sentence his visitor was out of the room. Father Crowley looked after him in mild surprise. He heard the front door slam and the sound of a car starting up.

When Loveridge reached his office, his first call was to the *Catholic Times*. A few words with Mr. Martindale confirmed his suspicions. There was no intention of writing about the Catholic Texts Translation Society, a body of which Mr. Martindale confessed that he had never heard, nor had any reporter been sent to interview them.

To make doubly sure, he spoke next to Mike Collins, who confirmed that Naylor was out of the office. "Had an appointment with his dentist," he said.

Suspicion hardened into certainty. The first thing was to alert Mr. Ligertwood. He grabbed the office telephone.

He encountered a check. Mr. Ligertwood, so his secretary informed him, had taken the midday plane for Paris, where he would make a connection with the Air France flight for Nice. She had the number of his hotel, but he would not be there much before eight o'clock. "Was it urgent?"

"Very urgent," said Loveridge shortly. He scribbled down the number of the hotel and got busy on the telephone. After that he started to do some savage thinking. He was a sound enough executive, who would carry out orders intelligently, but he was not good at standing on his own feet. He preferred ultimate responsibility to rest with someone else. And this was a case in which any premature or mistaken action might have the most unfortunate consequences. It was almost a relief when he was interrupted by Corkery.

His assistant seemed pleased with himself. He said, "I just had a message, sir, from my contact at West End Central, Sergeant Thomassen. Very sound man. He's got things set up."

The stress of recent events had driven the earlier matter from Loveridge's mind. It took him a moment to grasp what Corkery was talking about. Then he said, "Oh. Yes. Good. Tell me about that."

"It seems that the man we were after, Albert Rossall, otherwise known as Midge, has scarpered."

"Scarpered?"

"Taken himself off. His old man says they haven't seen him for a week and his wife says the same. She doesn't seem to be letting it worry her."

"That's not very satisfactory."

"Ah, but that's where Thomassen had a bit of luck. There's a couple of hard boys he knows, Frankie and Morrie Simmons. They're friends of Midge's, sort of."

"What does that mean?"

Corkery allowed himself a smile. He said, "What I understand it means, sir, is that Frankie Simmons is very particularly friendly with Midge's wife. If anyone knows where he's gone to, she will. And she'll tell Frankie."

"All right," said Loveridge. The question of Albert Rossall's whereabouts seemed of little importance beside the urgent problems presented by Naylor. The Hotel Tribunal at Nice had confirmed that they expected a Mr. Ligertwood that evening. They would ask him to telephone Mr. Loveridge as soon as he arrived. Loveridge had said that he would stay in his office until the call came through.

"I'll tell Thomassen to go ahead, shall I, sir?"

"What?"

"With the Simmons brothers."

"Oh, yes. Tell them to get on with it. Report back as soon as they've got any news."

John reached the Modern Bookshop in Barnard Street at half past three. He found Bill Rossall studying the racing news in the evening paper.

"Well," said Bill, "if it isn't Mr. Naylor. Nice to see you, sir. How are things with you?"

"I'm fine," said John. "What I wanted was a word with Midge. Is he about?"

"I'm afraid that's just what he isn't."

"What's happened to him?"

"He's gone into what you might call a retreat. It's not the first time. When there's been some trouble over one of the loads he was carrying, what he found was that when the police started asking questions about it, if he wasn't around to answer them, they'd have to get on to the people who employed him. They're the ones who reely oughter carry the can, if you follow me."

"Sound tactics," said John. "It's known in the army as making a tactical withdrawal to shorten your line. Was it bad trouble this time?"

"Middling. It was that chester droors."

"The one with the inlaid panels. I thought it was beautiful."

"Too beautiful by half," said Mr. Rossall gloomily. "One of France's national treasures, that's what they called it."

John said, "I think I read something in the papers about it. Is that the one the Victoria and Albert Museum have been getting steamed up about?"

"That's the very item. Used to belong to the French royal family. When they had a royal family, that is. And what's more, it seems it didn't belong to the party who sold it. It belonged to his aunt. She's about a hundred and ten and she's been raising the roof. You know what the French are like when they get worked up."

It seemed to John, however, that old Mr. Rossall was not unduly disturbed. A lifetime of driving odd loads around the Continent must have hardened the Rossall family to embarrassments of this sort. He said, "I did want to have a word with Midge. Not about the furniture. I wanted to find out if he ever did a trip for people called the Catholic Texts Translation Society."

"The Catholic Texts? Yerrs. He did mention they was a bit dodgy."

"Did he ever tell you what exactly was dodgy about them?"

Mr. Rossall hesitated. Then he said, speaking more seriously than he had so far, "What I'd like to know, Mr. Naylor, is what you're up to. Albert isn't a boy who opens his mouth wide about what doesn't concern him. But he did drop hints. Seems you might have a sort of war on your hands."

"It's a very private war," said John. "And I can assure you of one thing. None of the guns are aimed at Midge. The people I'm shooting at are an outfit called MBA. People who make computers and things like that."

"Bloated capitalists."

"I'm not sure," said John thoughtfully, "that I'd have described any of the ones I've met so far as bloated. But capitalists, no doubt about that."

"And you think Midge can give you something to shoot at 'em with?"

"If I can prove what I already suspect to be the truth of the matter, yes. It will give me just the ammunition I need."

"Well, this is only what he told me. He did two or three runs for the Catholics. The first one he did was to Klagenfurt. That's down in south Austria. The bit they call the Tea Roll. You know it, I expect. It was a two-day run, and when he stopped for the night—somewhere in the Black Forest or thereabouts—he thought he'd take a look at what he'd been landed with. He had a feeling there was more to it than met the eye. I mean, going all the way down to Florence to pick the stuff up and then running it half across Yurrup when it could just as well have gone by train—you follow me?"

"Exactly what I thought myself."

"Well, there was about a dozen of these big crates, all of 'em sealed with a certificate or something of the sort from some high-up in the Vatican, saying that they had holy works in 'em. But one of the crates had a special mark on it, which he'd been shown, and he was told that when he got to Klagenfurt that one was to be unloaded first and taken to an address he'd been given. Then the others would go to the Catholic headquarters. Midge has got a touch with seals, and he soon had this one open to see what was special in it."

"And what *was* in it?"

"Books."

"Just the same as the others?"

"Just the same, so far as he could see. Hundreds of 'em. Lives of blessed saints. But Midge isn't easy diverted, not once he's got his teeth into something. He'd got plenty of time on his hands. So what he did, he opened *all* the books, to have a look. And down toward the bottom of the crate he found half a dozen which weren't nothing to do with saints. I mean, they had the same pictures on the covers and they looked just the same, but what was inside them was different. It was bonds."

"What sort of bonds?"

Mr. Rossall had to think about this. He said, "I got a bit lost there. But what I think Midge said they were was Eurobonds. Does that make sense to you, sir?"

"Yes," said John. "Indeed it does. Very good sense. Eurobonds are bearer securities, which means you can turn them into cash at any bank in the world. Did Midge remember the denomination? I mean, how much each bond was worth."

"He told me that. A thousand dollars. Each book was made up with twenty of them."

"And six books. That makes quite a tidy sum."

"That's what he thought."

"You said he did several trips?"

"That's right. One was to Berne. That was just a day trip. The other was right down to Izmir in Turkey. Took him a week there and back."

"And on each trip there was one marked case which had to be delivered to a special address?"

"Right. He didn't bother to open them, because he guessed he knew what was in them."

"And he did nothing about it?"

"Of course he did. He trebled his expense account and they paid up like birds."

John laughed. Mr. Rossall said, "We couldn't either of us see the point of it."

"The point is that MBA have got sales centers and maintenance workshops in the six countries they sell to: South Germany, Switzerland, Austria, Greece, Yugoslavia and Turkey. These need regular infusions of cash to keep them ticking over. It had to come from Italy, but the Italians don't like money leaving the country. So it went out as the lives of saints. Foolproof cover, really. No customs officer would be anxious to break a papal seal, and if they did they'd have to open all six crates and examine about a thousand books."

"Smart," said Mr. Rossall. "But if you're going to use it against these computer people, you'll have to get it from Midge direct, won't you?"

"Certainly. Can you tell me where he is?"

"I know where he is," said Mr. Rossall slowly, "because it's where he always goes when things get rough. There's this friend of his, lives on the Kent marshes. He got blown up near Antwerp, at the end of the war. He was a kid of nineteen at the time and he's been crazy ever since. Not mad enough to put away, you understand, but suffering from delusions. One of them was that the Russians weren't going to stay put. They were going to come right on and invade England. He knew the way they were coming, too. They were coming up the Thames. His job in life was to stop them."

"What was he planning to do when they arrived?"

"Ring up the police, I suppose. Well, he got a job with an outfit that set up this factory on the marshes. They were producing a sort of peat substitute. You'll recollect that coal was in short supply for a bit after the war. Then the miners got stuck in and there was more coal than people wanted. I never understood why some years we've got no coal and other years we've too much."

"It's called the economic pendulum," said John. "But go on."

"Well, they had a lot of machinery there and, thinking the time might come when it'd be useful again, they didn't want to scrap it, so when they shut down and this chap said he'd stop behind and look after it, they jumped at the offer. Of course, the

179

real reason he stopped there was to keep an eye on the Russians."

"And he's there still?"

"That's right. No one's paying him. The company went bust years ago, and I expect they took away anything worth saving. But no one liked to turn the old boy out."

"And that's where Midge lies up when the heat's on?"

"Right. He parks his lorry there and lives snug in it."

"Then if you can give me directions—"

"It's what I can't do. I'm sorry about this, sir, but when he first found this place I gave him my word I'd keep it under my hat. Midge has got his head screwed on right. He knows that if you tell two people a secret you might as well tell two hundred. I'm not sure if he told Lois. He might have done. But if he did, it was me and her and no one else."

John said, "If you gave your word, of course that's the end of the matter. But it's a pity, because things look like coming to a head at any moment, and this might have been the decisive piece."

Mr. Rossall thought about it. He said, "Midge took to you right away, I could see that. And I'm sure he wouldn't mind you knowing. Tell you what I'll do. There's a lady looks after this shop for me sometimes. If I can get hold of her, I'll go down myself, tomorrow afternoon, and have a word with Midge. If he says yes, I'll give you the go-ahead right away."

"It's very good of you," said John. "Really it is. I've got no phone yet in my flat, but if you want to get hold of me, in business hours, this is the number." He wrote it down. "I'm in Mr. Collins's room. It's got an extension. If they ask who you are, say you're the Inland Revenue. O.K.?"

"O.K.," said Mr. Rossall. "I'm the Inland Revenue." The idea seemed to please him.

Loveridge's call from Nice came through at eleven o'clock that night. Mr. Ligertwood's mind was clearly on more important matters. He said, "Surely you can deal with Naylor yourself."

"Boot him out?"

"No. I don't think you can do that. Not without proof. We may get it from that chap in Scotland—what's his name? Layfield—when he comes down on Friday, or Ramage may have come through with something."

"You mean," said Loveridge, "that until then he can just wander round, asking questions?" To him the idea of a spy loose in the works seemed no safer than stabling a wolf in the sheepfold.

"You could keep an eye on him."

"Have one of my men follow him round? It wouldn't be easy."

"No need. All you have to do is get them to spread the idea, unofficially, that Naylor is a spy. Then no one will tell him anything."

"It's an idea," agreed Loveridge.

"If everything goes as well here tomorrow as it did this evening, I shall be catching the early plane back on Friday. I'll be with you soon after breakfast."

Thank God for that, thought Loveridge.

The old man sounded pleased with himself. He thought that things must have been going well.

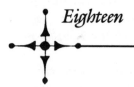

Eighteen

Thursday was not a pleasant day. It became increasingly unpleasant as it went on.

The first sign of something amiss was when Mike Collins was summoned out of the room by a telephone call, came back with a face like thunder and answered John's query as to what was up by swiveling around in his chair until his back was turned and refusing to say anything at all.

John decided that he must have had bad news of some sort, but couldn't see what he had done to provoke such treatment.

When he went along to the canteen the smiling West Indian woman was scowling, and she jerked his cup of coffee so abruptly across the counter that most of it went into the saucer. She did not apologize.

It was in the lunch break that matters became quite clear. When John had collected his food he moved, with his tray, to one of the large tables where there was an empty chair. The man sitting next to it saw him coming, picked up one of the cruets and put it down on the chair. He said, "This place is reserved."

John said, "All right. I'll go somewhere else." Two of his particular friends had been sitting at that table. They avoided his eye. No one said anything. John moved to a table that was empty and sat down. The table remained empty. The one next to it soon became uncomfortably crowded.

After his solitary meal, John went back to his room determined to have matters out with Mike, but Mike was not there. A note on his table said, *If anyone wants me, I shall be with the cashiers.* No one wanted him. The afternoon dragged past. John attempted to do some work but found it difficult to concentrate. He thought of going along for his normal tea at four o'clock but rejected the idea.

At six o'clock he'd had enough. His first idea was to go home. Then he said, "No. Why the hell should I? I'm damned if I'm going to be frozen out without making an effort to find out what it's all about."

He walked down to the Dolphin. The bar was already crowded. As he went in, all heads turned and all conversation stopped. John was wondering what to do when the door of the small private bar opened and the gatekeeper, Bob, came out. He beckoned to John. The crowd parted and he followed Bob in.

There were two other men in the room, the Scotsman, Red Rob, looking unusually serious, and one-armed Len. A hanging committee? It was Len who did the talking. He said, "We've had Loveridge and his goons spreading the word all day that you're up to no good. That you're some sort of spy. They said you'd come here under a false name, without any papers. That sort of thing. Not proof, you understand. Just suspicion. But it upset people."

Since something seemed to be expected of him, John said, "Yes. I can see it has."

"Some of the boys wanted to take your motorcycle to pieces, just for a start. Rob, here, stopped them."

The Scotsman said, "I told them we'd have nae Kangaroo Courts here. Like as not Loverboy had got the wrong end of the stick. It wouldna be the first time."

"Anyway, we've been told you're being turned away at the end of the week. Our advice to you is, Go now."

"Seeing as I've not been told to leave at the end of the week," said John mildly, "I feel I ought to put in a full week's work. Thanks for the advice, all the same."

He walked out into the public bar, shutting the door carefully behind him. "Either he's stark staring mad," said Rob, "or he's got a lot of guts."

Len said, "He's a New Zealander," as though that explained everything.

John considered the question of ordering himself a drink, decided it was unnecessarily theatrical, stalked across the crowded room and went out. No one had interfered with the Yamaha. He rode off slowly, trying to riddle out this new development.

His first idea was that it was a put-up job, organized by Loveridge to give them an excuse to sack him. If he failed to turn up tomorrow, without any legitimate reason, that would certainly allow them to hoof him out. But he rejected the idea. The feeling had been too genuine to have been artificially stimulated. And how had Len known that he was using a false name? He must have made some slipup there.

He stopped at the first telephone kiosk and rang Jonas Pickett's office. Jonas answered the phone himself. "What now, Mr. Naylor?"

"The sands are shifting," said John. "I want to talk to you, and I want to make a telephone call to Italy."

"Then come here. I'm alone in the office."

"It's the telephone call I'm thinking about. If it was traced to your office, you might get into trouble."

"All right. Come to my club. You know it. In Pall Mall. We've got about six thousand members. That should muddy the trail."

It was just turned six o'clock when Mr. Rossall got back to his shop. The gray-haired, middle-aged Welshwoman he had left in charge reported an uneventful afternoon's trading. As she was leaving, she said, "There were two men came in, looking for you. Just after you'd gone. They said they'd be back."

"What sort of men?"

"A pair of right sods, if you ask me," said the Welshwoman. "Could have been brothers."

Mr. Rossall said, "Ah," thoughtfully. He shifted his chair until it had its back wedged up against the bookshelves, with the width of the desk between him and the door.

Ten minutes later, as he was beginning to wonder if he should shut up for the night, the Simmons brothers arrived. Mr.

Rossall moved his right foot cautiously and pressed down with the toe.

Frankie walked through the front room to look into the annex at the back, came out and nodded to Morrie, who shot the bolt on the street door. Both then came and perched themselves one on each corner of the big desk.

"All right, Bill," said Frankie. "Let's keep it short. Where's Midge?"

"How'd I know?"

"Of course you know. He's your boy. He's ducked into the bushes, hasn't he? Same as he did when he had that trouble over the gold cups he brought in from Italy. Or so we heard."

"It seems to me," said Mr. Rossall, "that you know a lot more about Midge than what I do."

"Maybe, Bill. We hear stories. But there's one thing we don't know, and you do know, and we're here to find out."

"What do you want him for? You're not in his line of business."

Morrie, who was a lighter, thinner version of his brother, slid off the desk. He said, "We haven't got all night," and moved toward Mr. Rossall. Frankie held up one hand to check him. He said, "We've got nothing against Midge. You know that, Bill. All friends together. We just want a word with him. A bit of information he can let us have. It won't be any skin off his nose."

"Let's get this straight," said Mr. Rossall. "If I knew where Midge was, the last people I'd tell would be you and your brother. Why? Because I don't like you. And I've got a lot of good friends round here who think the same way as I do. Before you start anything, take a look out of the window."

Both men swung around. The shop window was not too clean and was cluttered with books, but they could see the policeman clearly enough.

Mr. Rossall got to his feet, lumbered across to the door, unbolted it and stepped out onto the pavement. He said, "Good evening, Mike. Nice to see you. Got two customers in here been

185

throwing their weight about. I'm not making any charges this time, but if they do it again you'll hear from me."

The Simmons brothers had emerged from the shop. The policeman, a large Irishman, looked at them without pleasure. He said, "Not asking for more trouble, are you, Frankie?"

"I'm not asking for anything. Not just at this moment. Some other time, maybe."

Mr. Rossall watched them as they swaggered off down the pavement, elbowing a man who was coming the other way. He said, "Ta, Mike. That was very friendly."

"It was a pleasure," said the policeman. "We've got our eye on that pair. Give us half a chance and we'll cool 'em properly."

Back in his shop, Mr. Rossall considered his next move. He was not afraid of Frankie and Morrie. As he said, he had a lot of friends. He had installed the alarm bell, which connected with the police station on the corner, after he had been attacked, with a knife, by a religious fanatic who objected to his line in bookselling. It was Midge, not himself, that he was worried about. He thought it very likely that the brothers, having failed to get the information out of him, would get it out of Lois. Clearly, the best thing to do would be to get hold of Naylor. The difficulty was that, while Midge knew Naylor's address, he did not. All he knew was that he had a flat somewhere up in Highgate.

He dialed the number Naylor had given him, but without much hope. A voice at the other end said that the office was shut. Could he take a message for Mr. Naylor? It sounded a bit unfriendly. Mr. Rossall said, No. It was all right. He would ring in the morning.

When John arrived at the club, Jonas was waiting for him in the foyer. He said, "You look fraught. Why don't we eat while you tell me about it."

John realized, suddenly, that he was ferociously hungry.

It had been a distressing day. He had had an unsatisfactory lunch and no tea. He followed Jonas into the dining room and looked with appreciation at the white tablecloths and the discreet table lights, under which the glasses and the silver winked in a friendly way. It seemed to him a long time since he had had a truly civilized meal.

While they ate and drank he brought Jonas up to date. He said, "I think I've been rumbled and I'm sorry about it. But I've got almost the whole story now. Hopefully, the last piece of the jigsaw will come to hand this weekend."

"And when you've got the whole story?"

"I shall write it. In triplicate. One copy goes into your strong room and the second copy to my bank."

"And the original?"

"The original goes to Sir Tom. In fact, I might send a copy to Ligertwood as well. There's a chance it'll give him heart failure. He's not a good life."

"And then—"

"When they've had time to digest it, I'll invite myself along for a little discussion."

"And in the course of this discussion you deliver your ultimatum. What's it going to be, exactly?"

John watched the solicitor as he refilled both glasses from the Burgundy in the decanter. Then he said, "I've been thinking about it a good deal lately, but I haven't changed my mind. I'll agree to suppress my memorandum if they will accept my conditions."

"And cleanse the Augean stable and live godly lives."

"No. I'm not asking for clean hands and a halo. A lot of the things they do are fairly near the knuckle. I've found out that they use the Scottish Nationalist party for their own purposes. A device expounded to me one evening by a character who quotes Burns. They take advantage of a loophole in the tax laws by making fictitious sales through Denmark, and I've just latched onto a neat line in currency smuggling carried out with the assistance—no doubt the innocent assistance—of the Pope. All right. I appreciate that an outfit fighting for its life in the international ring can't always observe Queensberry Rules. But what they must do is sever all connection with their bully-boy backers. And make an example of Faldo, if only as a warning to other people who may step into his shoes hereafter."

Jonas had listened in silence, sipping his wine. He said,

"You realize that Chervil is a hard man. He's most unlikely to accept either of your conditions."

"Then I shall publish my memorandum."

"Where?"

"I imagine there are one or two leftwing papers who would jump at it."

"With the possibility of an action for libel?"

"I've thought about that. I'm prepared to indemnify them. I'll write you out something here and now if you like."

"No hurry. They'd probably accept the risk, if you can produce proof of everything you say. And there'd be the obvious defense of these disclosures being in the public interest. Yes. I think I could guarantee publication. If it was posthumous it would be even more effective."

John grinned. He said, "I can't undertake to be slaughtered to make a Fleet Street holiday. That was a lovely Burgundy. Now lead me to your telephone. . . ."

When he reached her, Monica said, "I may be a little time. I shall have to slip out at the back and go some way to find a different callbox. I think the one I used before is being watched."

"No hurry," said John. "This is the number."

It was half an hour before the return call came through. Monica said, "Things have been moving out here. Mr. Ligertwood arrived last night. He was talking to Emile for hours, telephoning and making arrangements for a very high-powered meeting today. It took place in a hotel car park outside Menton. Both sides brought about six cars. Emile didn't enjoy it at all. He thought it was going to be an O.K. Corral shootout. But apparently Mr. Ligertwood was wonderful. Emile couldn't tell me what was arranged, but in the end they all went away happy."

"Good news for MBA, bad for me."

"Why?"

"When they were fighting each other, they hadn't got a lot of time to think about minor nuisances like me. Now all guns will be pointing in my direction."

"Look," said Monica. "Why don't you give it up?"

"I'm afraid that Battista wouldn't agree with you."

"Who the hell is Battista?"

"Battista Genzano. A simple Italian farmer. His children were kidnapped and he paid out over a year's profits to get them back. And I can tell you what he said. 'A man who does nothing in the face of wrongdoing is himself a wrongdoer.'"

"That was his fight. This isn't your fight."

"It's everyone's fight."

"You're impossible."

He could tell that she was angry and close to tears.

He said, "I'll be all right, Monica. I promise you I will."

"I wasn't only thinking about you. You're able to look after yourself. But if you stir things up, other people may get hurt. Had you thought about that?"

"No, I don't think I had."

"Then think about it now. Before any more bad things happen."

"All right," said John. "I'll think about it."

When he got back, Jonas said, "You're looking worried. Bad news?"

"Not really. I've been made to wonder whether I'm being selfish."

"In that case, I recommend a large glass of the club port. It's impossible to be introspective when drinking Warre Sixty-one."

"That's very good," said Chervil. "Very good indeed. I hope the trip wasn't too tiring."

"Air travel has taken most of the sting out of these excursions," said Ligertwood. "Nonstop this time. I had breakfast on the plane, and owing to the difference in the clocks I arrived almost before I'd started." He was clearly pleased with himself. "I've got another bit of good news for you, too. Ramage has laid hands on the Tolcom papers. They included a list of employees. Guess what? No one called Naylor ever worked for them."

"I'd begun to suspect as much," said Chervil. "Now that we know he made a false statement when applying for his job, we can sling him out without further ceremony. Or wait. Perhaps we ought to have a little ceremony. Hang him up outside the front entrance minus his trousers. Something entertaining like that."

Ligertwood was wondering whether he was serious when they were interrupted. His secretary said, "Mr. Layfield is asking whether you want to see him."

"Good heavens!" said Ligertwood. "I'd forgotten all about him. I'll have to apologize to him for bringing him up here under false pretenses."

"Who is Mr. Layfield?"

"He was the only one of the Benedict people we took on who had come to them from Tolcom. He's working in our Scottish office. We thought he might have been able to give us a line on Naylor. Won't be necessary, now we've got Ramage's report."

"And you brought him all the way down here for that?"

"He was coming anyway. For a sales conference over at Teddington. Oh, good morning, Layfield. I don't know if you've met Sir Thomas?"

"I haven't had that pleasure," said Layfield. He was a fattish middle-aged man. He looked badly shaken. More so, surely, than should have been the result of an unexpected meeting with his Chairman!

"Won't you sit down for a moment."

Layfield collapsed into the chair as though his legs were giving way under him. He said, "I'm sorry. I do apologize. I've just had a shock."

Both men looked at him. He did seem rather white about the face.

"Nothing personal, I hope," said Chervil kindly.

"No, sir. But I've just seen a ghost."

"Good gracious!"

Unbalanced, thought Ligertwood. Consider replacing him.

"It was as I was coming in. This man had his back to me. I was certain I knew him. Then, when he spoke, I was absolutely sure. No room for any doubt at all. It was Mr. Benedict. He always had that very slight New Zealand accent. Then I realized—"

There was a moment of absolute silence. Chervil said smoothly, "I can see it must have been a shock. But these things happen. The other day I met my old house beak from Eton in Bond Street. Actually shook him by the hand, before I remembered reading his obituary in the *Times*."

Some of the color had come back into Layfield's face.

Ligertwood said, "I've fixed a car to take you to Teddington. You'd better hurry along. Apologize to whoever's running the conference and tell him I kept you."

After the door had shut behind him, the two men sat for an appreciable time looking at each other. Ligertwood was the first to move. He picked up the office phone and said to his secretary, "Get me Eric Thorensen. Yes. The man at Flight Information. The number's in the book."

Chervil said, "It's quite incredible. But in a mad sort of way it does make sense. Ever since I was told about this character who was trekking across the Italian countryside mending people's cars for them, there was one point about him that rang a tiny bell in my mind. Only just then I was too busy to listen to tiny bells—"

"Hold it," said Ligertwood. "Hullo, Eric. How's the family? Keeping well, I hope. Good. Listen. There's one bit of information I wanted. I'm sure you'll be able to get it without moving from your chair. You remember the Tristar crash—just over a year ago?"

"I not only remember it, I attended the inquiry. Small firm called ABZ Charters. Lost their license after the crash, drummed out of business. Good thing, too."

"I couldn't agree more. What I wanted to know was this. On that particular flight, what were the scheduled stops?"

"Oh, the normal ones. Rome, Bahrain, Bombay, Singapore, Darwin and Auckland. Only, of course, they didn't get as far as Bahrain."

"I'm much obliged," said Ligertwood. "Remember me to your charming wife."

191

He replaced the receiver gently.

"Rome," he said. "That makes it possible. Suppose Benedict got off the plane for some reason at Rome. You remember some of the bodies were never identified."

"It's more than possible. It's almost certainly correct. I was telling you that there was something odd about this Italian trekker. I'd registered it subconsciously when I first heard the story. He called himself Gabriel."

"Well?"

"J. G. Benedict. I only once saw his name spelled out in full. It was on the sale agreement we both signed. John *Gabriel* Benedict."

"Good God!" said Ligertwood. "So we've had *Benedict* in this office for three weeks?" He was trying to assimilate the idea. "He seemed quite an ordinary man. Capable, of course, and pleasant enough."

Chervil said, "I met him three times. Once socially and twice on business. It wasn't until well on in our final business meeting that I realized the truth about him. The pleasant, easy-going bit is a facade. Inside, he's as tough as old boots. If I hadn't realized that, just in time, we'd have paid out a lot more money than we had to when we bought his business."

"What are we going to do about him?"

"Why don't we have a word with him. No time like the present. Ask your secretary to get him up here."

"Do you think that's wise?"

"We needn't tell him we know who he is. Ask him to explain the lies he's been telling and boot him out."

But Mr. Naylor, it appeared, was unavailable. The secretary said, "He wasn't in his office, so I asked around. The gateman told me he'd driven off on his motorcycle, not more than five minutes ago. He didn't say when he was coming back."

Ligertwood said, "Thank you. Let me know when he does get back." And to Chervil. "He'll have to be back sometime today if he wants his week's salary."

"You seem to forget," said Chervil dryly, "that the man we're dealing with is as near a millionaire as makes no difference.

What does a week's salary matter to him? If he doesn't intend to come back, he won't."

"We've got his address."

"His real address? Or phony, like his name."

"It's right enough. One of Loveridge's men checked it."

"Get Loveridge up here."

While they were waiting, Chervil sat quite still looking out of the window. The expression on his face was almost bland.

When Loveridge arrived he said, "We're having some trouble with one of our employees. A man called Naylor."

"Yes, sir. I know all about that."

"I believe one of your men checked his address."

"That's right, sir. He followed him home and had a word with the porter."

"I want that place watched, and when he turns up I want him kept under observation until I can be informed. I don't care if we have to bend a few rules and I don't care what it costs. You understand?"

"Yes, sir. I'd better take Corkery and Abbot off what they're doing. You remember, sir, they were looking for a man called Albert Rossall so that they could get the address out of him of a man he brought back in his lorry from France."

Chervil smiled bleakly. He said, "They can certainly be called off *that* assignment. It's no longer relevant."

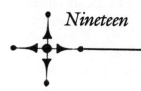

Nineteen

It had been shortly after ten o'clock that Friday morning when Bill Rossall succeeded in getting put through to John on the telephone.

He had been subjected to a number of obstructions and delays. First Mr. Naylor could not be found. Nor did anyone seem anxious to look for him. When he was found, he was said to be engaged. It was only by persistence and the use of language unusual in an employee of the Inland Revenue that he had managed, at last, to get his call through.

John detected the note of uneasiness behind his brusque manner.

"Lois was out late last night," he said, "and came home looking like a cat what's got at the cream. She wouldn't say where she'd been, but I didn't need three guesses. If she knew where Midge was laying up, and I think she did, Frankie would've got it out of her as quick as he'd get the cork out of a bottle. I think you'd better get down there. Here's the directions. . . ."

John went down to the vehicle park and collected his Yamaha. Bob swung the gate open for him and winked at him in a not unfriendly way.

Had enough, he thought, and clearing out. Showing some sense at last.

John concluded that it would be quicker, at that time of day, to go straight through London. There were moments in the West End when he wondered if it had been a sensible decision. It was nearly midday when he skirted Rochester. He was making for the Isle of Grain, the peninsula separating the mouths of the Thames and the Medway, a flat land, first stop for the east wind that blows in from Siberia.

"All Hallows is the nearest village," Bill had said. "From there you head due east for Yantlet Creek. It's not much more'n a farm road, but quite O.K. for wheels. The track you want is about a mile along on the left."

The signboard, though weathered and cracked, was still legible. THE ALTERNATIVE FUEL COMPANY LIMITED. STRICTLY PRIVATE. As he bumped along, he picked up the marks of wheels in the dried mud, some of them recent.

Over his right shoulder he could see, in the distance, the tall towers of the oil refinery. All around him were flat fields, broken by ditches of brackish water. One had been used as a dump for scrap. Thrust up in the middle, the nose of an old car looked like a sea animal coming up to breathe. A herring gull, sleek in its gray armor, rose from one of the ditches and screamed at him.

For the first few hundred yards the track rose toward a low ridge. As he topped it he could see, ahead of him, the gaunt framework of the fuel company's building and beyond that a cheerful slash of color where the waters of the Thames ran out to the North Sea.

He found Midge's van, tucked away out of sight behind the building. His hail was unanswered. He opened the van door and looked in. The remains of breakfast were laid out on the table. There was a piece of toast smeared with butter and marmalade and a cup half full of cold tea. John climbed down from the van and called again, more loudly. He was answered by the echo of his own voice.

He walked around to the front of the building. There was a huge rusted iron wheel up against the wall. It was at least six feet in diameter and was attached to a shaft which ran back through the brickwork. It was clearly many years since it had carried out whatever function of cutting or crushing it had been designed for. The only new-looking thing about it was a short length of rope hanging from one of the spokes.

There was a door beside the wheel. It appeared to be

locked, but it was so flimsy that a single resolute push lifted it open. John could now see the machinery to which the wheel was attached, as rusty and uncared-for as the wheel itself. A steep flight of wooden steps led up to a trapdoor in the ceiling.

It was at this moment that John first realized that he was not alone.

The ceiling was made of planks which had warped in their old age, allowing the sun to shine down through the cracks between them. As he looked, the line of light between two planks was obscured for a moment. Then it shone through again. There was no sound, but something or someone had moved in the upper room.

John hesitated for a moment, then started up the steps. When he got to the top he found the trapdoor immovable. There was no question of treating it as he had the outer door. It was a stout square of planks, bolted to crosspieces. Perched as he was on the top step, he could get no sort of leverage against it.

With a rasp of authority in his voice, he said, "Come along now. Open up. This is the police." A moment of silence. "If you don't open up, we'll have to break in." How? he wondered.

Another silence, then the squeak of bolts. John put his shoulder to the trap, lifted it and climbed through.

The upper room was furnished. There was matting on the floor, there were chairs and tables and an open cupboard crammed with utensils and tinned food. The midday sun shone down through a skylight. There were openings in two of the walls, but these were rough affairs, more spyholes than windows, cut, John guessed, by the old man who had fenced himself in between the largest table and the wall and was staring at him out of a tangle of white hair and beard.

John shut the trapdoor. He had the feeling that, given half a chance, the man would make a bolt for it. He was clearly scared silly.

In his normal friendly voice John said, "There's no need to be frightened. No one's going to hurt you."

The old man shook his head irritably, like a horse trying to dislodge a fly. Then he said, "You was fooling, mister, weren't you? You're no policeman."

196

"A sort of unofficial one. You might call me an inquiry agent."

"Whaddyer want?"

"I'm looking for a friend of mine. A man called Midge Rossall."

The old man started to shiver.

"You know the man I mean. That's his van outside. He often used to come and stay there, I believe."

The shivering grew worse. The hands, which were trying to hold the edge of the table, were jumping like castanets. John realized that if he made any sudden move, or even raised his voice, the old man might pass out altogether. He continued to talk, maintaining an easy conversational level.

"It must have been nice for you to have a bit of company. Particularly such a nice man as Midge. I haven't known him for very long, but I must say I've become very attached to him."

The old man's mouth opened. The sound that came out was horrible. Something between a whimper and a moan, the noise an animal might make when faced with the knife. But it had one positive result. It seemed to liberate his power of speech. The words now came tumbling out so fast that John could hardly keep up with them.

"This morning. They came this morning. Three of them. Dragged him out. Hit him. Tied him up to that wheel. Hit him with a hammer. They said, 'Tell us the address. Tell us the address.' When he wouldn't tell them, they hit him some more. Then he told them what they wanted. It was this address. That's what they wanted. When he told them, the two big ones stopped hitting him. Then the young one said, 'It's my turn now.' Frothing, he was. He hit him all over. Hands, arms and legs. Broke his bones. Horrible. When he was hitting him he said, 'You know how we got here? Your little wifey told us.' Midge didn't say anything. The young one said, 'Answer, can't you?' and hit him on the head. Then he was dead."

John was surprised that he could control his own voice. He said, "What did they do then?"

"Cut him down. Carried him down there." The old man

jerked his head in the direction of the river. "Threw him in, I expect. I didn't look. Then they went away."

Once he had spilled out these horrors the old man seemed easier. He peered out anxiously from the screen of his white hair. "You don't think I ought to have done something, do you? Tried to stop them."

"No," said John gently. "I don't think you could have done anything. It's up to me, now. Don't worry. I'll see they're paid."

It was a heavy bill. They had not only tortured Midge and killed him. In the final seconds of his life, as he hung barely conscious on the wheel, they had told him that it was his wife who had betrayed him. A thought to take into the shades with him.

As he climbed onto his machine, the old man ran up and grabbed him by the arm. "What shall I do if they come back? They'll know I told you. They'll kill me too."

John detached his arm. He said, "They won't come back."

As he bumped on his way down the path and out onto the road, he found that his mind was working with exceptional clarity. There were two problems. If the Simmons brothers now knew his address, he could not go back to his flat. And he would need help. He did not think he could deal with them single-handed.

In an odd sort of way, these two propositions, when put together, provided an answer.

"I'll get the Old Woman to help me," he said.

Having come to this conclusion, the next moves followed in logical sequence. He had got into the habit of carrying a fairly large sum of money with him, so there was no need to go to the bank or to involve Jonas.

When he reached London, his first stop was at a well-known sports shop in High Holborn. Here he bought a mountaineer's tent and sleeping bag, a solid-fuel stove and a few cooking utensils. These all went into one sack, which could be strapped to the carrier of his motorcycle. He then moved on to the sports section and spent some time in examining footwear. The young assistant who showed him around took an informed interest in John's choice. Together they turned over and examined a dozen different types of running shoe. So many of the tracks nowadays, said the young man, had artificial surfaces, that steel spikes were discouraged. In the end, John selected a pair of light shoes equipped with specially hardened rubber studs.

"Just the thing for the Old Woman," said John.

"The old woman, sir?"

"That's right. I'm buying them as a present for her."

The assistant looked at him to see whether his leg was being pulled, but John's face was perfectly serious.

He said, "How can you be sure that they'll fit her?"

"If they fit me," said John, "they'll fit her. That's for sure."

He paid for the shoes and put them into the sack along with the other stuff. After that there was nothing to keep him, and he turned his motorcycle toward the west.

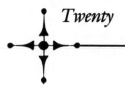

Twenty

On the afternoon of the following day, John turned his machine off the Tavistock road at Yelverton.

The part of Dartmoor lying north of the Dunsford–Two Bridges road is overstamped in red on the Ordnance Survey Map with the words DANGER AREA. This is a warning that it is under occasional fire from the Artillery Ranges at Okehampton and Willsworthy. But the more dangerous half of the moor lies to the south of that road. Ugborough Moor, Holne Moor and Penn Moor, Nakers Hill and Huntingdon Warren, Lud Gate and Childe's Tomb: a hostile country, of old mine shafts and prehistoric hut settlements, of disused pits and shifting bog, always under threat from the mist which hangs above the many tiny streams trickling down from secret sources in the heart of the moor.

There are human habitations on the outskirts and along the two roads that cross the moor, but only a sprinkling of villages on the moor itself. Calverscombe is one of the most remote and primitive.

Its inhabitants pride themselves that the name derives from the notorious Carver Doone, a sept of the Doone clan having come south when they were hounded out of Exmoor. Etymologists laugh at this, but the men of Calverscombe have little use for etymology. They prefer their own savage myths.

It was on his holiday excursions that John had come to know the long-haired, sloe-eyed, sharp-toothed people who lived there, half Iberian, half moorland gypsy. On one occasion he had managed to save a pony which had slipped into the upper waters of the Plym stream. This had gained him a measure of grudging acceptance.

From Yelverton a smaller road runs between Yellowmedd Tor and Gutter Tor. Calverscombe is at the end of this road. There are twenty cottages, a general store that is also a post office and, in the middle of the cobbled square that marks the end of all made roads, a public house called the Moorman.

The notice over the door announced that Rebecca Targett was licensed to sell intoxicating liquors for consumption on or off the premises. Rebecca was nearly eighty. The business of the house was carried on by her son Ezra and her nephew Amos, both of them widowers, their wives having been carried off by the lung disease which was endemic in those parts. The only other permanent resident of the house was the boy, Benno. Strangers assumed that he was the son of Ezra or Amos and sometimes referred to him as such. They were not corrected.

When John arrived, Benno was alone in the bar. His eyes lit up. He had helped John in his camping arrangements before.

John said, "I'll be using the same place, Benno." It was a patch of turf among a circle of stones halfway up Ditsworthy Tor: a fine campsite, when you reached it. The drawback was that the track up to it was so steep, and twisted so sharply among the outcrop of rocks, that there was no question of riding the motorcycle. It had first to be lightened of the bulky package on the carrier and then manhandled. This meant a further trip to carry up stores, and yet another for water, which went up in a jerrican borrowed from the pub. In all this Benno was a great help. His stringy body was wire and elastic. He seemed to walk uphill as easily as he walked down.

When the last of the stores was up, John turned his mind to provisions. He said, "When does the grocer from Yelverton get here?"

"Store van comes Mondays."

This required thought. The general store in the village was useful for household necessities from china and glass to needles and cotton, but it kept very little in the way of food. Bread could be got from the cottage which baked it.

"Get you some eggs," suggested Benno.

"All right. But buy them, don't steal them."

Benno grinned. He accepted this as a compliment. Some money passed. "Better get some milk, too. And when you've done that there's another job I've got for you. I'll tell you about it when you get back."

After he had gone, John set to work putting up the tent and building a fireplace under one of the larger rocks. The weather, for the moment, looked good.

It continued fine for the next few days. Benno seemed to spend all his time up at the camp. Ezra discussed this with Amos on Tuesday evening when they were sitting in the bar, waiting for the first customers.

"Benno's up there all day and every day," said Ezra. "Never don't see hide nor hair of 'm till after dark. What's he doing there?"

"Can't never tell what that boy's up to."

"You don't suppose—I mean—"

Amos, who was the older of the two, considered calmly the idea that John and Benno might be living in sin and dismissed it.

"They bean't neither of them that way inclined," he said.

"Then what do they do all day?"

"I dunno," said Amos. "But I saw him midday yesterday, came snucking through the hedge at the garden end. I was going to call out, when I saw the old lady was there. They had a talk about something, and he took away a lot of her special white stones. Ones she had round her herb garden."

"White stones?"

Possibilities of witchcraft passed through their minds. Rebecca was known to have dabbled in the forbidden arts at one time. She had been tolerated as long as she used them only for beneficial ends—curing cowpox and correcting squints.

"None the less, I'd like to find out what the boy's up to," said Ezra. "If he was a bit younger I'd belt it out of him."

Amos agreed that Benno was too big to be belted. The last time he had tried it the boy had whipped out a knife, and he would have used it, too.

"We'll find out sooner nor later," said Amos.

On Wednesday, coming down for water, John found that the postman had brought in the daily paper from Plymouth. An item in it caught his eye. A fire had broken out in a flat at Makepeace Mansions on the Holly Lodge Estate. The furniture and contents had apparently been broken up before being set alight. Fortunately the blaze had been noticed by the porter and the fire had been extinguished before any damage was done to the rest of the building. It seemed, said the paper, to be some sort of grudge job. Efforts to contact the owner, a Mr. Naylor, had so far proved unsuccessful.

John detected the hand of the Simmons brothers. If it had been an attempt to smoke him out, it had been a clumsy one. There was nothing of his in the flat to which he attached the least importance, and Jonas, as he knew, had the contents covered by ample insurance. The only people who would suffer from the vindictiveness of the Simmons brothers would be the insurance company.

Nevertheless, the news decided him. That morning he posted the letter he had prepared.

It was addressed to Lois Rossall, 24 Barnard Street, London, W.1, and was marked *Personal and Confidential*. Inside it was a second envelope, addressed to Albert Rossall. The letter to Lois simply said, *Could you see that this reaches Midge as soon as possible.* The enclosure was longer, and John had considered every word in it with great care.

> *Dear Midge,*
>
> *I am holed up, miles from anywhere, at a tiny place three miles out on the moor from Yelverton. There are two things I'd ask you to do, if you'd be so good.*
>
> *First, could you cash the enclosed check for £200. Get the money in fivers. If there's any difficulty with the bank, my solicitor will cash it for you. You've got his name and address.*
>
> *Second, more difficult and much more important, could you write out an account of what you did on Catholic Text trips. Bill gave me the outline, but I want as much* DETAIL *as possible and in your own words.*
>
> *Send the money and the account to me at the Moorman*

Public House, Calverscombe. They'll know how to get it to me. I've no real reason to call on your kindness in this way, but hope you'll oblige me.

Sincerely,
John Naylor

As he put the letter in the box, he made a calculation. Two days, he thought; more likely three.

Police Constable Mungeam, the police force of All Hallows, said to his immediate superior, Sergeant Pincott from Cliffe, "You know that old coot who roosts out at that factory?"

"The one who's waiting for the Rooshans?"

"That's the one. Well, I had him in here last night. Wanted me to find him somewhere to stay."

"I thought he was well fixed at the factory."

"So he was. Now he says he can't stay there. Something's happened to upset him, that's for sure."

"What did you do with him?"

"Told him to go into Chatham. See if he could find a bed in the Service Men's Club. He was in the army once, or said he was."

The sergeant approved of this. It seemed a neat way of passing the buck. He said, "What do you suppose upset him?"

"He didn't make much sense about that. But it wasn't the Rooshans. That I did make out. It might have been some rough characters from London. The man at the farm told me he saw a car *and* a motorcycle going down that way last week."

The sergeant thought about it. He said, "Suppose you walk down there sometime and have a look."

That, reflected Mungeam, was the sort of suggestion sergeants were fond of making to constables. As if he hadn't enough on his plate already. He said, "O.K., Sergeant. So soon as I've got a moment I'll do that."

It was Saturday evening, around eight o'clock, when the three men came to Calverscombe. They had left their car in a lay-by half a mile down the road. The evening was warm, and by the time they reached the village they were wishing they'd taken the car a bit closer.

They had left London very early that morning. The car they were driving was a stolen one, picked up for them by Gareth in the Borough High Street the night before.

"Might have chosen one with a bit more class," said Maurice. It was an old-fashioned Lancia tourer, slow and heavy to handle. They had made tolerable progress on the M 3 as far as it served them but had been badly held up by the summer traffic jams at Salisbury and Yeovil. Frankie Simmons was a bad-tempered driver. A few miles short of Exeter he had vented his mounting spleen on a Volkswagen, coming the other way, by driving it into the ditch. He had not stopped to inspect the damage.

"Bloody huns," he said. "Driving in the middle of the road. Think they own the bloody country."

Gareth, who was sitting beside him, said, "That's the stuff to give 'em, Frankie." Maurice, who had been sleeping in the back, had been less complimentary.

When they reached the Moorman they found Benno alone in the bar. The three men burst in like the spearhead of an invading force.

Frankie said, "We're looking for a man called Naylor. Right. Where is he?"

Benno got up slowly and moved across toward the bar.

"Come on, kiddo. You've got a tongue in your head. Try using it before we pull it out and give it to the birds."

Maurice said, "You know where he is. Don't frig around. Just tell us."

Benno looked him up and down before answering. Then he said, "Naw."

"And that's a fucking lie," said Frankie. "His letters are sent here. You know where he is, all right."

"Diddun say I diddun know. Said I wooden tell yer."

Maurice, who was much quicker and lighter than his brother, jumped forward and grabbed Benno by the coat collar.

205

He said, "We haven't got no time for monkey talk. You want to keep a few teeth in your mouth, speak up quick."

He gave the coat a shake. The next moment he found he was holding the coat but not the boy. Benno was at the other side of the bar.

"All right," said Frankie. "You've asked for it."

He then realized that they were no longer alone. The room was dimly lit and he could not see exactly where they had come from, but two men were now standing behind the bar. They were big men and looked solid. Also Frankie saw that one of them was holding something in his hand, under cover of the bar. A barman's persuader, he guessed. He moderated his approach.

"Didn't see you were there, chum, or wouldn't have spoken rough to the boy. All we wanted was a bit of info."

Amos said, "Ah." Ezra said nothing.

"We're looking for a man called Naylor. Said to be hanging out somewhere around here. Camping, maybe."

Amos said, "Ah," again.

"Well, if so be you happen to know where he can find him, we'd be obliged."

Amos came out from behind the bar, walked in silence to the door and went out. After a moment's hesitation, the three men followed him. He pointed.

On the hillside above the village they could see a spark of light which might have come from a campfire.

"Up there, is he?" said Frankie.

Amos said, "Won't be far off. Sprained his ankle, the boy said."

Frankie said, "Tricky place, this moor, for getting about on, innit?"

Amos said, "Ah."

The three men started up the path.

"Bloody chatty, aren't they?" said Maurice.

"If it's right he's wrecked his ankle, no need to hurry," said Frankie. They were finding the path hard on their London shoes and stopped for a breather at a place where a naked wooden post pointed at the sky.

"Remember," said Gareth, "it's me who's got the score to pay off. Twisted my arm, didn't he? I'll twist him, the big bully."

"Take him on single-handed if you like," said Frankie with a grin.

"I'm not sure I could quite manage that, even if he has twisted his ankle."

"I'm bloody sure you couldn't," said Maurice contemptuously. "He'd eat you. When we've knocked him about a bit you can jump on him if you like. Keep quiet now."

They plodded upward.

When they reached the campsite their first impression was that it was deserted. Then they saw their quarry, standing, as though undecided, twenty yards away.

"Perfect," said Frankie. "Grab him."

John swung around and ran. For a man with a sprained ankle, he seemed to cover the ground fairly fast. He was following a beaten track in the heather. They pounded after him.

The track rose gradually until it became a causeway, leading out into an open area of mud and water. As he reached the end of the causeway John's progress changed. He was no longer running but was jumping from tussock to tussock. Maurice, more active than the others, was hard on his heels. The tussocks seemed to be stepping-stones across a sodden piece of ground. Tricky, but he reckoned that he had only to step where his quarry stepped and he would be safe enough.

They were nearly halfway across when he made his first and only mistake.

The distance between two of the tussocks was so wide that it called for a special effort to jump it, but he noticed a third tussock, conveniently placed, halfway between the other two. It was when he landed on it that he realized that it was only a patch of weeds and grass afloat on the treacherous surface. The force of his landing took him into the mud up to his waist.

John heard him scream but did not dare to look around.

He had been practicing this crossing for a week, coached by Benno, who had dropped a white stone on each of the safe landing places. But he was still scared of it. Like a difficult rock climb, it had to be done with rhythm and momentum. And once you started, there was no stopping. The spiked shoes he wore, Benno's careful instruction and his own skill at jumping: these were advantages. But always at the back of his mind was the thought that if he made one mistake, hesitated when he should have gone on, jumped too far or not far enough, the Old Woman, deepest and most treacherous of all Dartmoor's morasses, would have him in her claws. She would not let him go.

At the moment when Maurice went in, Frankie and Gareth were some way behind and were advancing cautiously. The scream made Frankie check and swing around. His feet had no grip on the slimy edge of the embanked path, and before he could stop himself he had tobogganed down into the ooze.

He said, "Bugger that for a lark." He had no idea that he was in any danger. He had only gone in up to his knees, and the path was within reach. "Give us a hand and pull us out."

Gareth bent forward cautiously. He disliked the look of the mud, which had started to bubble and heave at the point where Frankie had gone into it. He was determined to run no risk himself. He got his hands onto the lapels of Frankie's coat and pulled. Frankie gave a series of violent kicks. When they stopped he was farther down in the mud than when they had started.

He said, "You've got to do better than that, boyo. Get down on your fucking knees, get your hands under my arms and fucking *heave*."

"I'm doing my best." It was a whine, part anger but mostly fear. "If I get too close I'll be in myself."

They heard Maurice scream again, a scream which was cut off suddenly. The sound chilled Frankie. He realized for the first time the danger he was in. He said, through clenched teeth, "That was Morrie. You heard him. I guess he's gone right in. So what happens to you if you *don't* get me out? You'll be on your own, won't you? And when that bloody Naylor comes back, he'll pick you up by one leg and toss you into the middle."

Gareth said, "All right, Frankie. All right. I'll try. It might be better if I lie down."

He felt that he would be safer with the whole width of the causeway under his body.

Frankie had already sunk in up to his waist, and this put his shoulders within Gareth's reach. He locked his outstretched arms under Frankie's arms and pulled.

After a minute of agonizing effort, he said, "It's no good. I can't do it." He had felt himself sliding toward the mud.

"You're not bloody trying."

"Oh, I am. Honest I am." The pathetic whimper seemed to make Frankie's mind up. The mud had reached his chest, but he still had the full use of his arms. He said, "We'll have one more shot at it. Hold out your hands. Quick now."

Gareth found his wrists held.

Frankie's lips were drawn back so far that his teeth showed in a death's-head grin. He said, "I can tell you one thing, little man. If I don't get out, you're coming in here with me."

Gareth said, "Oh, please. Please don't do that. Please." He tried to release himself, but his wrists were gripped in steel shackles. Then Frankie gave a jerk, using all of his considerable strength. The effort pushed him lower, but it sent Gareth slithering over his shoulder, head first into the mud.

When John climbed out, he had to make a wide circle to get back to the camp. He approached it cautiously. He was certain that the man behind him was finished, but he was not yet clear about the other two.

After listening for a few minutes, he made his way back along the path into the morass. Here, too, there was nothing but the piping of night birds and—faint, but just audible—the sound of the liquid mud settling down.

The evening must have been cooler than he thought. It was making him shiver.

When he got back once again to the campsite, he found that Benno had completed the packing. John strapped one load onto the back of the motorcycle, Benno shouldered the other and they started down. He saw that Benno had already nailed back into place on the post the notice which warned people of the danger of approaching too near to the morass.

When they were almost at the village, Benno swung off

onto a track on the right. He said, "I found where they dumped the car. No need to go through the village."

This seemed to John to be a sound idea. He was not afraid of tongues wagging. The villagers of Calverscombe were noted for failure to cooperate with the authorities. There had already been trouble over a convict, on the run from the prison at Princetown, who had lived there, unreported, for nearly six months. But children sometimes talked, and the less anyone saw of his departure the better.

He found that the stolen car had a trunk with a lid which opened outward. This solved his main difficulty. He had to force the lock, but once the lid was fully open he and Benno were able to hoist the motorcycle into the car. The lid could then be partly closed and secured with ropes. It made a clumsy and conspicuous package, but night was now closing down and he was not planning to carry it far.

He started the engine. Benno watched the operation carefully, memorizing it for future use. John gave him a handful of notes, which he stuffed into a pocket in his ancient coat. They would not stay there long. He would bury them on his way back to the inn.

John drove off carefully. It was not an occasion for accidents. He expected no traffic on the side road to Yelverton and met none. From there he took the old road that circled the moor, northward past Okehampton and Crediton. By the time he reached Tiverton it was pitch dark, with a slight mist. This had the useful effect of forcing the few drivers who passed him to concentrate on their driving and not on him.

From Tiverton he went north again, toward Dulverton and the southern fringes of Exmoor. A few miles beyond Bampton he found the sort of place he was looking for.

It was a private park, belonging to a big house, marked on his map as Priory Court. The condition of the gateway and the unkempt appearance of the park suggested that the house was either empty or little used.

The padlock on the gate looked formidable. After inspecting it, John got a big spanner from the Lancia's tool kit and used it to snap two of the rusted crossbars. He was then able to lift the chain clear of the uprights and open the double gates. Once he was safely inside he unloaded the motorcycle. This was a more difficult feat without Benno to help him, but he accomplished it in the end and propped the machine up out of sight. Then he got back into the car and drove toward the gloomy and unlighted house which stood, dimly visible, at the far end of the drive.

He thought it was empty, but he had no desire to be proved wrong, and he was relieved to find a path that led off the drive. He assumed it went around to the back of the house and the kitchen quarters. Some way along, at a point where the laurels and rank holly almost met overhead, he stopped the car by stalling the engine and got out. He used a torch to make sure that he had left nothing of his own in the car, slammed the lid of the trunk hard enough to wedge it shut and walked back to the gate.

What would happen when the car was discovered?

Nothing much, he hoped. He was reasonably confident that the police would not be able to tie it in with him. He had taken the precaution of wearing gloves while he was in it.

He wheeled his motorcycle back onto the road, replaced the useless chain, put on the motorcycling kit that was stowed in his haversack and set out, heading back the way he had come.

At midnight he was bypassing Taunton and heading for Glastonbury and Midsomer Norton. After that came a long haul up the A 429. By this time there was very little traffic, even on the main road, but he felt that the sooner he got on smaller roads the better. He was making for the old Roman road, known as Akeman Street, which forked off the Fosse Way at Cirencester.

As he rode through the night under the circling stars there were moments which reminded him of that other night drive, through France, but there was not the same sense of strain. This time he knew where he was going and what he was going to do.

As he approached Woodstock, the light was coming back into the sky. He turned off into a coppice and stretched out on the ground to ease the cramp in his legs. The sounds made by the machine as it cooled competed with the birds that were tuning up for the morning overture. There were things to be done, and he would devote a few minutes to thinking about them. . . .

When he woke, with a start, he found that it was past eight and the sun was well up. He wheeled the machine farther into the trees and set about boiling some water on the solid fuel stove and constructing the best breakfast he could manage out of the remains of his stores. After breakfast, he washed and shaved carefully. He was entering an area north of Oxford which had a high respectability rating.

He had chosen it because he felt certain that he could find the lodging he required. In its villages there were cottages and small houses which put up fourth-year students from Oxford, men reading for fellowships or the Foreign Service who found it convenient to be a mile or two outside the city. Now, in the middle of the long vacation, many of them would be free.

He was lucky at his second attempt. Mrs. Shuttleworth of Owls Pen, Woodeaton, scrutinized him and decided that he passed muster.

"You'll be studying, I expect," she said. The fact that he was a lot older than the average undergraduate was no surprise to her. Since the war she had accommodated all sorts: a middle-aged enthusiast from Birmingham who had returned to the university to study speleology; a Rhodes Scholar as black as her kitchen stove, but no trouble at all.

"Actually," said John, "I'm writing a thesis."

This sounded a respectable sort of undertaking. John explained that it might take a week or two. Terms were agreed.

Mr. Claxton was the sort of lodger she liked. There was a look of real kindness in his eyes. A bit tired at the moment, which was hardly surprising if he had ridden down all the way from London that morning, but he looked, she thought, like a man who was at peace with himself.

Twenty-One

Bill Rossall stormed upstairs from his bookshop. Lois was finishing breakfast. She took one look at his face and jumped up.

"What is it?" she said. "What's happened?"

"What's happened?" said Bill thickly. "What's happened? You're asking me what's happened."

"But, Dad—"

"Don't call me Dad, you sodding little bitch. Sit down and listen."

"If you'd only explain—"

"Sit down."

Bill was shouting now.

Lois collapsed into her chair and stared up at a face she had never seen before.

"All right. Now listen."

At least his voice had come back under some sort of control.

"I've had the police round from West End Central. They've had the word from the ones in Kent who found Midge's van. But Midge was gone."

Lois opened her mouth and shut it again.

"That's right. Don't say anything yet. I'll tell you when to talk. Like I said, they found the van, where Midge parked it. And his breakfast, half eaten. And no one else there at all, because the man who hung out there had run off and was living at a hostel in Chatham. And all he would say was that he was— scared."

Bill put such force into the last word that his voice started to rise again. Lois said, "Dad, please—please don't shout."

"If I feel like shouting, I'll shout." He picked up the coffeepot and brought it down with such force on the table that it cracked. A brown flood started to spread over the white cloth. Lois made no move to stop it.

"You haven't asked me why the old toe-rag was scared. Go on. Ask me."

"Why—why was he scared?"

"He was scared of three men who'd come down. And you bloody well know who they were. He said they pulled Midge out of his van and done something to him. He wouldn't say what they done. He couldn't say it. He was too frightened. Frightened they might come back and do it to him. How do you like the story so far?"

Lois tried to speak, but no human sound came out.

Bill leaned across the table and said, in a voice which was quieter, but more deadly for its quietness, "So now you can guess the question I'm going to ask you: *How did Frankie and his chums know where Midge was hanging out?*"

As he asked this, Bill pushed the table, hard, at Lois. She scraped her chair back, until it met the sideboard. The table followed. She was now pinned between the two pieces of furniture.

Bill put one hand out and picked up the saw-edged bread knife. He said, "I'll ask you once more. Then, if you don't speak up, you lose some of your face. Did you tell Frankie where Midge was?"

Lois said, "Yes. But I never thought—"

"Never mind what you didn't think. Next question. Did Frankie say why he wanted to know?"

"Yes, he did," said Lois eagerly. "It wasn't nothing to do with Midge, really. He'd got nothing against Midge. He wanted to know Mr. Naylor's address. That was all. Honestly it was."

"And why did he want that?"

"Well—because of what happened in the pub, I suppose. When he roughed up Gareth."

Bill gave a short dry laugh. "Roughed him up? He put one finger on him and told him to sit down. That's all the roughing up he did to that nasty little fairy." He broke off for a moment and seemed to be thinking. "Of course, Midge wouldn't tell them what they wanted to know. Midge was like that. Then they'd start in on him, and if Gareth got worked up and threw one of his fits he wouldn't be able to stop. That's about the strength of it."

He was talking to himself now, not to Lois. She said, timidly, "What are you going to do about it?"

"Do? I'm going to set the police onto those three characters and see they get what's coming to them. And listen. If they ask you the same questions as I've asked you, you'll give them the same answers. Yes?"

"Yes," said Lois faintly. If he'd known about that letter! Pray God he never found out.

"It's a shambles," said Detective Sergeant Thomassen. "A bloody shambles." He was staring gloomily out of the window of the private bar in the Eagle and Child public house. "I tell you, I wish I'd never touched it."

"That's not like you, Tom," said Corkery. "What's the difficulty? Surely you can head the old bugger off."

"Head off Bill Rossall? I'd as soon try to head off a Sherman tank in overdrive. He's mad. Stark, staring mad."

"But what can he do?"

"Do? You're asking me what he can do? I'll tell you what he can do. He can walk right up Victoria Street to Scotland Yard and blow his top."

"Yes. I see," said Corkery. He was starting to work out how this development might affect him and was not liking it much. "Just what is it he wants you to do?"

"Oh, that's very easy. He just wants us to lay hold of Frankie and his brother and the mad teeny-bopper and charge 'em with murdering Midge and have 'em sent down for thirty years apiece. He might settle for twenty-five, but thirty's what he's after."

Corkery got up, walked over to the hatch and rang the bell. When the girl appeared, he ordered two more pints of best bitter. He wanted time to think. He said nothing until the drinks had been paid for and were on the table and they were alone again. Then he said, "Let's get one or two things clear. What *we* asked you to do was locate a certain character, name unknown, who'd been picked up by Midge on one of his continental trips. *You* handed the job to Frankie, because he was, in a manner of speaking, a friend of the family, the idea being that he could get the info we needed. That's the story as far as we know it. Right?"

What he meant was, that's the extent of our involvement. He didn't need to put this into words.

"Suppose you go on from there."

Thomassen, who was also thinking in terms of involvement, chose his words carefully. He said, "We passed the message on. Just like you said. All we wanted was info. The trouble was, Midge had gone to earth. He'd got this hideout, down in Kent. Frankie found out about it."

"How?"

"From Midge's girl, Lois."

"She admitted that?"

"Under pressure, I gather. Yes. She admitted it. So we know that it was Frankie and company who went down there that morning. The next bit's not too clear, because the only person who saw it was this old coot who was living there, and it sent him right round the bend and he won't talk about it, but it's not hard to guess."

"Midge wouldn't cough up the details they wanted, so they knocked him about and found they'd gone too far and finished him off."

"Right. And the river was very handy. I've talked to the local boys about it. There's a fast scour running. Drop someone in with a few weights attached, and by dark he'd be rolling around on the bottom of the North Sea."

Both men thought about this.

"What it comes to," said Corkery, the relief clear in his voice, "is that apart from Frankie and company, who won't want to talk about it, there's no one left knows anything about it."

"Except Mr. Naylor."

"For God's sake," said Corkery, really startled. "How does *he* come into it?"

"How he comes into it is that when old Rossall guessed that Lois might have split, he rang him up and advised him to get down there quick. Which he did, but he must have been too late."

"But—" said Corkery. He now knew some of the truth about Naylor's true identity but realized that this particular piece of knowledge was best kept to himself. So he changed his mind and said, "But what I'd like to know is where Frankie and company are now."

"That's what Bill wants to know. And that's what he wants us to get busy and find out."

"And you've got to do it?"

"We've got to make an effort, yes. It's all right, Corky, I know just what you're thinking. And I'm thinking it too. It'd be better for all of us if we didn't find them. Because if we do, they'll talk. And the first thing they'll say is that I sent them down there. And I shall have to say that you told me to do it. And you'll say you got *your* instructions from your boss at MBA. And then we shall all be in the shit."

This accurate summary of the position seemed to cause Corkery no sort of pleasure.

Sir Thomas Chervil greeted Detective Superintendent David Lowes warmly and directed him to one of the more comfortable of the office chairs. Some years before, when he was in the Foreign Service, he recalled that he had been asked to help the police in a matter of organized smuggling from the Middle East and had encountered Lowes, then an inspector. He mentioned this, and Lowes responded with a smile and settled himself more comfortably. It was the same gesture of settling down for a cozy chat, the same friendly smile Chervil remembered from the previous occasion. It had deceived the organizer of the smuggling ring and had led him to a long cold term of imprisonment.

Chervil was not deceived. He knew the department in

which Lowes now served. It was not a department staffed by fools.

"Well, now," he said. "What can I do for you?"

"It's an odd case," said Lowes. "A murder hunt in which the presumed victim and the presumed killers have both disappeared."

"Interesting," said Chervil.

"You might be able to help us in one particular, so let me give you the story, as it appears to us. It starts on the Friday before last, with three men going down to a place on the North Kent Marshes. . . ."

Lowes described the Alternative Fuel Company, its abandoned premises and their odd guardian. He spoke deliberately, not wasting time, exactly, but filling in the picture with careful detail.

"There seems to be no doubt who the three men were. They all have criminal records. Maurice Simmons, a number of convictions for criminal assault and grievous bodily harm. Gareth Peters for car thefts and soliciting, and Maurice's brother, Frank Simmons. He has only the one actual conviction, arising out of a brawl in a public house. It involved an elderly man, called William Rossall, who keeps a bookshop in Soho and a second, rather mysterious character, who happened to be staying with the Rossalls at the time."

"The Rossalls?"

"Sorry, I should have introduced them. They all play a part in this story. There's William's son, Albert, who runs a van on continental trips, and Albert's common-law wife, Lois. The van parked behind the factory was Albert's van. And he seems to have been the victim. But I am doubtful whether we shall find his body. The river is very handy at that point."

"I believe that a murder charge *can* be brought without a body."

"It can be. And has been. But it's not easy."

Chervil decided to force the pace a little. He said, "What reason had these three characters got for killing young Rossall? If they did."

"Well, now," said Lowes, "I've had rather different explanations from different people. Lois says that they were inquiring about the mysterious character I mentioned."

"The one who was involved in the brawl in the pub?"

"Correct. William Rossall maintains that they didn't simply want to locate him. They had very definite and disagreeable ideas about what they were going to do to him when they caught up with him. Arising out of that same brawl."

"I see. And Albert refused to answer their questions and got beaten up and killed."

"That's the assumption we're working on. Though I'm not sure the killing was originally intended."

Chervil thought about it.

Pursuit of a private vendetta. It would, from his point of view, be a very convenient explanation of why the three men went down there. It left MBA in the clear. If he had been less experienced he might have fallen into the trap of agreeing too readily. Instead, he said, "It all seems a bit farfetched to me, Superintendent. There must have been something else behind it. Surely the man you need to get hold of is this mysterious stranger. How did he get involved?"

"It seems that William Rossall got hold of him and asked him to go down."

"Got hold of him? How?"

"By telephone."

"Then you have his number."

"Laleham oh-four-seven-four."

It was nicely done, but Lowes had made the mistake of playing his cards too slowly. Chervil had guessed what was coming and was ready for him.

"In that case," he said in tones of calm triumph, "I believe I can tell you his name. John Naylor. Correct?"

"Perfectly correct," said Lowes with a tiny smile. "Of course you'll have deduced from the telephone number that he was one of your own employees. But please explain how you knew which one."

"Simple. Naylor walked out on the Friday you're talking about and hasn't been seen since."

"I see." If Lowes was disappointed at the way things were

going, he managed to conceal it. "I was hoping you might be able to tell us something about him."

"A certain amount. We checked up on him very carefully, of course."

"Oh? Why?"

"We suspected he might be a spy, planted by our rivals."

"I imagine you do suffer from that sort of thing."

"We try to deal with it when it arises," said Chervil grimly. "We checked his address: One forty-one Makepeace Mansions, Highgate."

Lowes looked up sharply and said, "Interesting. Tell you why in a moment. Please go on."

"We took two references. A bank and a solicitor."

"And both of them will clam up as soon as I talk to them," said Lowes. But he wrote down the names and addresses.

"The other information he gave us, about his previous firm and connections, was false. We'd just found that out. That's why we were going to sack him. Only he beat us to it by walking out."

"Nothing else?"

"He made one or two friends while he was with us. A man he shared a room with, Mike Collins. And there were men he used to drink with in the evenings. He might have told them something. I'll certainly inquire."

"Anything would be helpful."

"I'm afraid it's rather a dead end." Chervil made the very slight move that could have been a cue for the ending of the interview, but Lowes did not appear to notice it.

He said, "Perhaps, so far as Naylor is concerned. But we've recently had some information about the Simmons crowd."

Chervil said, Damn, but said it to himself. The last thing he wanted was for that trio to reappear.

"A car was found abandoned in a private park near Dulverton. The national computer identified it as one which had been stolen in the Borough last Friday. It had been suggested at the time that young Peters might have been the thief. It was his line, and he had been seen hanging about there earlier. So I thought it was worth pursuing. We had the car given a proper going over, and sure enough we identified the prints of all three men."

"Dulverton, you said."

"In Devonshire. South of Exmoor."

"But why on earth—?"

"Why, indeed. It makes no sense at all. If they went to Devonshire to look for Naylor and found him and killed him, this was the last place they'd have left the car. To start with, it was fifteen miles from the nearest railway station."

"Perhaps they had some place handy to hide up."

"Three Soho villains in the wilds of Devonshire? They'd have stuck out like a sore thumb."

"Yes. It was a stupid suggestion."

Chervil's mind was working at speed as he turned over the possibilities of this latest development. Was it good for him, or was it bad? When in doubt maintain pressure.

He said, "I'm an amateur, Superintendent, and you're a professional. So shoot me down if you want to. But aren't you making the mistake that Napoleon warned his generals against? He called it painting pictures. You're basing all your suppositions on the idea that the trips to Kent and to Devonshire were motivated by hatred of Naylor. Isn't that rather thin? There might be quite a different explanation."

Lowes said, "That's true. But there has been one piece of positive evidence to support it. When you mentioned that address in Highgate, I recalled that on the Tuesday after the Kent visit, three men paid a visit to that particular flat, wrecked it and set it on fire."

"There's a smell of private vengeance about that," Chervil agreed. He was careful to keep the relief out of his voice. "Well, I don't know that I can help you any further." He half rose in his chair. Lowes got up as well. "I'll make those inquiries. If I get anything useful about Naylor, you shall have it."

As soon as his secretary had shown Lowes out, he grabbed the telephone. When Ligertwood answered, he said, "Jump into your car and come up here quick."

221

"Is it important? I've got our German man coming to see me."

"It's damnably important. And I can't move from here. I'm expecting a call from Lambert Mather at any moment. He's coming here to see me. Whether it's this afternoon or tomorrow morning depends on a date he's got with the Minister."

"*He's* coming to see you?" Ligertwood was sufficiently conscious of government protocol to appreciate the significance of this.

"Right."

"I'll be with you as soon as I can. . . ."

When he arrived Chervil said, "It's been quite a day. Not only Lambert Mather. Our lawyers are already in touch, and his visit may clinch things."

"Excellent."

"Which, as you say, is excellent. The other two developments are—unhelpful." Chervil was not given to overstatement. He said "unhelpful" when another man might have said "disastrous." Ligertwood knew this and listened anxiously to the story of Lowes's visit.

When he had taken it in and thought about it, he said, "Then the only people who could connect us with this unfortunate business are Loveridge and Corkery. They're both professionals. They won't talk out of school."

"And the man at West End Central who made the contact for them."

"Him least of all. It would cost him his job."

"I agree. But shut all three mouths and do it as quickly as you can."

Ligertwood nodded. He was not unduly disturbed. He said, "The only other people who might upset the applecart are Naylor—or Benedict, I should say—and the Simmons lot. The idea seems to be that they followed him to the West Country, caught up with him and finished him off. If that's right, he can't talk and they won't. If they did, they'd be connecting themselves with the earlier killing."

"An admirable analysis," said Chervil dryly.

Ligertwood looked up sharply.

"There's only one thing wrong with it. I told you there had been *two* developments." He unlocked the drawer in his desk and took out a small sheaf of papers: not more than half a dozen pages, typed on one side only and neatly stapled at the corner. It was headed THE BIRTH OF A GIANT. "Have a look at this," he said. "It won't take you long."

As Ligertwood started to read, his expression changed. First it went red, with simple anger. Then, as he tore into the third and fourth pages, Chervil noticed a grayish tinge in his face. He said, "Come on, Henry, it's not as bad as all that." He fetched a bottle from the corner cupboard, poured some of the contents into a tumbler and handed it to Ligertwood, who continued to read and drink at the same time, putting down the glass as he turned the pages. He finished reading and drinking at the same moment.

"Bad," he said thickly. "It's—it's damnable. The bloody little creeping sneaking spy."

"Posted yesterday in Oxford," said Chervil.

The flat unexcited tone in which he said this had the effect of a rebuke. Ligertwood recovered some of his normal poise.

"What are we going to do about it?"

"As I remarked before, one thing we are not going to do is lose our heads. What were we taught in the army? When in doubt, put yourself in the enemy's shoes. There was no letter with this. That means that the next move is with Benedict. He will have to say what he wants from us, for suppressing it. That, I imagine, was the object of sending it to us in advance."

"Or to make us sweat," said Ligertwood.

"Yes. No doubt he'll wait a bit to make us sweat. That's the technique in these cases, I believe. But he's got to make contact sooner or later. By telephone or letter, I should guess. And when that happens we shall have to think carefully. Because"—and here Chervil spoke so slowly that there seemed to be a gap between each word—"he is a very dangerous man."

"I'm sure you'll think of something," said Ligertwood. It comforted him that Tom Chervil should be facing this problem in the same way that he had faced so many other problems in the early days of their enterprise. It gave him an illogical feeling that everything would come out all right in the end.

Chervil went on, in the same level voice, "He's doubly dangerous. First because, on his track record so far, he doesn't look like a man who could be easily frightened. And secondly, since he's got more than enough money for his needs, it's clear that he can't be bought off. We may be forced to listen to his terms and see if we can agree to them."

A gleam of hope had appeared in Ligertwood's eyes. He said, "You mentioned just now that he might keep us waiting. Suppose he keeps us waiting too long."

"Meaning?"

"If we can sign up with Lambert Mather tomorrow, it'll be too late for Naylor—I mean Benedict—to produce his precious document. They'll be committed."

"My dear Henry," said Chervil, with a note of real affection in his voice. "Try not to be simplistic. We're not contracting with private people. We're entering into an arrangement with the Government. And you know as well as I do that the Government can, and will, back out of any arrangement which looks as if it might be an embarrassment."

"Then you think we're really in Benedict's hands."

"To an extent," said Chervil easily. "But I do possess one weapon that he doesn't know about. I won't discuss it now because it's not a very nice weapon, and I hope I shan't have to use it. We shall see."

"Well, that's very satisfactory," said Lambert Mather. "The Minister was quite clear. He has decided that, on its record and achievements to date, MBA is the horse we ought to back. And I hope we shall see it galloping past the winning post and leaving all its competitors many lengths behind."

"With the benefit of the very generous subsidy you mentioned, I think they will be weighted out of the race."

"We don't want that. Not entirely. Competition is an excellent thing in all walks of life. But there has to be a leader in every field. A pacesetter, to make other competitors run harder."

"Of course." Chervil felt that Lambert Mather's metaphor

was becoming a bit tangled. "I imagine there will be a certain amount of paperwork to get through."

"Alas, yes. There is always paper. Our people are in touch with your lawyers, and they will no doubt dot a lot of *i*'s and cross a lot of *t*'s. But the principle is decided. That's the great thing."

"It is indeed," said Chervil. He helped Lambert Mather on with his coat, steered him to the door and out through the ante-room where his secretary sat.

"Don't bother to come down," said Lambert Mather. "A man who can find his way through the corridors of Whitehall will not lose his way in this simple straightforward building."

As his secretary closed the door she had been holding open, Chervil said, "A little pompous, don't you think, Lucy?"

"A bit orotund," agreed his secretary, who had been educated at Roedean and Oxford. "I didn't like to interrupt you, because I knew how important your discussion was. But there's been someone waiting to see you for nearly half an hour."

"Has he got an appointment?"

"No, but he said he thought you'd like to see him. It's a Mr. Benedict."

For a moment, but only a moment, Chervil was taken aback. Then he said, "Mr. Benedict. Yes, we have one or two things to discuss. Show him in."

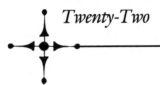

Twenty-Two

"I expected to hear from you," said Chervil blandly. "But not so soon. And not, I must confess, in person."

"Once you had read my memorandum," said John, "there was no point in hanging about. And it seemed better that our negotiations—if you are prepared to negotiate—should be personal and verbal. Letters sometimes get into the wrong hands."

"By negotiations, I take it you mean that you might be prepared, in certain circumstances, to suppress your remarkable memorandum. I hope, by the way, that this is not the only copy. It would be a tragedy if it was accidentally destroyed."

"There are other copies."

"With your solicitors and bankers? Very wise. With instructions to publish if anything should happen to you."

"Certainly. That's why I had no hesitation about coming to see you personally."

"An unnecessary precaution. I am not, myself, a man of violence."

"You prefer to entrust violence to paid professionals."

"Of course. Just as I entrust legal matters to lawyers and financial matters to merchant bankers. But to business. I shall not pretend that the publication of your memorandum, at this particular moment, would not be damaging."

"I imagined that it might be," said John. "Particularly when I succeeded in identifying the gentleman who preceded me here this morning."

"Then we start without illusions. Yes. It will be valuable to us to have this document suppressed. What do you ask in return?"

"Two things. First you must sever all associations with the Mafia in Italy and the Union Corse in France. I have sufficient contacts in both your factories to know when this has been done. It must apply equally to any offshoots or rivals of these organizations. And it must be permanent."

"Dealing with that last point first, I can assure you that once we severed our association with the Mafia no lesser body would be tempted to step into their shoes. They would recognize the danger of doing so. As for the severance being permanent, of course. These are not the sort of people you can say 'goodbye' to one moment and 'help me' to the next."

"Then you agree to it?"

"I'd like to hear your second condition first."

"My second condition is that you sack Sergio Faldo. I say sack, to make it clear that I don't mean that you retire him with a handsome redundancy payment. I mean you throw him out. And let it be known that he is being thrown out because of what he allowed to happen at the Paoli farm. I want to see him starving in the gutters of Naples."

"You hate him as much as that?"

"As much and more. But personal feelings apart, I want it done in that way as a warning to any of his successors who might be tempted to imitate him."

"And if I agree to your conditions, all copies of this document will be destroyed."

"No. They will remain in existence. But they will not be published as long as you abide by your side of the bargain. I realize, of course, that time is on your side. It would be extremely inconvenient if it were published today. Less so in a year's time. In five year's time, possibly not at all. In business old sins are easily forgotten."

"In five years' time, if we succeed, as I hope we shall, we shall not have the least incentive to sin. You must have noticed that it is emergent organizations that break the rules. The established ones are tiresomely insistent on their being observed.

227

Very well. I understand your conditions. If I agree to them, I have to rely on your word that you will keep your side of the bargain."

"In our negotiations last year," said John coldly, "I seem to remember that you were prepared to take my word on a number of important matters. You will know, by now, whether it is reliable or not."

Chervil thought about this and nodded his head as though coming to a decision. He said, "I agree, fully and without reserve, to both your conditions."

"Then that is an end of the matter." John started to get up.

"I wish it was," said Chervil. "I shall have to ask you to be patient while I touch on one further point. The fact that I am raising it at all must be taken as a considerable compliment. It's a proof of my conviction that you are not a man who will go back on his word once it is given."

John sat down again slowly.

"There are two sorts of conditions. Lawyers describe them as executory and executed. As the words imply, executory conditions are things which have to be done in the future. Executed conditions are ones which have already been done."

John sat very still. He wondered what was coming and had a suspicion that he was not going to like it.

"Both your conditions," Chervil continued, "have already been fulfilled. Recently, as I think you know, Henry Ligertwood went out to Nice. He found that a dangerous situation had arisen."

"You're referring to the dispute between the Mafia and the Union."

"That is so. Your sources of information seem to be surprisingly good. Yes. It was already boiling up to a point where a bloody confrontation was possible. I need hardly say that the people at the top of both organizations would have done a lot to avoid it."

"As I understand it," said John, "all that was needed was for one of them to pay a sum of money."

"Exactly. *But which of them?* The sum was not large. It would hardly have caused a ripple in either budget. But the group who paid would be knuckling down and admitting that they were in the wrong. What was at stake was not money. It was something much more important to them. It was prestige."

"Awkward," agreed John.

"Awkward for them. But, as Ligertwood shrewdly perceived, useful for us. If the money happened to come *from a third party,* the face of both organizations would be saved. Accordingly, he offered to hand over to the Union the equivalent in lire of fifty thousand pounds, to be used to compensate the family of Paul Rocca. But there was a condition. This sum was to be regarded as a signing off—what you might call a parting present to both organizations. We were not to call further on them. They were not to call further on us."

"Do you think they will observe this?"

"It was fixed at such a high level that I am confident it will hold."

John thought about it. He said, "Very well. And Faldo?"

"What happened there was inevitable. I had this cable this morning." He passed the blue form across the desk. "The news will be in the Italian press tomorrow and no doubt in the English papers as well, though they may not give it so much space."

While he was speaking John was reading the cable. He looked first at the signature.

"Giacomo," said Chervil, who had followed his eye down. "When Faldo disappeared two days ago, we gave him the temporary job of stand-in managing director."

The cable recorded that, on the previous evening, a car had been found, burnt out, on the flank of Monte Forcuso, above Carile. The body in the driving seat had been identified as Sergio Faldo, who had disappeared, on the day before, from his house. Faldo had been attached to the steering wheel of the car by a steel chain and padlock. Inquiries were proceeding.

Driven to a high place, thought John, and set on fire so that the flames could be seen by all in the area.

Chervil was looking at him curiously. He said, "I realize it must be a disappointment to you that you have been deprived of the satisfaction of forcing your conditions on us. Irritating, at first sight, that fate should have done your work, not you. But, after all, is that a correct analysis? You are an engineer and well used to tracing the sequences of cause and effect. In this case, if you look at the matter logically, it *was* you who brought about the fulfillment of both conditions. You did it when you opened the door of the lift in that French hotel. That led to the destruction of Rocca and led, in turn, to the quarrel between the two organizations, which gave us an opportunity of getting rid of them. As soon as the protection of the Mafia was removed, Faldo's life was forfeit."

"I expect you're right," said John. It was over and done with. The past was unimportant. It was the future that mattered now.

"And what," asked Chervil, with no more than an appearance of polite interest, "are your own plans?"

"I shall continue the travels on which I started out rather more than a year ago."

"You are going back to New Zealand?"

"Yes. I hope there will be no further interruptions to my journey."

"I see no reason why there should be," said Chervil.

His secretary had noticed that the importance of a visitor was nicely graded by the distance that Sir Tom went to show him out. Lambert Mather, for instance, he had escorted as far as the door of her room. With the imperious Mr. Benedict, who had not even had an appointment, he walked right down the stairs and out into the street, talking pleasantly as he went. . . .

To Ligertwood, who had come up to learn the result of the morning's work, Chervil said, "A most remarkable man. I've got a feeling, with no evidence to support it, that he and those three thugs went down to the West Country with the same idea in mind. Both intended to finish off the other party. Since Benedict has returned alone, it's just possible that we shall hear no more of that trio."

"That would be good news," said Ligertwood.

"It solves one problem. But this"—he pointed to the cable—"leaves us with another. I'm afraid there's no alternative. You'll have to go out there, Henry, and take over."

"But, Tom—"

"Until our headhunters have found us a replacement, or the Five fifty-five is on the production line."

"But that might take months. Who's going to look after Laleham?"

"Laleham's less important than Italy."

Ligertwood said, "Why don't we offer the post to Benedict? He's ideally qualified for the job."

"It's a lovely idea, Henry. But I shall feel much safer when he's at the other side of the globe."

Ligertwood recognized the logic of the decision. In fact he was not unhappy at the idea of a short spell of active command, with its different problems and challenges.

As he rose to go, he said, "By the way, I've been puzzling over something you said last time we met. If Benedict had been totally unreasonable, you implied that you had a weapon you could use."

"Monica St. Aubyn."

"Lytaudy's assistant?"

"I noticed that Benedict seemed extremely well informed about all that was going on in our French factory. I'm sure that Lytaudy himself was absolutely discreet, so I assumed that the culprit was Miss St. Aubyn."

"And you think that a threat to her would have moved Benedict."

"Yes. Though exactly what it would have moved him to do is something I don't care to contemplate. Fortunately, it didn't arise."

"I'll stop over at Nice on my way out to Italy," said Ligertwood, "and see that she is removed."

"Let me hazard a guess," said Chervil. "I rather think you will be too late."

Twenty-Three

It was three weeks before John finally caught a plane to Nice. There had been much to arrange. Jonas had been pleased when he heard that John intended to take over the farm in New Zealand. It seemed to him to be an admirable arrangement, and he had dispatched the necessary cables to set it in train.

There were visits, also, to the Secretary of the Bishop of London.

John and Monica were married in the little English church in the hills above Nice. The first chaplain there after the war had been an Eighth Army man. Overcoming some stuffy ecclesiastical resistance, he had succeeded in ornamenting the lower panel of the east window with colored representations of Eighth Army divisional signs: the jerboa and the hawk, the mailed fist and the battleax. It seemed to John a happy portent that when they knelt in front of the altar the morning light should have struck directly onto them through the green fern of the New Zealand division.

The farm, when they got there, was in a shocking condition. They said goodbye to the temporary manager without regrets on either side and soon found themselves as happy as two well-suited and very busy people could be.

There were moments, as in all marriages, when feet were close to the edge of the cliff. On one occasion Monica found John staring out of the window at the peak of Mount Cook emerging from the morning mist. He said, "Three thousand seven hundred and sixty-four meters. *Not* three thousand seven hundred and sixty-three."

She nearly asked what he was talking about, but being a woman of intuition she refrained. Did she realize, perhaps, that they were walking over a grave?